Different Kinds of
DEAD
and Other Tales

Other Five Star Titles
by Ed Gorman:

Night Kills
Such a Good Girl and Other Crime Stories

Different Kinds of

DEAD

and Other Tales

ED
GORMAN

Five Star • Waterville, Maine

First Edition
First Printing: July 2005

Published in 2005 in conjunction with
Tekno Books and Ed Gorman.

Set in 11 pt. Plantin.

Printed in the United States on permanent paper.

Library of Congress Cataloging-in-Publication Data

Gorman, Edward.
    Different kinds of dead and other tales / by Ed Gorman.
    —1st ed.
      p. cm.
    ISBN 1-59414-213-0 (hc : alk. paper)
    1. Suspense fiction, American.   I. Title.
PS3557.O759D54 2005
  813'.54—dc22
                                        2005005998

To my beautiful, talented,
and enormously patient wife
CAROL

Contents

Introduction

I grew up in the waning days of the magazine boom which had lasted from approximately 1870 to 1960. But then came paperbacks and television. It was unthinkable that such magazines as *Collier's*, *The Saturday Evening Post*, and *American* would die.

But die they did, their advertising revenues fleeing to TV. And for all their unhappy fiction readers, who could no longer read short stories and short novels in their pages, there were new twenty-five cent mass-market paperbacks. And on TV you could find any kind of fiction you wanted, from westerns with Hopalong Cassidy and Matt Dillon; funny tales with Lucille Ball and Jackie Gleason; and crime stories with Jack Webb and Raymond Burr as Perry Mason.

The pulps had become smaller in size and page count, and year-by-year their circulation figures fell even further. Today, there are maybe six genre magazines—science fiction, detective, the occasional western—left on the newsstands. And they are nowhere near their peak in circulation figures.

All this has created a real problem for people who like to read and people who like to write short stories. Most of the tales here come from anthologies rather than magazines. And even anthologies, which remained strong during the previous two decades, have declined in number considerably.

Virtually all of the stories collected here fall into the category of suspense. But not just contemporary suspense. You'll find historical suspense, as in westerns; and future suspense as in science fiction; and dark suspense as in horror. Stories are stories. At least to me.

These particular pieces span twenty-five years in their composition and a variety of sources in their publication. There are too many editors involved to thank by name. A few of them have passed from the scene from age and infirmity; far more have passed from the scene because there are simply no magazines left to employ them. To those readers who've e-mailed me asking when my next collection would appear, here it is. I hope you find it worth the wait.

—Ed Gorman

Muse

1

There were a couple of things you learned pretty quick at the *Skylar Times*. One was that you weren't ever going to own a BMW if you stayed in newspaper journalism. And two was that the cosmically desirable Dulcy Tremont, editor of the weekly Entertainment magazine, was the property of publisher Cal Rawlins, husband, father, and tireless exponent of Family Values.

This was how things were on the day a few years ago when David Osborne came strolling into the newsroom one fine spring morning, direct from his recent guest shot on Jay Leno's show, and from his even more recent appearance on the cover of *Rolling Stone*. Not too long ago, Osborne had sat at the desk next to mine, cranking out copy and, like the rest of us males and probably at least one female, dreaming uselessly of possessing Dulcy Tremont. Osborne and I had another passion in common. We both wrote songs.

Osborne had had it particularly bad for Dulcy. They were both part-time jazz musicians and singers who worked in Chicago most weekends. They sang and played well, but without any particular distinction. Unfortunately, a whole lot of people sing and play well. Plus he spent half his time at the newspaper working directly with Dulcy. That had to be a special kind of hell, if you were in love with the lady. Forget her looks for a moment. I'd never met a woman who *smelled* as good as Dulcy. Her scent alone could drive a man to testicular frenzy.

But now it was Dulcy, standing in the doorway of her office—a real office, not a cubicle, or just a battered desk in a sea of battered newsroom desks—now it was Dulcy who did the gaping. Gone was all her imperious blondeness. She was now just a celebrity-struck prairie girl with her eyes fixed upon somebody whose name could be found every other week or so in the pages of *Entertainment Weekly*.

There was just enough left of Osborne's old face so that you recognized him. But cosmetic surgery had turned an average-looking guy into something resembling a movie star. Same with the body. He was twenty-five pounds lighter. And he covered what was left in the kind of Southern California Casual that you just don't see here on the Illinois edge of the Mississippi River. He'd previewed the new face on the *Rolling Stone* cover. But it was a lot more startling in person. How could this be the pudgy, pasty, shy kid who'd always deferred to me as the newsroom ass bandit, which I pretty much am by default. All this means is that I bathe regularly and have had my acne under control for some years now.

If lording your success over former colleagues had been an Olympic event, Osborne would have won the gold and silver on the spot. He was like the Pope making his way through a throng of unwashed peasants.

Me, he left till last. Amidst all the computer keyboards clacking away, amidst all the phones ringing and the fax bells going insane, amidst all the earthquake rumble from the basement where the giant presses were being fired up for the day, he swaggered over and said, "You have time for a coffee break?"

"Not right now, Dave. Maybe in an hour."

He smiled. There was a little bit of Elvis' old sneer in that smile. Maybe the plastic surgeon built the sneer capacity into Dave's new face.

"We'll go now."

"But I've got to finish—"

He put up a halting hand. "I'll take care of it with Rawlins." Then: "By the way, it's 'David' now. Not 'Dave.' "

He made a point of not looking at Dulcy. He just let her slump against her doorframe, spent in an almost post-coital way. It was a wonder her hair wasn't mussed up and she wasn't smoking a cigarette. But at least a part of her considerable mind, the part that wasn't receiving sexual charges from the mere presence of a Star in the newsroom—at least a part of her mind had to be remembering all the ways she'd snubbed Dave—pardon me, David—over their working years together. She had treated him as she had treated everybody else, male and female alike—as if we were silly little people whose lives didn't interest her in the least.

He walked all the way to the back of the newsroom, where Cal Rawlins' vast, baronial office stretched across the length of the entire southern wall. The door was open and moments later the tall, solid red-bearded man in a blue custom-made suit appeared and bellowed out "David!" as if he hadn't spent all of Osborne's years here bullying him as he bullied everybody else. Rawlins slid his arm around Osborne's shoulder and they vanished inside the office that was filled with huge black and white photographs, very artsy you know, of Rawlins killing every kind of animal that moved. He dispatched them with gun, bow and arrow, and even, on one of those Africa veldt safaris for American tourists of the faux macho persuasion, hurling a spear into the side and hide of a rhino lumbering its way to a small lake.

13

The only thing impressive about all these kills, as he called them, was that his blood alcohol levels were probably setting Guinness Book records while he was doing in all the poor animals. He had some issues, as they say, with the bottle.

Rawlins always made a point of slamming his door. Kept the troops awake, he always joked. It can scare the hell out of you when you're concentrating on your work. Shell-shocked.

He slammed the door extra-hard for visitors. Maybe someday somebody'll take a photo of him doing some door-slamming. He could add it to his office wall collection.

"You know, he's really a pretty decent guy when you give him a chance."

We were eating lunch on a veranda overlooking the Mississippi. There was a soft river breeze, sweetened by the scents of blooming spring. I looked with boyish longing at the craft on the water, everything from tugs to small yachts to bully-boy speed craft. Nothing spoke of freedom the way the Mississippi did. Just get on a boat and follow the river wherever it flowed.

Claire's was the restaurant of choice for those thirty-somethings who had been led to believe that they were important in the Skylar scheme of things. This meant lawyers, bankers, land developers, the mayor and the city council people, and a cross-section of doctors, visitors, TV station managers, and various hangers-on and wanna-bes. I was here only because Osborne had insisted on it. Everybody knew who he was, of course. He gave little flickering, dismissive waves to everybody who said hello.

"You're talking about the Great White Hunter?"

"Yes. Believe it or not, he was downright charming this morning, Jason."

"Was he ever charming to you all the years you worked for him?"

"No. But obviously he's changed."

Osborne had become a peacock, that was for sure. But one thing about him hadn't changed. He was still naïve about people. That was his chief failure as a reporter. He wasn't skeptical enough. He could be conned too easily.

"He hasn't changed, Dave."

"David."

"David. He hasn't changed at all. He's only being charming because you're a famous songwriter now."

"He invited me to his club. That's pretty impressive."

"You'll be his trophy guest. You really can't see that?"

He smiled. "I'm not a complete dunce, Manning. I know he's being nice because I'm somebody now. But that doesn't mean he can't be charming, does it?"

He checked his gold Rolex. "Listen, Jason. I've got maybe a half-hour window here. If we're going to do an interview, now's the time."

We did the interview while we ate. The recorder I used was about the size of a paperback. The smaller the better. Even people who are frequently interviewed get self-conscious if a big machine is grinding away.

Just about everybody in Skylar knew the story. Mild-mannered young reporter turns out to be brilliant songwriter. And not of Top Ten trash but real, true popular music on the level of the great writers who had served two audiences—the big Broadway and radio audience; and the more refined, hipper jazz audience. You've never heard Porter or Kern or Larry Hart, until you've heard them done by great jazz singers and musicians. Then you'll find out just how rich their music really is.

That was about the only thing Osborne and I ever had in

common. Our love of jazz. Her highness Dulcy Tremont let us both write many articles on Chicago jazz for her Entertainment magazine, the city being only two hours down the Interstate. We wrote several articles about the origins of Chicago jazz during WW I, when the so-called Great Migration brought Southern blacks up from the South because the need for workers was so enormous. To give you an idea of how serious the migration was, in less than three years, seventy-five thousand blacks came to the city, where they found not only good wages but jazz legends such as Jelly Roll Martin and Erskine Tate already in place. New Orleans jazz merged with Chicago jazz and a new form was born. Then the era of Charlie Parker. And Miles. And Oscar Brown, Jr. All of them making significant contributions to the evolving genres.

We also covered the contemporary scene, too. Improv jazz and fusion jazz and avant garde jazz. The Hungry Brain, the Myopic Bookstore, the Deadtech, the No Friction Café. So many cool venues. So much great music.

The contemporary scene was how Dave Osborne became the star feature writer for the paper. Before he gave Dulcy a chance to break his heart, he fell in useless love with an elegant, young jazz singer named Eve Caine, the live-mate of famously-jealous horn player Sam Reed. Osborne was no threat to Reed, which was obvious to everybody except Osborne. One night, after having snorted a couple lines of coke behind better than a pint of vodka, Reed sees Dave in the wintry parking lot of a jazz club talking to Eve. Reed yanks a .45 from the pocket of his Burberry and opens fire. Remember, wintry. The parking lot is covered with ice. Both Osborne and Eve try to dive for cover. But Eve dives exactly the wrong way. Right into the path of two bullets. Both of them entering her skull.

Reed is never seen again. All sorts of speculation in the months following Eve's death. Suicide. The West Coast. The East Coast. Europe.

Osborne becomes a local celebrity.

The way the media handle it, you'd think he and Eve had been hot and heavy. He is the Other Man in a story that involves a beautiful young woman, a psycho horn player, and murder. Is this a story or is this a story? And the man right in the middle of it just happens to be a newspaper writer.

Osborne not only wrote a number of articles, he also wrote a screenplay and a book. They didn't do great business but they did reasonable business, the book and the film. But they made him some serious money, anyway. And then he started writing songs. Correction: then he started writing *good* songs. He'd been writing songs since I'd met him. Bad ones. I'd do my best to support him by bringing my lady of the moment to whatever tiny club he was moonlighting in. But it wasn't easy. He was pretty bad.

The talent agency that had handled his screenplay and book deal had a music division. When he sent a tape of six of his new songs to them, the head of the music division flew him to Hollywood, where four of the songs ended up in a romantic drama that won two Oscars, one for leading lady Cameron Diaz and another for best song, written by David Osborne.

That was pretty much the last we saw of him. It seemed that every singer of any note wanted a David Osborne song. He even recorded his own CD and won a Grammy for it. Following his cosmetic surgery, he became a perennial on Most Desirable Bachelor lists. He had a Malibu house, more than enough ladies, and, to be fair, a gift for creating music that was both elegant and memorable. I loved his stuff. He was as modern as Elvis Costello and as timeless as Duke Ellington.

This was what we covered in the interview. He was clever enough to always put a modest spin on all the major turning points in his life, attributing it to "luck" and "good timing." Best to let the reporter brag on you, rather than you bragging on yourself. He even admitted to the fear that someday it would all leave him—the talent, the glitz, the celebrity. "All things end," he said three times in the course of that interview.

If only he'd known how prescient his words would prove to be.

2

There was an e-mail waiting for me when I got back to my desk that afternoon. Actually, per usual, there were *many* e-mails waiting for me when I got back. But only one that made me curious enough to open it right away.

> *Jason—*
> *Please stop by my office as soon as you can.*
> *Dulcy*

The e-mails I could ignore. The phone calls, I couldn't. They had some urgency to them. A reporter works on any number of stories at a time—the way a detective works on any number of cases—and two of them seemed to be off the respirator and breathing on their own again. I spent half an hour catching up on them. And then it was time for Dulcy.

The men of the newsroom resented her because she always made it clear that they were not worthy of her attention.

The women disliked her because she inhaled most of the sexual air available. Her natural gifts were only enhanced by her clothes, all of which she bought on frequent trips to Chicago. Not even the most lavished-upon Gold Coast mistress dressed any better than Dulcy. Made you wonder, and frequently speculate in coffee-break moments, exactly how much the Great White Hunter was paying her.

Today she wore an emerald green summer dress that displayed her body with wondrous ease: flowing, hugging, defining her with every step she took. She wasn't in her office when I got there. But just as I reached the doorway to leave, I saw her and that dress moving in a ballet of tasteful sexuality among all the worker bees in the newsroom. She was headed to her own office. And to me.

"I really appreciate this, Jason," she said, walking past me into her office. As Cal Rawlins' office was a hymn to his prowess as a hunter, hers was a hymn to her prowess as an Important Personage. Each wall was a museum of photos showing her with various other Important Personages, including Bill Clinton, George Bush, Gwyneth Paltrow, and two Illinois governors, at least one of whom would soon enough be in prison, which was too bad because he was actually a rather decent guy. No matter who else shared the photo with her, the eye went instantly to Dulcy. She never showboated or flaunted. She didn't need to. She was a surprisingly quiet and even somewhat reticent woman by inclination. She didn't need any tricks to attract or sustain attention.

"How was lunch?" she asked once the door was closed and we were seated.

I shrugged. "Fine. I think I got a good interview for the magazine."

"Thanks, I appreciate it." Then, "Gosh, I barely recognized him when he walked in." I'd never been able to figure

out if her "goshes" or "gollys" were her preferred word
choices or simply affectations of innocence.

"I didn't either."

"So how did he sound? Pretty much as he always was, or
kind of a star?"

You have to understand how unlikely this conversation
was. This was maybe the fourth time I'd ever been in her
office. This was also about the longest conversation I'd ever
had with her. Back in the days when Osborne and I were
writing all those jazz articles—we stopped doing them even
before he left for the coast; except for reviews of current
acts, we'd pretty much covered all the highlights of Chicago
jazz history—she dealt with Dave; I dealt with her assistant,
who always conveyed Dulcy's thoughts on revisions.

But this afternoon she spoke as if we were friends, or at
least amiable associates, who did this sort of thing quite often.
There was even a non-sexual kind of intimacy in her tone.

"Oh, about half and half, I guess. Sometimes he was like
the old Osborne. Sometimes he was definitely a star."

"I was wondering if you'd do me a favor."

So now we'd come to it. The reason for the meeting.
The reason for the cordiality.

"Sure, if I can."

"I was wondering if you'd invite him to dinner tonight."

"Can't. I've got a date."

She shook her gloriously blonde head. "Not dinner for
you two—dinner for David and me."

"Ah."

"I know it's stupid—it's just I'm—uncomfortable—
calling him myself. We were never—while he worked here, I
mean—we were never, you know, close friends or anything." She paused. "I mean, I know what people say about
me. That I'm not always as warm as I could be." I didn't

even try to contradict her. "And there's another thing."

Those pure blue eyes shifted eastward for the moment. Eastward from her desk meant the office of the Great White Hunter. "This has to be strictly between us. Certain people—Well, I don't need to go into the whole thing, do I? Certain people wouldn't necessarily be happy if they found out I had dinner with David. I wouldn't want to hurt anybody's feelings over this."

I'd been reluctant to make the call for her. It was sort of high school. Adults tended to make their own calls when they wanted dates. But I hadn't thought of how a dinner date like this would rankle Cal Rawlins, an arrogant man who badly needed rankling.

"I'll have him call you. If he's agreeable, I mean."

Her smile was almost oppressively sweet. "That's so nice of you, Jason. Why don't you start feeding me some ideas for the magazine again? I can probably get you some pretty decent freelance money, if the pieces are major enough."

"I'd really appreciate that."

Twenty minutes later, on his cell talking to my cell, Osborne said, "You know how many sex fantasies I had about that bitch?"

"Not any more than I had. Have. I don't live in Malibu, so the Dulcy Tremont Fantasy Theater is still open for me. You, she's asking out to dinner."

"I played it pretty cool with her today. Didn't look at her once."

This was the old Osborne. Hurt, vindictive, childish. You know, just like the rest of us.

"You need the phone number?"

"I didn't say I'd go."

"Sure, you'll go. Because you want to see what happens."

"Bitch better come through for me if I go."

21

"Well, that part of things, you'll have to handle for yourself. Can't help you there."

"I should plant a video camera in my hotel room. Tape us going at it. And then put it on the Net."

"Yeah, that's pretty classy."

"It may not be classy, Jason. But think back to how she treated us all those years. Lording it all over us. Running to Rawlins every time she was unhappy. Never speaking when she walked past. She wasn't real classy herself, when you think about it."

"No, she wasn't. But things are different now. You're famous. And rich."

"And handsome. I paid a lot of money for this face, man."

"I didn't want to mention your new face. You being so humble and all, I thought it might embarrass you."

He had the grace to laugh, anyway. "I laid the star trip on everybody pretty heavy this morning. Sorry, Jason. I really do consider you a friend."

I'm easily swayed. He probably didn't mean it, but it was damned decent of him to say it.

"Call her, David. And then tomorrow, I'll expect a full report."

"Lunch'll be on me again. And don't be surprised if I show up with a video."

After a conversation like that, the rest of the afternoon was pretty dull. But I'm a mule. Any time, any place there's work to be done, I do it. I just plug my brain in and proceed. Time goes a lot faster when you're working than when you're just watching the clock and waiting for the day to end.

I played racquetball after work, then went to Pizza Hut with Suki Zimmerman afterward. For nearly six months, Suki and I had lived together. We had both decided that it was time to get Serious about somebody. We were pretty much equally matched as to brains, interests, wit, and looks. And the sex was mighty fine. There was just one problem. We never fell in love. We kept expecting to wake up next to each other one fine sunny morn and be absolutely ga-ga over each other. But it never happened. That was a few years back. Between Serious Relationships, we still got together sometimes, which was one of the things I admired about both of us. We did our share of sleeping around, but we were faithful when we were involved with somebody. I hadn't cheated on her once when we'd lived together; I don't think she cheated once on me, either. That seems hard to come by these days.

The sex was always good and it certainly wasn't any different tonight. Very good, in fact. Afterward, we got sentimental about each other, but that ended when the phone rang and it was a woman I'd been seeing occasionally. Reminded Suki we'd moved on, I guess. She didn't stay over. She ran her own three-woman public relations agency these days. To keep the cash flow coming, she got to the office at seven a.m., six mornings a week. She wanted her own bed and her own shower.

She was just leaving when the phone rang again—"Popular guy," Suki said at the door—and Dulcy Tremont sobbed into my ear, "Somebody shot him, Jason! Somebody killed him!"

She didn't need to drop a name on me. I knew who she was talking about.

3

The national TV folks hit town before dawn. A number of producers phoned me at home to find out what I knew.

They seemed surprised I was asleep. Dulcy and I had ended up in a franchise restaurant pouring down hot coffee and going over all the details she'd gone over with them for more than three hours . . .

They'd turned the lights down in most sections of the nearly-empty restaurant. The few remaining customers didn't seem animated in any way. Like props or zombies. I wondered if the franchise made them put lifelike early-morning dummies in place to give an impression the restaurant was busy. But these were zombies designed by Edward Hopper. Not scary zombies—lonely ones.

Dulcy claimed she was convinced that the person who'd fired the shot from the darkness was some old enemy of Osborne's from his days on the newspaper. I was convinced that she was saying that because she didn't want to admit there was at least a chance that the killer had been Cal Rawlins. I mostly listened as she described her date with Osborne, a date that had gone well enough to conclude in a most passionate way on her stately couch in her stately living room. Osborne had been hoping for consummation. But she'd held off. Said why didn't they talk about it tomorrow night. She mentioned that four times in the three hours they'd been in her apartment the phone had rung. She'd picked up all three times. But then the caller had hung up immediately. She had Caller ID but the number had been blocked from the other end.

"I got tired. It wasn't that late—it was about what, eleven when I called you?—but I was tired and Cal wanted me to be at the Chamber of Commerce right at seven-thirty for this breakfast. So we decided we'd take up where we'd left off tomorrow night. Then he left. He was yawning. He said he was tired, too, all of a sudden. I'm not much for sleepovers, so I didn't ask him to stay. I assume you know all the stories about Cal and me. Well, there's no sense lying about them now. It's bound to come out. In fact, it already has. Chief Feller asked me—very tactfully, of course—if I might have a jealous boyfriend somewhere in the background. He meant Cal, of course, but he wouldn't say so. He's afraid of Cal. Just about everybody is. The newspaper can be a powerful weapon."

I said it. "Do you think it could have been Cal?"

She surprised me. "Oh, God, I'm trying not to think about that."

"Did he know about your date?"

She hesitated. "Maybe I shouldn't have done it."

"Done what?"

"Told him."

"So he did know?"

"I guess I just thought that it'd be worse if he found out about it from somebody else. Somebody was bound to see it and bring it up. David is big news. Was, I guess I should say. God, that sounds so unreal: 'was.' "

"Did you tell the police you told Cal?"

"I had to, didn't I?"

I couldn't help it. I smiled.

"I don't see anything funny here. Poor David is dead."

"It's not Dave. I'm sorry he's dead, too. It's Cal. He's such an arrogant bastard. I pity the cop who has to question him. Cal'll try to get the guy fired."

Even she had a brief smile for that one. "Cal at somebody else's mercy—I'd love to be there for that. He'll probably take out one of his guns and shoot the guy." Then, realizing the implication of what she'd just said: "I don't think he killed David. I really don't."

I looked up at the clock above the cash register. Nearly

four a.m. "Well, I need to get a little sleep, anyway."

"Me, too. I just hope I can sleep when I actually get to bed." She did something so unlike herself—or at least my impression of her—that I watched as if a miracle were unfolding before my eyes. It was a tiny little thing you see people do all the time. People. Not goddesses. She took a mincing bite out of a fingernail. And then spit with great tiny delicacy. The way a goddess would spit. "I wish they'd let you smoke in here. I'm going to ruin my fingernails."

"C'mon, let's get out of here anyway."

"Is it all right if I smoke in your car?"

"I guess I didn't know you smoked." I took her down a peg for smoking. It felt good. "But sure. You can smoke. Just roll the window down."

Cal Rawlins wasn't in yet, and it was already eleven. Work was getting done sporadically. It was difficult to concentrate when a story like David Osborne's murder was still breaking. The city desk had four reporters at the police station alone. I couldn't ever recall that happening before.

Dulcy wasn't in yet, either. I was working on a story about the prospect of a new sports center for the poorest side of town. It contained all the usual elements. Funding was the big problem, of course. The last two tax referendums had failed to pass. The prospects for this one looked grim. The yea and nay sides were predictable in their arguing. All these kids have to do is get on a bus and ride over to the west side, where there's a perfectly fine sports center. That perfectly fine sports center, said the yea side, was in fact eighteen miles away, on the farthest edge of the city limits, and was already overcrowded anyway. The yea side implied that there was an undertow of racism here, the nay side not caring if minority kids had a sports center or not. I sometimes got tired of the race issue being applied to so many issues, but here I thought it was appropriate. Just last year the nay side had started talking about a second sports facility being built on the west side due to the over-crowding. Pretty hard not to see racism at work in this particular case.

Dulcy got in at one thirty. She looked pale, even gaunt. She was perfectly groomed as always, but even that didn't help. She closed her office door immediately.

Rawlins got in at three o'clock. He set another Guinness record for door slamming. The entire floor seemed to tremble.

I was just picking up the phone to call a black minister involved in the steering committee for the proposed east side sports center, when a "Buddy" message came up on my screen. Simple message. *The Rendezvous at four thirty. D*

The Rendezvous was a bar out near the largest of our four shopping malls. It served food of a kind—not a good kind—and was basically a hang-out for mall employees. Because of the eighty-seven-degree heat, the owners had decided to see how close to winter the air conditioning could get. We sat in the back. Nobody knew who we were and nobody cared, except for the men trekking back and forth to the john back by the bumper pool table. Their eyes always got hung up on a glimpse of Dulcy. Even pale, she was a stunner.

She explained why she was late getting to the paper. "He came over about nine this morning. He told me that he'd been with his lawyer since six o'clock. He told me that I shouldn't mention to anybody that I'd told him about my date with David. He could see what I was thinking. He went out of his way to convince me that he didn't kill

David. And then he just came apart."

"That doesn't sound like Rawlins. The Great White Hunter coming apart?"

"You don't know about his family situation. His older brother Richard was supposed to take over the paper. That's what Cal's father wanted. Cal had cancer when he was small. Leukemia. Very few people know about that. He almost died, two or three times. His mother smothered him. Really overprotected him. She wouldn't let him go out for sports or hang out with any 'rough' kids or even go to summer camp. She was terrified that something would happen to him. So Cal's father thought he was a sissy. He used to make cracks sometimes that his wife had finally gotten the daughter she'd always wanted. He never even considered turning the paper over to Cal.

"But then the father died of a heart attack. Cal was at Yale when that happened. He changed a lot there. His roommate took him hunting and Cal loved it. He even started boxing. He loved that, too. He started womanizing and drinking and spending a lot of time in New York at the dance clubs. This was before AIDS, so the times were pretty wild. His mother was horrified, of course. She felt betrayed. She's a very melodramatic woman. She was always sending him these long, ranting letters. She even had him followed around by private detectives from time to time. One of them got hold of his medical records and found out that he'd gotten the clap twice. Cal laughed when he told me that. He said he could just imagine his mother's face when she found out about that. 'Absolutely stricken,' was how he put it: clutching her bosom and screaming for the maid to bring her a vodka tonic. Anyway, she saw that the only way he might settle down was to make him the publisher. She even had the proper young woman lined up for him to marry. Strictly Junior League, though the times I've met her—and believe it or not, Jason, I feel damned guilty about her—she seemed like a very bright, very decent woman. I feel sorry for her and so does Cal. She loves him very much. She knows about me now but still doesn't want a divorce. That part of it's very sad."

"When did you learn all this?"

"That's what we were doing all day. Sitting in my apartment, drinking pot after pot of straight coffee, talking about Cal's past. He's been publisher for eleven years now. His brother hasn't spoken to him in all that time."

"Is his brother in town?"

"Chicago. He's a very high-power corporate attorney. And Cal—" She frowned. "Cal has just now realized that all the drinking and hunting and running around—he's been trying to become the kind of man he thought his father would like."

"Is his brother that way?"

"Very much so. He's on marriage number three."

"Well, thanks a hell of a lot," I said.

That beautiful head of hers gave a tiny backwards jerk. She looked shocked at what I'd said.

"You've just managed to turn the guy I hate most in the world into a somewhat sympathetic human being. Cal had cancer? An overprotective mother? A macho jerk father? Now I can't even hate him anymore."

Her smile was radiant. "So you do have a heart, after all. You're so cynical and hardboiled all the time. And by the way, you've probably slept with half the girls who work at the paper. So you don't have any right to criticize Cal. Or even his brother."

"One difference, babe. I'm not married."

She shrugged. "Does that really matter these days? It

seems as if just about everybody I know is on marriage number two or three."

I could see what she was doing. Or not doing. She was avoiding the subject that had brought us together.

"You realize, of course, that Cal may have killed him."

"I know. He—cried. He was talking about everything—it was like this real long shrink session—and then he just started sobbing. Put his face in his hands. His whole upper body was shaking. I tried to comfort him but he was inconsolable. But when I was holding him that's all I could think about. Maybe this whole thing—telling me all about his past and all—was really a long roundabout way of working up to telling me that he'd killed David."

"Did he ever say that or even hint it?"

"No. But he did say that he was afraid that the police were looking at him very carefully. They found out about something that happened over in Dubuque one night. At this little jazz club there. Some jerk was really coming on to me. I was just trying to be polite to the guy, but Cal was so drunk he thought I was coming on right back. Before I could stop him, he grabbed the guy and took him out on the sidewalk and really beat him. Thank God I was sober. I took the guy to the ER and then convinced him that there'd be a sizeable check for him if he didn't go to the police. He got a couple teeth knocked out and a black eye. Could've been a lot worse. We worked out the financial arrangement and it was kept out of the news."

"So now the police know about it. And they've got proof that Cal is one very jealous dude."

"Exactly. That's what he's so scared about. He also feels terrible for what this will do to his family."

"Dear old Mom."

"Not her. His wife and kids. The kids are all in their

early teens. This kind of scandal'll be very hard on them. And he has genuine affection for his wife. He cares about her. He just kept saying, 'She sure doesn't deserve this,' over and over."

"So you think it's a possibility. All this talk we've had comes down to one thing. You think it's a possibility that Cal killed Dave."

She sighed. "I feel disloyal saying it, but yes, I do." Then: "And disloyal about one other thing, too, since I'm 'fessing up all this stuff. I plan to move to L.A. in two months. I woke up on my thirty-second birthday six months ago and saw what I was. A powerful man's mistress in a little, nowhere city, where I was just going to fade away if I didn't do something and pretty quickly. I've got a good voice. I probably could have made a living playing clubs in Chicago. I even got offered a CD contract. I met Cal at a club. When he found out that I was already working for a newspaper, he made me an offer. I couldn't make *that* kind of money playing clubs. I had a lot of college loans. Plus credit cards. So I took Cal up on his offer. I knew what his 'offer' really meant but I pretended it was just a regular job."

"Have you told Cal you're leaving?"

"No. And now," she said, "now I'm afraid to. He really loves me. I'm afraid of how he might react."

"The way he maybe reacted to you and Dave going out?"

"Exactly," she said.

4

The manila envelope was in my mailbox when I got back to my apartment. I happened to get there around six o'clock,

31

just when everybody else in my building arrived.

There were the usual conversations in the vestibule. The single men and women were discussing the evening that lay ahead, those who didn't have dates sighing that they'd have to settle for TV or catching up on their bills or just going to bed early after a long, hard week. The frenzied, single working mothers had collected their one-point-two children and were hustling upstairs for dinners that would come from freezers, cans, or boxes.

There were a few old people. They looked the most relaxed and comfortable. The sex wars and the raising children wars were behind them. They could look at the rest of us with a certain superiority; or with a certain melancholy, some of them probably missing the wars, especially the sex wars. Or simply missing youth itself. I'd be there myself someday.

Once inside my apartment, automatically clicking on the local TV news, I opened a bottle of beer and the manila envelope. Sitting there in an easy chair, I gradually began to lose all contact with the external world. I was completely involved in the loose pages inside the envelope.

Sheets of music. Everything had been hand-done in pen and pencil. There were erasures. There were even a few strike-overs. The pages were old enough to be yellowed along the edges. There were five songs. Each one of which had helped turn young Dave Osborne into the new Cole Porter or the new Jacques Brel or the new George Gershwin. Take your pick.

I was tired enough that I didn't get the significance of the yellowed, handwritten pages until I'd drained most of my beer. It came down to mathematics. Osborne had claimed to write most of his hit songs in a burst a few years ago. Yet these pages had to be at least ten years old. Maybe even fifteen. Osborne would have still been in high school. Or maybe even junior high.

There was no return address on the envelope. No letter or note inside. My first impulse was to call Dulcy. I always kept my trusty cell next to me on the chair. Reporters get calls 24/7. I started to punch in the numbers but stopped myself. What if Cal Rawlins was there when I called? I needed my job. I had all sorts of daydreams about having the same kind of success Osborne had had. But in the meantime, I needed to eat the same kind of freezer meals those single mothers served their little ones every night.

I went through the sheets again. This time I noticed it. Just a pair of tiny initials in the upper right-hand corner on one of the back pages: SR. Once again, it took me a while. I watched some tepid TV entertainment show filled with grinning robots and endless, noisy commercials. And I was fixing my eyes on a particularly fetching pair of real breasts (they sure did look real, anyway, but then maybe plastic surgeons were finally learning subtlety or there was a shortage of silicone), I made sense of the initials.

SR. Sam Reed. The man who'd mistakenly killed his girlfriend while aiming at Osborne. Why were his initials on a song that Osborne had written? Or was I missing the point? Why had Osborne claimed to have written a song that had been written long ago and had Reed's initials on it?

I tried Dulcy's home number. Got the machine. Tried her office number. Got the machine. It was difficult to just sit there and stare at the pages in front of me. I needed to talk to somebody about all this. I examined the envelope three different times, looking for any clue as to who had sent it. None. My name and address in ballpoint pen. Three stamps. Local postmark. No other clue.

I tried reading, watching TV, reading again. Didn't

work. Too fixed on the envelope and what it might mean. Not only was it some sort of challenge to the authorship of Osborne's songs, it might even bear on who'd killed Osborne. And why.

I called Dulcy three more times before deciding to try and sleep. I didn't want to leave a message, in case Rawlins came in with her.

A few minutes after I settled into bed with a paperback, the phone rang. I snapped up and grabbed the receiver.

"I sent you an envelope. You should've gotten it today." Woman's voice. Middle-aged. No hello. No name.

"Yes. I did get it."

"He didn't write them songs. That friend of yours."

"I need to know who I'm talking to here."

There was a long pause. "My husband had some trouble with the law down South. This was a long time ago."

"He jump bail?"

Another long pause. "Yes."

"What was he charged with?"

"Armed robbery. But nobody was hurt."

Though she was reluctant to say much, her words sounded truthful. If her husband had killed somebody, I'd feel bound to turn him over. If I got a name from her, I'd run a check on the last name anyway.

"Why do you care?" she said.

"Just trying to figure out who I'm dealing with."

"Sam Reed was my husband's cousin."

"I see."

"Fifteen years ago, when he first come to Chicago, he stayed with us. We had a nice house. Got the basement all fixed up for him. He had his piano down there. He wanted to be a songwriter but he never had nerve enough to play anybody his songs. Which was kinda funny, him bein' arrogant and all. Me and the mister always told him he should play his songs for somebody but he never did. Only reason we'd heard 'em was because he was right downstairs. You know what I mean?"

"Yes."

"So after a while, he got to be such a well-known musician, he quit writing songs." Another pause. "What happened was he got to be a cokehead. And then he got involved with that damned girl. That Eve. She couldn't handle his coke thing. She was always breakin' up with him. Made him crazy."

She'd tried to make Eve sound unsympathetic. But living with a junkie wasn't easy.

"He started getting crazy jealous. That's what happened with your friend. Osborne. Sam thought they was getting it on. That's why he tried to kill him. But he killed her by mistake."

"You say Osborne took his songs."

She laughed bitterly. "You afraid to say the word?"

"What word?"

"What word? He stole 'em, man. He didn't just 'take' them. He stole them. He tried to buddy up to us while he was writing all his articles for the newspaper and then for his book. He wanted us to give him Sam's personal things to look through. But we wouldn't. About a month after he started bothering us, we went on vacation. My folks have a little house out near Phoenix. We stayed there a couple of weeks. When we came back, we knew right away something was wrong. Somebody'd been in here. In the basement, I mean. Where Sam was still living. He was getting so bad off on dope, he needed somebody to take care of him. We took care of him, my husband and me."

"Things were missing?"

"Not missing—just not where they'd been. He must've

forgotten where things belonged exactly."

"Did he take the songs?"

"No. But later on we figured out what he did do. He Xeroxed them. There were a lot more songs, too. He was probably going to release them one at a time, so it'd look like he was writing them fresh. He must've known how good the songs were, even if Sam hadn't had no confidence in them. And then Osborne starts playin' them in clubs around here."

"You're calling from Chicago, right?"

"Right. So Osborne plays them around here and then all of a sudden he's this big star. He's on the tube all the time. He's in *People* magazine. His CDs are selling big-time. And there's nothing we can do about it."

"Why not?"

"He checked us out. Found out my husband was still wanted. He knew we wouldn't come forward, couldn't. Same with Sam. Nothin' Sam could do, either. He's still out there hiding someplace. And no, I don't know where he is. He calls every once in a while, but just to say hi. From a pay phone. Which is how I'm calling you. The FBI has our phone tapped, for sure."

I asked the most logical question of all. "So why're you coming forward now?"

"Because Osborne's dead. Because now's the time to tell the truth. As long as our names aren't involved. Sam isn't any sterling character, but he should at least get credit for the songs he's written. You just leave our names out of it. You've got the originals now. Write your story about Sam. You can maybe even get a book out of it." Then: "I gotta go."

And go she did.

I sat there not knowing what to do. Sam Reed, killer and songwriter. David Osborne, jazz composer wanna-be and fraud. Big-time fraud.

I went uselessly to bed, taking two big shots of whiskey with me. I even smoked a joint, so Mr. Sleep would appear sooner. I smoke maybe three or four joints a year and always for the same reason—to relax enough to fall asleep. A recreational pot smoker, I'm not. Disorientation is not one of my favorite experiences.

It was odd what I did first thing next morning. I sat at my portable electric piano, playing two of the songs Osborne hadn't gotten around to introducing yet. I liked them even more than the ones he'd been celebrated for. Both of them had the feeling of "Laura," which happens to be my all-time favorite song, whether done by Charlie Parker or Frank Sinatra or Chet Baker. That melancholy, tender, aching feeling that comes especially on lonely Saturday nights when you walk the neon streets, looking not just for any woman but *the* woman. You don't think of killers as having tender moments. But obviously Reed had them. His songs had the power to devastate me. Especially those two new ones.

As my fingers played the notes, I imagined that they were *my* notes, *my* lyrics. I imagined what it must have been like for Osborne. All that fame and adulation. Maybe by the end he'd convinced himself that they really were his songs. Maybe by the end he'd driven Reed from his mind entirely. He had all these other songs to draw on. He had had an entire career ahead of him.

5

"You're late."

She said it in a nasty way. I hadn't had enough sleep. I was irritable.

"You're forgetting something," I said as I slid into the Perkins booth across from her.

"What's that?"

"You don't get to be a bitch anymore. At least not around me. We're sort of partners in this thing. Whatever the hell it is. So knock off the crap."

"And good morning to you, Mr. Manning."

And then brought her menu up to cover her face and disappear.

We didn't talk for the first ten minutes. The waitress could sense it. She kept looking back and forth between us, the way people watch a tennis match. She took our orders and left.

"I'm sorry I called so early."

"I was up anyway, actually." Then I said: "Sorry I was so bitchy when I came in."

"I was bitchy, too." She smiled. "Face it. I *am* a bitch. My father spoiled me when I was a girl and a number of men have spoiled me since I grew up." She laughed. "And I want them to keep right on doing it."

"So how's good old Cal?"

"Good old Cal is ready for electro-shock. He doesn't have an alibi. But even if the police find the real killer, his whole life is going to be spread all over everywhere. He's always taken shots at the Chicago papers, how we're actually a better paper because we're not beholden to 'special interest groups,' as he says."

"That's a crock and always has been. His delusion. The *Trib* and the *Sun-Times* are about a thousand times better than we are. And I don't know what 'special interests' he's talking about. His family owns half this town and he runs the newspaper. If that isn't a special interest, I don't know what it is."

"Believe it or not, he's worried about his family, Jason. He may be every bit as bad as you say, but he does care about his wife and children. He really does."

It was kind of funny sitting there and talking to her in the lemon-colored morning sunlight of an early workday, the coffee smells so good, nearly everybody's face still a little pinched from sleepiness, God turning the celestial crank to get the town going for another day. Sitting there, I realized that for the first time, I liked her. It was a testament to gonadic truth that I could feel such profound lust for her for such a long time without every really caring for her. But this morning, now that we'd both gotten through our usual bitchiness, I saw an aspect of her that I liked. Actually liked.

So I told her about the manila envelope and the woman who'd called me last night. What I didn't tell her about were the extra songs.

When I finished, she said, "Wow. What a story this is going to make."

"It sure is."

"You might even get a book out of it. The same way David did."

"I know. That would be really nice. I'd have some money for a change. Maybe I could even start selling books on the side. That's all I ever wanted to be anyway. A writer of some kind. Didn't matter much what kind, either. I just liked being a 'writer.' That's why I got into newspapering. Closest I could get to it. Being a reporter, I mean."

"Is that why you got up so early? Have you already started writing the story?" Then: "If I fixed you a very nice dinner—and I'm a good cook, I really am—do you suppose you'd let me break it in the magazine? People never think of a magazine section having a news scoop. We'd probably

39

have to double the number of pages just to have run for all the extra ads. We could warn the advertising department that the magazine was going to carry the most important breaking news of the whole year."

"Sure. The magazine. That would be very nice. I could kind of get the whole story down in general, to show it to a book publisher."

"Thank you. I really appreciate it."

She didn't seem to notice that there wasn't much enthusiasm in my voice for any of this. Which was good because that meant she hadn't guessed the thoughts I was having. If Dave Osborne had been able to pass those songs off as his own . . . why couldn't I pass of the remaining songs as *my* own? Make it sound as if I'd been writing songs with Dave as my mentor, which is why the songs might be a bit like his. Who could object? Certainly not Sam Reed, who was still running for his life. Certainly not the woman who'd called, her husband being wanted in the South. And certainly not Dulcy, who didn't know the songs even existed.

This time, I made sure to sound pleased with her ideas.

"Do I get to choose the dinner you make?"

She gleamed, she beamed. "Oh, it'll be so great. I'll be able to use this whole thing when I move to L.A. On job interviews, I mean. Show them the scoop I came up with, thanks to my good friend Jason Manning, who is now about to become a published author."

"Writer. Not author."

"What's the difference?"

"Oh, I just think of an author as some dusty old guy they make you read in high school. You know, Victor Hugo or whoever wrote *Silas Marner.*"

"Yuck. *Silas Marner.*"

"See, that's exactly what I mean. 'Writer' sounds a

lot more vital. Contemporary."

"Jason Manning, writer." That wonderful smile. "I guess I can see what you mean."

I paid for the bill at the cash register and left a thirty percent tip on our table. As we were walking out, Dulcy took my arm and slid it through hers, guiding it so that it brushed lovingly against her breast. Did I dare imagine that this dinner she was talking about would also include a very special dessert?

I spent the entire day trying to see Cal Rawlins. No luck. I couldn't get within ten yards of his secretary's desk. She'd never cared much for me, anyway. She shared Cal's attitude that the newsroom people were at best flunkies, and at worst a subspecies that smelled rank and terrible. All she did was shake her head. She did it quickly, curtly, so as to enhance the dismissiveness of it. Which would send me scuttling back to my desk.

Lawyers came, lawyers went. They were the only ones permitted into Rawlins' inner sanctum. At least there weren't any cops to make the story even juicier for the newsroom. Midafternoon, worn out from speculating on would he or wouldn't he be arrested, somebody wondered aloud what would happen once Cal's affair came out with Dulcy. Would that force him to resign? Who would take over the paper? Would it be his mean brother? And if it was his mean brother, would everybody presently working here be fired and replaced with people Mean Brother had personally selected?

Here's how it works. How it works in offices of every kind in every country of the civilized world. Cal's resignation becomes speculation. *Would he really resign?* Then it becomes gossip. *Of course he would really resign. In fact, it was*

now known that he had discussed resigning this very morning.
And then speculation and gossip become hard fact. *He secretly resigned at three this afternoon and has now surrendered to
the police for the murder of David Osborne.*

By late afternoon, it was said, all over the building—in
the newsroom, coffee rooms, meeting rooms, and even
above the roar of the presses—that within two hours Mean
Brother would be landing in a black helicopter on the roof
of the building and that the entire existing staff would be
gassed by men in radiation-style suits.

Finally, the gossip getting crazier and crazier, I knocked
on Dulcy's door. A muffled word or two on the other side
of the door caused me to turn the knob and walk in. Dulcy
was smoking a cigarette in a violently No Smoking building.

As soon as I closed the door, she said, "Have you heard
all the crazy stories that are going around in this place?"

I smiled. "Cal was electrocuted by lethal injection
twenty minutes ago."

"God," she said, taking a deep, quick hit on her cigarette, "I'm sure somebody's actually saying that by now.
These are supposed to be intelligent people. They *are* intelligent people. How can they *say* all this crap?"

"Because they're scared. People like security. This is a
very insecure time. Especially for the people with families to
support."

"Poor Joyce Lafferty," she said. "Four kids."

"And Paul Arnold. Leukemia. What happens if he loses
his insurance?"

She sighed. Nodded for me to sit down.

After I sat, she said, "He called me from his cell. Cal. He
was sitting in his car. He had a gun with him. He said he
was thinking of killing himself."

"I knew *something* good had to come of this."

"That's not funny, Jason. You keep insisting he's this really bad guy. Which, I'll grant you, he is in many respects. But he's not *all* bad. He really does care what happens when all this comes out on the news tonight."

"Chicago news?"

"He got a tip from somebody. Six o'clock news. Lead story. Respectable newspaper publisher outed as unfaithful husband. I saw a van parked across the street when I left for lunch. No logo. But a porthole. I'm sure they were shooting video of me. They'll probably super a big A across my chest, just to let people know who the scarlet woman is."

"You don't really think he'll kill himself, do you?"

She smirked. "So, there is a little humanity left in you after all."

"Just that I want to see him alive. To suffer."

"Just admit it, Jason. You don't want to see him kill himself."

I shrugged. "I guess you're right. I hate him, but not that much."

"Anyway, it's four o'clock. I'm going home now to start drinking martinis. I want to be good and soaked before the six o'clock news comes on. And then I'm going to unplug my phone and put the cell in the linen closet, so I can't hear it ring. Because dear old father from dear old Oak Park will be calling me to see if his daughter is really the other woman the way they said on TV. My dear old father will be at his girlfriend's apartment—after telling my mother that he has to work late—and when he sees the news, he might go into cardiac arrest, his heart having survived two different attacks in the last four years. At which point my goody-goody country club sister will lead a lynch mob of her friends to my apartment. They'll all be holding torches like in that old Frankenstein movie—and shouting for me to be burned at the stake." She stabbed out her cigarette.

"This'll just make my news story all the better."

She glared at me. "You know, Jason, earlier today I thought you and I might wind up in bed some wintry night. But now I know that's never going to happen. Now get the hell out of my office."

The gossip kept on coming. Cops had searched Rawlins' house, hunting cabin, and three classic cars last night. The police were looking for the murder weapon. Turned out Osborne had been killed with a rare variant on the standard .45 caliber handgun. Most of the hysteria was kept in check now. Nobody was talking about Mean Brother or mass firings. They were back to bitching about the usual things: salaries, expense accounts, other reporters not present, and the diminishing number of available parking spaces in the city lot most of us had to use.

It was funny. Despite the mood all around me, I kept humming the melodies of the two songs I'd taken to the piano this morning. Even in the grind of the workday, they lingered melancholy and romantic in my mind.

I had a trashy tabloid fantasy. Me on the arm of some beautiful starlet beneath the headline: "Brooding, handsome composer searches for the 'mystery woman' of his songs." I felt duly ashamed of myself, of course. But I wondered if you ever got so old that you didn't have fantasies like these. Maybe there were people so content with their lot, so absolutely fixed to reality, that they didn't need these kinds of fantasies. They might dream of a new riding mower, a new plasma TV set, a new Chevrolet. But they'd never be callow or silly enough to dream of fame. Maybe there really were people like that.

I was eager to have the workday over with.

★ ★ ★ ★ ★

Just before quitting time, Rawlins called a surprise meeting. He addressed the entire newsroom. You could see that it had all worn him out. It had also beaten the arrogance out of him. His voice, relative to his usual slavemaster bellow, was gentle and soft.

He said, "I'm going to sound like Richard Nixon did when he said, 'You need to know that your president is not a crook.' Well, you need to know that your publisher is not a killer. And I hope the police will be able to prove that very soon. But even if I'm not a killer, I'm not a very good man. I've destroyed a marriage, I've been pretty damned callous as a boss, and I've never been properly grateful for everything the good Lord has given me. I'm hoping I can save my marriage. And I'm hoping I can save my reputation here in the newsroom. You people have a lot to teach me. You're the professionals here, not me. I sit in my office and play at being publisher. But I couldn't report a story or take a photo or transcribe an interview if my life depended on it. I'm going to try and change these things. I'm also going to try and be a better man as a boss. I'll never be a touchy-feely sort of guy, that's just not my nature. But I sure as hell can keep my door open to any of you who want to come in and talk. And I sure as hell can be a lot more sympathetic to you folks as people and as employees."

He just stopped, as if his internal word machine was suddenly empty. There was a very long silence and then the applause started, light at first but then heavier and heavier, so much so that at its peak it was louder than I would have thought possible. Men and women alike had tears on their cheeks. It wasn't that he'd been all that eloquent. It was that he'd been that honest. Maybe he'd go back to being a bastard if and when the police found the real killer. But at the moment, that didn't matter. He had humbled himself. But it hadn't been a showy humility. It had been simple and believable and therefore moving. I'd never liked him much, but between what Dulcy had told me about him and what I'd just seen and heard, I had to allow him membership in the human race. Which was damned big of me, I thought.

"If I get done early enough, how about I stop by with Chinese for dinner?" Dulcy said as we walked back toward my desk.

"I can see you're deeply moved by his little speech there."

She leaned close to me. Smelled wonderful. Her cologne. Felt wonderful. Her breast. "I told you he wasn't as bad as you think." She held me even tighter. "And I'm sorry I said that about saying you and I won't ever wind up in bed together." She laughed. "Who knows?"

By the time I got home, I was almost ready to call Dulcy and say let's make it another night. It was a night for Domino's, a couple of cold brews, and watching a little telly in my boxers. I wasn't even daydreaming about being a famous songwriter any more. I just wanted to hang out with myself and go to bed early. I was drained.

I had just closed and locked the door of my apartment, and was about to hang my suit coat in the front closet, when I heard it. Sometimes odd sounds identify themselves readily; other times you have to guess what they are. This was the former. The unmistakable noise a bureau drawer makes when it's being closed with no particular finesse.

About two seconds after I heard it, I walked right into the coffee table in front of the couch. That made a louder sound than closing the bureau drawer did.

Somebody was in my apartment, somebody who hadn't

heard me come in apparently, but who now knew for sure that I was home.

I wasn't feeling brave. What I decided to do was get to the door, run down the hall to the stairs, and then get outside. The intruder had only two ways to get out. He could take the same path I did, or he could climb out the bedroom window and go down the fire escape.

About the time I was punching in numbers on my cell, he'd be escaping. But so be it. That was better than confronting him, whoever he was.

But before I got three steps toward the front door, I found out who he was.

He came out of the bedroom with a .45 in his hand. I'm no gun expert but the paper runs a syndicated gun column once a month. When I run out of other stuff to read in the john, I turn to the gun column. The only thing left after that is Religious News.

He wore a white button-down shirt and chinos. His blonde hair, graying at the edges now, was expensively cut. There was something private school about him. But then there always had been. It had always made him stand out in the Chicago jazz clubs where I listened to him play. He'd been damned good. I hoped he wasn't as good with a gun as he was a horn.

"Hi, Sam. You probably don't remember me."

"Sure, I do, Manning. You were always in the clubs with Osborne. Sniffing around all those chicks who used to laugh at you."

"You just talked yourself out of an invitation to my next birthday party."

"Shut up and give me the music."

"What music?"

I was coy because I didn't know what else to be. Facing the gun put me into a state of denial. If I kept things light, the gun might not actually come into play. But I knew I couldn't stay coy long. My bowels were doing terrible things and my right hand was twitching.

He started walking toward me. "I killed your friend Osborne. And I'll be happy to kill you, too." He shook his head as if in pity. "He was so lame he had to steal my material. I suppose you've got the same thing in mind. But it's not going to happen because you're going to turn those songs over right now."

He moved so fast, so unexpectedly, I didn't have a chance to ready myself. He grabbed me by the wrist and flung me up against the apartment door.

I slammed my head so hard I acted on instinct. I cracked him hard across the jaw with my right fist. My knee was coming up hard when he pounded me on the jaw with the barrel. That opened a painful wound, a wound that shut me down at least temporarily.

"Where the hell's that music?"

"In the closet."

"I looked in the closet."

"It's under the rug. In a hiding place. You have to know where to look."

He poked the muzzle of the .45 into my forehead. "Then we'll go get it. And right now."

As he yanked me away from the door, using my wrist again, I thought I heard some faint noise, but then I didn't have any time to figure out what it was because he was shoving me across the living room toward the bedroom.

"I worked hard on those songs," he said, "and that schmuck friend of yours gets all the credit. He wins a Grammy. A Grammy—on my work."

He was talking to himself more than he was to me. The words were familiar to him. I'll bet he'd said them to himself a thousand times over the years he was running: seeing Osborne on TV, hearing him on the radio, staring up at his banner in music departments. But he couldn't come forward, of course. Not ever.

I wanted another crack at him. Either my pride or my death wish had kicked in. I was assuming he was going to kill me. The thought was so overwhelming I couldn't deal with it. The only thing I could cling to was the hope that I'd get my hands on him. I wasn't tough, but I was tougher than he was.

He pushed me into the walk-in closet, so that I scraped my head against the doorframe. That only increased my now unreasoning need to hurt him. Really hurt him.

There was no sense in trying to deceive or dissuade him in any way. Not even any reason to stall. He wanted his songs. He would have his songs. "I have to take my keys out of my trouser pocket," I said, down on my hands and knees in the far corner of the closet. I'd pushed all the clothes back in the other direction, so finding the hidey hole wouldn't be any problem.

"Why?"

"I use a key to pull up the carpet edge."

"Just watch what you do. You understand?"

That wasn't worth answering. I took my keys out slowly and with great delicacy. I even held them up for him to see. "Keys. No reason to get excited."

"Just get the songs."

The carpet lies flat against the wall. A knife can pull it up easily. Below the carpet there is a trap-door-like compartment the size of a hardcover book. It runs twice that length inside.

"This could be a set-up," he said. "Maybe you've got a gun down there."

"Yeah. Or a tank."

By this time I'd guessed that his state of extreme agitation owed to a cocaine addiction that wasn't working out very well at the moment.

"Just calm down, all right? There's no gun, there's no knife, there's not even a rock. It's just a place to put valuables. So don't start shooting yet, all right? At least let me get the songs out first."

The denial state was wearing off. I was sweating so much that drops were standing on my face, as well as my arms and chest and legs. He was going to kill me. I'd never been up against that particular fear before and wasn't quite sure what to do. I knew that in a few minutes I'd start begging for my life. All the smart-guy patter had left me. I didn't want to beg but I would.

Actually retrieving the songs was anti-climactic. I unhinged the trapdoor. I pulled it up. I reached down inside. I felt the papers. I gripped them. I lifted them up.

He snapped them out of my hand before I could turn around and hand them to him. "Even if you copy them, it won't matter. I have the originals. I can prove I wrote them. I don't give a damn about royalties. I just want the credit I deserve."

"If you contact anybody, the cops'll be able to track you."

"No, they won't. Not if I use a lawyer to verify how old these pages are. And not if the lawyer makes the presentation to the right people. He can tell them where I was. But I'll be long gone before the cops can find me. Now get up and go over to that bed and lie face down."

I struggled to my feet, trying to avoid cracking my head against the clothes bar. I got turned around and walked out of the closet.

At first I didn't realize the significance of him having me

lie down. Maybe he'd just bind and gag me, leave me for the super to find me sometime.

But as my knees came in contact with the mattress, I glanced at the pillows at the head of the bed and knew what he had in mind. The pillows would absorb the noise of the gunshots. The bedroom window opened on the fire escape. Simple. He'd be gone seconds after shooting me.

He hit me so hard across the back of the head that I was unconscious for a few moments there. I wasn't completely conscious when I felt the pillows being slapped across my shoulders and neck. The jab of the barrel against my skull jolted me. He was going to do just what I'd imagined. Execute me, the pillows muffling the noise.

I wish I could tell you exactly what happened next. But I was face down, two pillows covered the back of my head, and my ears were still ringing painfully from where he'd struck me with the gun.

A familiar voice shouted: "Reed! Leave him alone!"

And then Reed started swearing. The pressure from his hand on the pillow vanished. And then two guns started blasting away.

All the stuff you hear on the screen, this was nothing like it. The gunshots don't thunder, they bark. And they come so hard and fast, they sound like they're spitting. And they smell. And there's so much clamor between the cursing and the screaming that it's impossible to make even a good guess at what's going on—without seeing it, I mean.

Then it was done. I heard a body hit the floor. A heavy, ugly noise.

I flung the pillows from the back of my head and jerked myself to my feet. And there she was in the doorway. Slumped against it, as if totally exhausted. For a long moment, the gun dangled from her fingers, then she let it drop to the floor.

51

The one and only Dulcy Tremont.

"I went downstairs and got the super to give me the key. I'd been at the door, listening to it all. I brought the Chinese over which, by the way, is getting cold in the hallway. I called the cops on my cell. Listen—you can hear the sirens now. But I was afraid he'd kill you by the time they got here. So I came in and—"

She nodded to the man on the floor. She'd shot him twice in the head. He wasn't pretty anymore. The odd thing was that even in death, though, he looked arrogant. That isn't real easy to do.

And then the cops were piling up the stairs, shouting. And she was falling into my arms, crying. And everything was crazy in the most exciting way of my life.

6

"Ever sleep with her?"

"Nah."

"Ever come close?"

"Not really."

"But you went out with her?"

"Well, it's kind've a long story. Kinda personal, too."

"Man, she is some beautiful chick. And she can sing, too. And those songs she writes—"

I didn't know his name. I never knew any of their names. But when I'd be in one of the jazz clubs in Chicago, the bartender would invariably tell the guy on the bar stool next to me that I'd known the one and only Dulcy Tremont.

Tonight we all had a special treat. She was on Jay Leno. Two songs. Sam Reed's songs, of course.

This place had one of those huge screens. She looked so

impeccably beautiful all I could think of was Grace Kelly at the exact peak of her beauty.

In all the confusion in my apartment after the shoot-out, I didn't see her take the songs. Didn't even really think about them until the next morning. I hadn't mentioned them to the cops. I'd told them Reed had it in for me because he thought I'd slept with his girlfriend, too, the way he'd thought Osborne had.

So when I called her apartment and got no answer, I went to work expecting to find her there. But her secretary told me that she'd quit. That she'd given the police all the information they'd needed. She'd also given them her sister's address in Los Angeles. The secretary said it wasn't very far from Malibu.

That was a year-and-a-half ago.

You probably thought you had this ending figured out. You know, all nice and pat. Dulcy and I hand over the songs, good citizens that we are; and then start an office romance at the paper, which is now resided over by a happily-married Cal Rawlins; and then find a nice little starter house for ourselves somewhere on the edge of the boonies and then fill her tummy with the first of two or three kids.

That's what I figured, too. I called her somewhere around a hundred times the first three months she was staying with her sister. I even flew out there. But within twenty-fours she got a judge to issue a restraining order against me.

As I say, that was a year-and-a-half ago. Next month, we'll see if she wins any of the four Grammys she's up for. And in the fall, we'll see how good her acting skills are. She's got the third lead in a Julia Roberts picture. The tabloids call her "Demolition Dulcy," because of all the homes and hearts she's wrecked. Her fans seem to love the imperious side of her nature. They're very forgiving of her ways and wiles.

"Maybe you should go out and visit her some time," the guy next to me said. "Maybe she'd take you to some of those Hollywood parties."

"Yeah," I said. "Those Hollywood parties."

Then he clapped me on the back. God, I hate being clapped on the back. "And who knows, you go out there and spend a little time with her, maybe you'll finally get lucky and get in her knickers."

7

The legal charge was assault and battery. Cost me $500 and a night in the drunk tank. His dental bill was another $1000. But it was worth it. Well worth it. I really hate getting clapped on the back that way.

Riff

Just before dawn, I wake up and listen to the hushed sounds from the room next to mine. When I hear these particular sounds at this particular time on a cancer floor in a hospital—three or four rushed whispering voices; faint squeaks of gurney wheels; and then elevator doors opening down the hall, eight floors down to the basement and the morgue—I know what's happened.

Charlie Grady died. I'd see him a couple times a day on my little walks up and down the hall. The nurses don't make me walk. I do it on my own.

I sort of knew Charlie wasn't going to hang on much longer. His wife was talking to a hospice woman, but I figured Charlie wouldn't make it even that long. He was a nice old guy, real estate rich, never asking me the standard questions I get about my so-called fame. In fact, he said right-out one day that he didn't care much for jazz. And he hoped that didn't offend me. His kind of money can give you that kind of confidence. He didn't give a damn if it offended me or not.

His wife is a weeper. She came twice a day to see him—his lung cancer and his eighty pounds overweight were shaping up to bring on one massive heart attack—and she never left but she was wailing. I sure don't blame her. She loves her man. But that doesn't make it any easier to take when you're in the room next door and trying to deal with your own problems. Health-wise, I mean. And every-other-wise, for that matter.

I have a 7:00 a.m. visitor, right after the doc making his rounds leaves my room. Guy named Larry Donnelly. Kind of a fix-it guy for jazz folk. Very serious jazz cat, Larry is. Really got into it in the slam, where he served ten years for torching a building with a janitor still in it. Larry had no idea, of course. I called Larry a couple of days ago, asked him to stop up. He hesitates in the doorway now. Some people get like that about cancer. Scared. Like it's a plague you can pick up. "C'mon in, Larry."

He's only there ten minutes. And is kind of junkie-twitchy all the time. Can probably feel the cancer working its way through his veins as he stands there trembling. Then he's gone.

I fall back asleep and wake up for a second time. This time it's the nurse with the rattling breakfast cart. They keep telling me to eat, but my appetite has gone with all the rest of it. I'm in pretty much the same shape as Charlie Grady was. Except mine's in the pancreas. I'm hoping I'm as lucky as Charlie. A heart attack like that, you're one lucky man. And so are your loved ones. Quick and clean. Instead of hanging on.

Hanging on.

That's what I've done with my wife Karen the last five years. Met her in a jazz club in Chicago. She was a singer, then. Not much of one. But she had the Look. That slender body, that melancholy face, the dark eyes, the tumbling dark hair. She was from Omaha but she made you think international. Paris in spring, where I gigged with Brubeck. And London in autumn, where I gigged with Miles. Milan, baking in the summer while we were working on my live album. I dumped wife number four for her, just as I'd dumped all the old ones for new ones. I never said I was proud of myself. But you get on the road, you're six, seven months out from seeing the wife and the kiddies, you're just naturally going to fall in love with somebody else.

What I didn't know that night in Chicago was that it was payback time. I'm sitting in the back of this tiny, drafty club and people are coming up asking for my autograph and, if she isn't singing, they ask me did I dig playing with Brubeck, was Miles as much of a diva prick as people said, was my label ever going to do a box set of my music—and hey, that was one fine article in *Time*, "The Legend of the Saddest Sax in Jazz History: Mike Thorne." It was actually the usual thing, that *Time* piece, how I'd managed to survive and prosper in a music world dominated by rock and rap, and how I was the Chet Baker of my time—handsome, media-friendly, and probably the best sax man of the past two decades. Thank God, the article concluded, that I never got hooked on junk the way poor Chet had. You read about Chet, man, and you want to cut your wrists.

So, I'm sitting there trying to be nice to the people who come up, but I'm paying more and more serious attention to this singer Karen Miller. The clarity of her beauty is astonishing.

Between her sets, I ask her over to my table for a drink. I can see how flustered she is. Mike Thorne, fifty-three-year-old jazz legend, asking a twenty-two-year-old nobody to have a drink with him.

I get to play the cool dude that night. I'm properly humble when she's flattering me, I'm properly appreciative when we talk about her own performance, and I'm properly matter-of-fact when I drop some big jazz names I'm meeting later that night for drinks. What I am really is so smitten I'm like I was at the tenth-grade dance when I could never quite work up nerve enough to ask Marietta

Courtney to dance slow with me.

But that wasn't what was really going on at all. Subtext they call it. You know, where it seems like you're really saying this but you're really saying that, just below the surface.

What I was really doing was setting myself up for payback. For every time I'd ever cheated on a woman, for every promise I'd broken to my three daughters, for every heartbreak I'd caused—old numero uno was about to get his. Maybe this Karen Miller from Omaha couldn't sing worth a damn. But she sure knew how to lie, cheat, steal, betray, and humiliate you.

If there is a Green Beret unit of heartbreakers and ballbusters, Karen Leigh Miller of Omaha, Nebraska was Commander-in-Chief.

Thirty-eight years I play clubs. When I'm in my prime, I'm hitting Letterman and Leno and guest-playing on albums by big rock stars who want the cachet of having a jazz star on their CD. They don't know diddly about jazz, but they think it sounds cool to the reviewers.

This is when I start collecting jazz memorabilia. I'm in places where Satchmo and Charlie Parker and Gerry Mulligan and people like that have played, and so I start buying up things they left behind in the clubs and that the club owners might otherwise throw out in a box in the back.

This is also the time I get the critics on my back for playing Vegas. Just once, for God's sake. I don't have a right to make a fucking living? I can't take the scorn. A serious jazz musician playing Vegas as the opening act for some jiggle-titted TV star who thinks she can sing? Karen digs it, of course. Me being in Vegas. While I'm on stage, she's sitting at a table out front with Cameron Diaz and

Bruce Willis, who are in town shooting a picture together. Your regular jazz clubs—the kind I usually play in—you don't get Cameron Diaz and Bruce Willis, let me tell you.

Sam Caine is with them, too. Sam is my agent and manager. I met him twenty years ago when he was just one of the many hungry young men you see running up and down the halls of William Morris in search of clients who might have stumbled and fallen and would appreciate the hungry young man who helped pick them up.

Sam was then the assistant to my agent. By the time I decide to do a lot of my own bookings, Sam was a full-fledged agent who is just about to open up a small shop of his own. He wants clients, I'm sick of big agencies. I handle most of the small gigs; he books the big ones. He's a failed actor, our Sam. You always hear about how many beautiful, failed wanna-be actresses there are in Hollywood. There are an equal number of beautiful, failed wanna-be actors.

Sam has no interest in jazz. He's a club lizard. If you can't hustle chicks while it's being played, Sam doesn't want to hear it. But he's funny and shrewd and gets me bookings I couldn't get for myself.

The years go by, my CDs aren't selling the way they used to, Letterman and Leno's people don't return Sam's calls, and you know what? By now, I don't care. I'm married to Karen.

The fourth year of our marriage, I learn three things.

1) Karen has spent most of the nearly two million dollars that was for my retirement. You should see our house, our cars, her clothes. It sounds like a joke, but two million isn't what it used to be. My accountant keeps saying you gotta do something about this, Mike. But I never do. I'm scared she'll leave me. That started the second year, the way she'd get whatever she wanted by saying, just kind of off-handed,

"I've gotta be honest, Mike. Sometimes, I wonder if we did the right thing." And of course I'd give in and say, sure, baby, buy whatever you want. She went right straight through my money.

2) I find a note that she threw away in the tiny basket next to her dressing table—you could land a fighter jet on that table; an aircraft carrier should be so lucky to have that room—and right away I see what it says. And right away I recognize the handwriting. Now, I know she's had little nights when she's strayed. A couple of her boys got so hot for her they even broke the rules and called the house for her. I listened in on the extension. The first couple of times, I literally rush to the john and throw up. Now I know what I put all those women through. This time somebody else is holding the gun. But I don't confront her. It's the same with the money she spends. If I confront her, she'll leave me. But this time it's different. This time it's Sam and in the note he talks about how much they're in love. I do a lot of throwing up for several days running. And that's not so unheard of, you know. They say when Sinatra caught Ava Gardner cheating on him, he started puking around the clock, lost his voice, and ended up trying to kill himself.

3) I start losing weight. My skin color changes. Nothing drastic. But there's a peculiar faint yellow tone. The maid— of course we have a maid—she's the first one to say any-thing. She says I should see a doctor right away. All I can think of though is Karen and Sam. It was only a week ago that I found the note. The maid is insistent; and then Karen starts in on me about how I'm looking all of a sudden. I go to the doctor, there are so many tests I lose count at twelve, and the diagnosis is pancreatic cancer.

Now I'm in the hospital. I hear Karen and the lady from the hospital in the hall the other day. "A cancer like this," the hospice lady says, "it never takes long, Mrs. Thorne."

Karen says, "You really look good in those pajamas, Mike."

"Thanks for getting them for me, honey."

Night. You know how it is, night in a hospital. You can always tell the rooms where death has no dominion. There's laughter and maybe grandkids and a lot of plans about what's going to happen when the patient finally gets out of here. But the other rooms—there's a whispery quality and a tension and long, terrible, aching silences, and both sides prepare themselves for the flap-flap-flap of house slippers that come down the hall in the middle of the night. An elderly, obscene gent who puts his gnarled, papery hand in yours and leads you into a world you cannot fathom.

Sam says, "You sound a lot better than you did last night."

"Yeah, I thought I'd go dancing later."

Karen laughs, leans over, and gives me a little kiss. They're on opposite sides of my bed. "Oh, honey, it's so good you've kept your sense of humor."

Sam looks at his watch. "Well, guess I'll push off, Mike. But I'll be back tomorrow."

They've been here fifteen minutes. Talk about strained conversations.

What he's going to do, of course, is go downstairs and wait for her. She'll stay another ten, maybe fifteen, minutes and then leave.

I notice the strain on Sam's face. The strain isn't entirely because of the situation with Karen. He's lost his three biggest clients this year. The sniffling sounds he makes—nobody wants a cokehead for an agent. Sam's deep in debt. Deep.

"Take care, Mike," he says and leaves the room.

"He's such a good friend to you," Karen says after he leaves.

"Loyal," I said. "Nobody more loyal than Sam."

I say that staring right into those elegant, violet eyes of hers. She looks uncomfortable. "Yes, loyal."

The tone sounds. Visiting hours will be over in ten minutes.

As she bends over to me for her goodnight kiss, I see a moment of distaste in her eyes. I got a glimpse of myself this morning. I'm a lurid dirty-yellow color. Even my eyes have a yellow tint to them. I've lost twenty-six pounds in just under seven weeks.

"You're all I think about, babe," she says.

"Yeah," I said. "You're all I think about, too."

"You're such a good husband," she says. And the tears come right on time. FedEx delivers them. You can order them in pints, quarts, or gallons. "Such a good husband."

Fondling her hand. "And you're such a good wife."

The tone rings again and she says, "I'll see you tomorrow night. I thought I'd run up the coast tomorrow. See Shirley."

The good friend "Shirley" she's been talking about for three years. I've never met "Shirley" because she doesn't exist.

She gives me a peck on the cheek and then gives me another look at those pure, glistening tears you order from FedEx. And then she goes.

Larry calls just after nine. He knows better than to say anything meaningful. He just says, "Just wanted to say it was good seeing you today, Mike. Guess I'll have me a beer and watch the news."

"Sure wish *I* could have a beer," I say. "Guess I'll just have to settle for the news."

It's the fifth story on the ten o'clock news. "The home of jazz legend Mike Thorne was destroyed by fire tonight. First estimate is that everything was destroyed, including his collection of jazz memorabilia, said to be worth between two and three million dollars."

Good job, Larry.

Karen and Sam would've sold the memorabilia first. The collection would've brought more like four, instead of the three the anchorman said. The house was worth another million-and-a-half by now, with all the improvements she put in it. Insurance money is sweet.

But I canceled the policy last week. No insurance on the house, no insurance on my memorabilia.

I wake up near dawn again. Sweet Ruth Andrews this time. Two doors down. Breast cancer. The gurney, the whispers, the elevator to the morgue downstairs.

I lie in darkness, waiting my turn.

A Girl Like You

He knew they were in trouble and he couldn't eat. He knew they were in trouble and he couldn't sleep. He knew they were in trouble and he couldn't concentrate.

Not on anything except his girl Nora.

His name was Peter Wyeth and he was eighteen, all ready to enter the state university this fall, and he'd met her two-and-a-half months ago at a kegger on graduation night. He'd been pretty bombed, so bombed in fact that she'd driven him home in the new Firebird his folks had bought him for graduation.

That first night, she hadn't seemed like so much. Or maybe it was that he'd been so bombed he didn't realize just how much she really was. The truth was, Peter pretty much took girls for granted. He could afford to. He had the Wyeth look. There was some Dartmouth about the Wyeth boys, even though they'd lived all their lives here in small-town Iowa; and something Smith about the Wyeth girls. Between them, they broke a lot of hearts hereabouts, and if they didn't seem to take any particular pleasure in it, still they didn't seem to care much either.

Nora Caine was different somehow.

He'd never seen or heard of her before the night of the kegger. But he asked about her a lot the next day. Somebody said that they thought she was from one of those little towns near the point where Iowa and Wisconsin faced each other across the Mississippi. Visiting somebody here. It was all vague.

He ran into her that night at Charlie's, which was the sports bar on the highway where you could drink if you had a fake ID. Or if you were a Wyeth. She was dancing with some guy he recognized as a university frosh football player, something Peter himself had planned to be until he'd damaged his knee in a game against Des Moines.

He didn't like it. That was the first thing he noticed. And he realized instantly that he'd never felt this particular feeling before. Jealousy. He didn't even know this girl and yet he was jealous that she was dancing with somebody else. What the hell was that all about? Wyeths didn't get jealous; they didn't need to.

He watched her for the next hour. If she was teasing him, she was doing it subtly. Except for a few glances, she didn't seem aware of him at all. She just kept dancing with the frosh. By this time, Peter's friends were there and they were standing all around him telling him just how beautiful Nora Caine was. As if he needed to be told. What most fascinated him about her physically was a certain . . . timelessness . . . about her. Her hairstyle wasn't quite contemporary. Her clothes hinted at another era. Even her dance steps seemed a little dated. And yet she bedazzled, fascinated, imprisoned him.

Nora Caine.

She left that night with the frosh.

Peter spent a sleepless night—the first of many, as things would turn out—and knew just what he'd do at first light. He'd go looking for her. Somebody had to know who she was, where she lived, what she was doing here in town.

He met her that afternoon. She was sitting along the peaceful river, a sleek black raven sitting next to her, as if it was keeping guard. Her apartment was only a block from here. The landlady, impressed that she was talking to young

Wyeth, told him everything she knew about Nora. Girl was here for a few weeks settling some kind of family matters with an attorney. The frosh football player a constant visitor. Nora listening to classical music (played low), given to long walks along the river (always alone), and painting lovely pictures of days gone by.

"You remember me?"

She looked up. "Sure."

"Thanks for driving me home the other night. How'd you get home?"

"Walked."

"You could've taken a cab and just told them to put it on my father's account."

"He must be an important man."

"He is." Then: "Mind if I sit down?"

"I sort of have a boyfriend."

"The football player?"

"Yes." She smiled and he was cut in half, so profound was the effect of her smile on him. He wanted to cry in both joy and sorrow, joy for her smile, sorrow for her words. He felt scared, and wondered if he might be losing his mind. He'd been drinking too much beer lately, that was for sure. "The funny thing is, I don't even like sports."

"I'd like to go out with you sometime."

"I guess I'm just not sure how things're going to go with Brad. So I really can't make any dates."

A few weeks later—well into outrageous, green, suffocating summer now—Peter heard that Brad took a bad spill on his motorcycle. Real bad. He'd be in University hospital for several months.

He'd tried to distract himself with the wildest girls he could find. He had a lot of giggles and a lot of sex and a lot of brewskis and yet he was still soul-empty. He'd never felt like this. Empty this way. Empty and scared and lonely and jealous. What the hell was it about Nora anyway? Sure, she was beautiful, but so were most of his girls. Sure, she was winsome and sweet, but so were some of the girls he'd dated seriously. Sure, she was—And then he realized what it was. He couldn't have her. That was what was so special about her. If she'd ever just give in to him the way the other girls did . . . he wouldn't want her.

She was just playing games like all the other girls (or he'd always imagined they were playing games anyway) and he was—for the first time—losing.

He did a very irrational thing one rainy night. He parked in the alley behind her apartment house and watched as she left the house. He climbed the fire escape along the back and broke into her room and there he saw her paintings. They were everywhere, leaning against the walls, set in chairs, standing on one of the three easels. As silver rain eeled down the windows, he stood in the lightning-flashes of the night and escaped into the various worlds she had painted. They looked like magazine cover illustrations from every decade in this century—the doughboys of World War I, the hollow-eyed farmers of the Depression, the dogfaces of World War II, a young girl with a 1950s hula hoop, an anti-Vietnam hippie protester, a stockbroker on the floor, Times Square the first night of the new century. There was a reality to the illustrations that gave him a dizzy feeling, as if they were drawing him into the world they represented. He'd have to give up smoking so much pot, too. It obviously wasn't doing him any good.

Then she came home, carrying a small, damp sack of groceries, her red hair bejeweled with raindrops. The funny thing was she didn't even ask him why he was here. She just set down the groceries and came to him.

Not long after that, a local newspaper editor, Paul Sheridan, came up on the street to him and said, "I see you know Nora Caine. She's going to teach you a lot." As always, the white-haired, ruddy-cheeked Sheridan smelled of liquor. He was in his sixties. As a young man, he'd written a novel that had sold very well. But that was the end of his literary career. He could never seem to find a suitable subject for a second novel. His wife and daughter had died in a fire some time ago. He had inherited the newspaper from his father and ran it until his drinking caused him to bring in his cousin, who ran the paper and did a better job than Paul ever had. Now Paul wrote some editorials, some reviews of books nobody in a town like this would ever read, and did pieces on town history, at which he excelled. There was always talk that somebody should collect these pieces that stretched back now some twenty-five years but as yet nobody had. Sheridan said: "If you're strong, Peter, you'll be the better man for it."

What the hell was Sheridan muttering about? How did he even know that Peter knew Nora? And how the hell did anybody Sheridan's age know Nora?

It was two weeks before she'd let Peter sleep with her. He was crazy by then. He was so caught up in her, he found himself thinking unimaginable things: he wouldn't go to college, he'd get a job so they could get married. And they'd have a kid. He didn't want to lose her and he lived in constant terror that he would. But if they had a kid . . . When he was away from her, he was miserable. His parents took to giving him long, confused looks. He no longer returned the calls of his buddies—they seemed childish to him now. Nora was the one lone, true reality. He would not wash his hands sometimes for long periods; he wanted to retain their intimacy. He learned things about women—

about fears and appetites and nuances. And he learned about heartbreak. The times they'd argue, he was devastated when he realized that someday she might well leave him.

And so it went all summer.

He took her home. His parents did not care for her.

"Sort of . . . aloof," his mother said.

"What's wrong with Tom Bolan's daughter? She's a lot better looking than this Nora and she's certainly got a nicer pair of melons," his father said.

To which his mother predictably replied, "Oh, Lloyd, you and your melons. Good Lord."

They avoided the old places he used to go. He didn't want to share her.

There was no intimacy they did not know, sexual, mental, spiritual. She even got him to go to some lectures at the University on Buddhism and he found himself not enraptured (as she seemed to be) but at least genuinely interested in the topic and the discussion that followed.

He would lay his hand on her stomach and dream of the kid they'd have. He'd see toddlers on the street and try to imagine what it'd be like to have one of his own. And you know what, he thought it would be kinda cool, actually. It really would be.

And then, this one morning, she was gone.

Her landlady told him that a cab had shown up right at nine o'clock this morning and taken her and her two bags (they later found that she'd shipped all her canvases and art supplies separately) and that she was gone. She said to tell Peter goodbye for her.

He'd known they were in some sort of trouble these past couple of weeks—something she wouldn't discuss—but now it had all come crashing down.

A cab had picked her up. Swept her away. Points unknown.

Tell Peter goodbye for me.

He had enemies. The whole Wyeth family did. Whenever anything bad happened to one of the Wyeths, the collective town put on a forlorn face of course (hypocrisy not being limited to Madison Avenue cocktail parties) and then proceeded to chuckle when the camera was off them.

A fine handsome boy, they said, too bad.

He wasn't a fine boy, though, and everybody knew it. He had treated some people terribly. Girls especially. Get them all worked up and tell them lots of lies and then sleep with them till a kind of predatory spell came over him and he was stalking new blood once again. There had been two abortions; a girl who'd sunk into so low a depression that she had to stay in a hospital for a time; and innumerable standard-issue broken hearts. He was no kinder to males. Boys who amused him got to warm themselves in the great presence of a Wyeth; but when they amused him no longer—or held strong opinions with which he disagreed or hinted that maybe his family wasn't all that it claimed to be—they were banished forever from the golden kingdom.

So who could argue that the bereaved, angry, sullen, despondent, boy who had been dumped by a passing-through girl . . . who could argue that he didn't deserve it?

His mother suggested a vacation. She had family in New Hampshire.

His father suggested Uncle Don in Wyoming. He broke broncos; maybe he could break Peter, who was embarrassing to be around these days. By God, and over a girl too.

He stayed in town. He drank and he slept off the drink and then he drank some more. He was arrested twice for speeding, fortunately when he was sober. And—back with his friends again—he was also fined for various kinds of childish mischief, not least of which was spray-painting the F-word on a police car.

Autumn came; early autumn, dusky ducks dark against the cold, mauve, melancholy, prairie sky, his friends all gone off to college, and Peter was more alone than he'd ever been.

His father said he needed to get a job if he wasn't going to the university.

His mother said maybe he needed to see a psychologist.

He was forced, for friendship, to hang out with boys he'd always avoided before. Not from the right social class. Not bright or hip or aware. Factory kids or mall kids, the former sooty when they left the mill at three every afternoon; the latter dressed in the cheap suits they wore to sell appliances or tires or cheap suits. And yet, after an initial period of feeling superior, he found that these kids weren't really much different from his other friends. All the same fears and hopes. And he found himself actually liking most of them. Understanding them in a way he would have thought impossible.

There was just one thing they couldn't do: they couldn't save him from his grief. They couldn't save him and booze couldn't save him and pot couldn't save him and speed couldn't save him and driving fast couldn't save him and fucking his brains out and sobbing couldn't save him and puking couldn't save him and masturbating couldn't save him and hitting people couldn't save him and praying couldn't save him. Not even sleep could save him, for always in sleep came Nora. Nora Nora Nora. Nothing could save him.

And then the night—his folks at the country club—he

couldn't handle it any more. Any of it. He lay on his bed with his grandfather's straight razor and cut his wrists. He was all drunked up and crying and scared shitless but somehow he found the nerve to do it. Just at the last minute, blood starting to cover his hands now, he rolled over on the bed to call 911 but then he dropped the receiver. Too weak. And then he went to sleep. . . .

He woke up near dawn in a very white room. Streaks of dawn in the window. The hospital just coming awake. Rattle of breakfast carts; squeak of nurses' shoes. And his folks peering down at him and smiling and a young woman doctor saying, "You're going to be fine, Peter. Just fine."

His mother wept and his father kept whispering, "You'll have to forgive your mother. She used to cry when you two would watch 'Lassie' together," which actually struck Peter as funny.

"I'll never get over her," he said.

"You'll be back to breaking hearts in no time," his father said.

"She wasn't our kind anyway," his mother said. "I don't mean to be unkind, honey, but that's the truth."

"I still wish you'd give old Tom's daughter a go," his father said.

"Yeah, I know," Peter said. "Melons." He grinned. He was glad he wasn't dead. He felt young and old; totally sane and totally crazy; horny and absolutely monastic; drunk and sober.

He went home the next day. And stayed home. It was pretty embarrassing to go out. People looking at you. Whispering.

He watched "Nick at Night" a lot. Took him back to the days when he was six and seven. You have it knocked when you're six and seven and you don't even realize it. Being six and seven—no responsibilities, no hassles, no doom—is better than having a few billion in the bank. He stayed sober; he slept a lot; every once in awhile the sorrow would just overwhelm him and he'd see her right in front of him in some fantastical way, and hear her and feel her and smell her and taste her, and he would be so balled-up in pain that not only would he want to be six or seven, he wanted to go all the way back to the womb.

March got all confused and came on like May. My God, you just didn't know what to do with yourself on days like this. Disney had a hand in creating a day like this; he had to.

He started driving to town and parking and walking around. He always went midafternoon when everybody was still in school. He never would've thought he'd be so happy to see his old town again. He took particular notice of the trolley tracks and the hitching posts and the green Model T you could see all dusty in Old Man Baumhofer's garage. He sat in the library and actually read some books, something he'd never wanted to do in his whole life.

But mostly he walked around. And thought thoughts he'd never thought before either. He'd see a squirrel and he'd wonder if there was some way to communicate with the little guy that human beings—in their presumptuousness and arrogance—just hadn't figured out yet. He saw flowers and stopped and really studied them and lovingly touched them and sniffed them. He saw infants in strollers being pushed by pretty young moms with that twenty-year-old just-bloomed beauty that flees so sadly and quickly; and saw the war memorials of three different conflicts and was proud to see how many times the name Wyeth was listed. He looked—for the first time in his life he really looked at things. And he loved what he saw; just loved it.

And one day when he was walking down by the deserted

mill near the newspaper office, he saw Paul Sheridan just leaving and he went up to him and he said, "A while back you told me Nora was going to teach me things. And that if I was strong, I'd be a better man for it."

For the first time, he looked past the drunken red face and the jowls and the white hair and saw Sheridan as he must have been at Peter's age. Handsome and tall, probably a little theatrical (he still was now), and possessed of a real warmth. Sheridan smiled: "I knew you'd look me up, kiddo. C'mon in the office. I want to show you something."

Except for a couple of pressmen in the back, the office was empty. Several computer stations stood silent, like eyes guarding against intruders.

Sheridan went over to his desk and pulled out a photo album. He carried it over to a nearby table and set it down. "You want coffee?"

"That sounds good."

"I'll get us some. You look through the album."

He looked through the album. Boy, did he. And wondered who the jokester was who'd gone to all this trouble.

Here were photographs—some recent, some tinted in turn-of-the-last-century-fashion—of Nora Caine in dozens of different poses, moods, outfits—and times. Her face never changed, though. She was Nora in the 1890s and she was Nora today. There could be no mistaking that.

Goosebumps; disbelief.

"Recognize her?" Sheridan said when he sat down. He pushed a cup of coffee Peter's way.

"Somebody sure went to a lot of trouble to fake all these photographs."

Sheridan smiled at him. "Now, you know better than that. You're just afraid to admit it. Sure, they're real."

"But that's impossible."

"No, it's not. Not if you're an angel or a ghost or whatever the hell she is." He sipped some coffee. "She broke my heart back when I was your age. So bad I ended up in a mental hospital having electroshock treatments. No fun, let me tell you. Took me a long time to figure out what she did for me."

"You mean, did *to* you?"

"No; that's the point. You have to see her being with you for a positive thing rather than a negative one. I was a spoiled, rich kid, just like you. A real heartbreaker. Didn't know shit from shinola and didn't care to. All I wanted to do was have fun. And then she came along and crushed me—and turned me into a genuine human being. I hated her for at least ten years. Tried to find her. Hired private detectives. Everything. I wrote my novel about her. Only novel I had in me, as things turned out. But I never would've read a book; or felt any compassion for poor people; or cared about spiritual things. I was an arrogant jerk and it took somebody like her to change me. It had to be painful or it wouldn't have worked. I was bitter and angry for a long time, like I said, but then eventually I saw what she'd done for me. And I thanked her for it. And loved her all the more. But in a different way now."

"You don't really believe she's some kind of ghost or something, do you?"

"The photos are real, Peter. Took me thirty years to collect them. I went all over the Midwest collecting them. I'd show a photo to somebody in some little town and then they'd remember her or remember somebody who'd known her. And it was always the same story. Some arrogant young prick—rich or poor, black or white, didn't matter—and he'd have his fling with her. And then she'd move on. And he'd be crushed. But he'd never be his arrogant old self again. Some of them couldn't handle it and they'd kill themselves. Some of them would just be bitter and drink themselves to death. But the strong ones—us, Peter, you and me—we learned the lessons she wanted us to. Just think of all the things we know now we didn't know before she met us."

The phone rang. He got up to get it. Peter noticed that he staggered a little.

He was on the phone for ten minutes. No big deal. Just a conversation with somebody about a sewer project. You didn't usually get big deals on some town newspapers like this one.

Peter just looked at the pictures. His entire being yearned for a simple touch of her. In her flapper outfit. Or her WW II Rosie-the-Riveter get-up. Or her hippie attire. Nora Nora Nora.

Sheridan came back from the phone. "I didn't expect you to believe me, Peter. I didn't believe it for a long time. Now I do." He looked at him for a time. "And someday you will, too. And you'll be grateful that she was in your life for that time." He grinned and you could see the boy in him suddenly. "She had some ass, didn't she?"

Peter laughed. "She sure did."

"I got to head over to the library, kiddo."

Sheridan said goodbye to the pressmen and then they headed out the door. The day was still almost oppressively beautiful.

"This is the world she wanted me to see, Peter. And I never would've appreciated it if I hadn't loved her."

They crossed the little bridge heading to the merchant blocks. Sheridan started to turn right toward the library.

"The next woman you love, you'll know how to love. How to be tender with her. How to give yourself to her. I

76

can't say that my life has been a great success. Peter. It hasn't been. But I loved my wife and daughter more than I ever could've if I hadn't met Nora. Maybe that's the most important thing she ever taught us. Peter." And with that, Sheridan waved goodbye.

Six years later his wife Faith gave birth to a girl. Peter asked if they might name her Nora. And Faith, understanding, smiled yes.

The Brasher Girl

For Stephen King

I guess by now you pretty much know what happened the last year or so in the Valley here—with Cindy and me, I mean.

All I can hope for is that you'll give me time to tell my side of things. Nobody ever did. Not the cops, not the press, not even my own parents. They all just assumed—

Well, they all assumed wrong, each and every one of them.

It took me nineteen dates to have my way with Cindy Marie Brasher, who was not only the prettiest girl in Central Consolidated High, but the prettiest girl in the entire Valley, though I will admit to some prejudice on that particular judgment.

Night we met, I was twenty-three and just out of the Army, and she was seventeen and about to be voted Homecoming Queen. She was not only good-looking, she was popular, too.

Consolidated being my own alma mater, I went along with my sixteen-year-old brother to the season's first football game, and afterward to a party.

Things hadn't changed much, as far as high school rituals went. There was a big bonfire down by the river and a couple kegs of Bud and a few dozen joints of some of the worst marijuana I'd ever smoked. Couple hours in, several of the couples snuck off into the woods to make out more seriously than they could around the bonfire, at least ten different boys and maybe two girls rushed down to the riverbank to throw up, and two farm boys about the same size got into a fistfight that I let run three, four minutes before I stepped in and broke it up. One thing you learn in the Army, drinking and fistfights can lead to some serious damage.

Now it'd be real nice here to tell you that Cindy took one look at me in my Army clothes (face it, might as well get some mileage out of my paratrooper uniform) and fell right in love with me. But she didn't. For one thing, she was the date of Michael Henning, whose old man was president of the oldest bank in the Valley. And Michael himself was no slouch, either—took the basketball team twice to state, and had a swimming scholarship waiting for him at any of three Big Ten schools.

No, she didn't rush into my arms, but she did look me over. Subtly. Very subtly. Because that was her style. But a few times our gazes met over the flickering flames and—there was some mutual interest. No doubt about it.

She left early, and on Michael Henning's arm, but just before she vanished into the prairie darkness surrounding the bonfire, she looked at me a last time and I knew I hadn't been imagining things earlier.

Three weeks went by before I saw her again, during which time I carried her in my mind like a talisman. Always there, burning brightly.

Autumn had come to our small town. On sunny mornings, I walked down to the State employment office to take aptitude tests and to see if they'd found anything for me yet. Then I'd drift over to the library and check out a book by Hemingway or John Steinbeck or Robert Stone. They were my favorite writers. Most of the time, I'd read in the town square, the fierce, fall leaves of red and gold and bronze scraping along the walk, pushed by a chill wind. The bandstand was closed for the season and even the two men on the Civil War statues appeared to be hunkering down for winter.

That was where I had my first real talk with her, sitting on a park bench reading Steinbeck's *In Dubious Battle*.

She was cutting through the park on her way back to school. I heard her and looked up.

She looked quickly away, but I could tell she'd been staring at me.

"Hey," I said, "you're Cindy Brasher, right?"

She grinned. "You were at the bonfire party? You're Ted's brother, right?"

I walked her back to school. And after school, I just happened to be sitting in Lymon's, which is the Rexall drugstore downtown where the kids all go, and where Cindy had told me she just might be if I stopped in. Unfortunately, I'd no more than picked up my cherry Coke and started walking back to the booths than Michael Henning showed up and sat down next to her.

Things went on like this for another month. I got a job selling men's clothes, just a temporary sort of thing, at Wallingham's Fine Fashions, and I also got a loan from my Dad so I could pay down on a three-year-old Pontiac convertible, a red job that shined up real well.

Of course, my main interest remained Cindy. We saw each other three, four times a week, but always in a sneaky kind of way—one time we sat in the grassy railroad tracks behind G&H Supermarket—and there was never anything romantic. She told me that she was in the process of breaking up with Michael Henning and that he was having a hard time with it. She said he cried a lot and one time even threatened to kill himself. She said she felt terribly guilty and responsible and that Michael was a fine person whom people disliked just because he came from money and that she wished she still loved him but she didn't and that nothing between us could happen until her break with Michael was final and official and she wouldn't blame me if I'd go find somebody else, having to wait around like this and all, but of course she knew better. By now there was nobody else for me and never would be.

To be honest, I felt a little guilty about Michael Henning, too. From what Cindy said, she'd been drifting away from Michael before I got back from the Army but that my presence certainly accelerated things. Back in eleventh grade I'd been going with Laurie McKee, a very appealing blonde, and she dumped me for a senior named Sam Hampton. I didn't take it well. I drank a lot and got into a lot of fights and one night I even ran away from home, loading up my car and taking off down the highway like a character in a Kerouac novel. Came back four days later, broke and aggrieved and scared as hell of just about everything. That was why I finished up my high school at St. Pius, the Catholic school. My folks weren't all that crazy about papists but they knew I'd never make it through Consolidated, having to see Laurie every day. Far as that went, that was no magic formula, either, I was still depressed a lot, and still occasionally hinted that I'd like to take my Dad's hunting rifle down and do a Hemingway on myself, and still had notions of taking Sam Hampton out into the woods and kicking his ass real good.

So I pretty much knew what Michael Henning was going through and, believe me, that's not something I'd wish on anybody.

The break-up didn't come until after Christmas. The

kids all joked that she'd wanted to drag it out so she could get a nice Christmas present, but in fact when Michael gave her that brand-new coat rumored to have cost $500, she told him that it wasn't right that he'd give her something like this, and would he please take it back.

Same night he took it back, he showed up on my parents' doorstep and asked me if I wanted to go for a ride. I had a lot of quick, spooky premonitions. He might have a gun in his car and blow my brains out. Or he might drive us both off a cliff up at Manning State Park. Or he might drag me over to Cindy's house for a real humiliating scene.

But I went. Poor bastard was shaking so bad I couldn't say no; big, lanky, handsome kid who looked real scared.

Christmas night, the highways were empty. You saw the occasional cannonball sixteen-wheeler whooshing through the Midwestern night but that was about all. We drove west, paralleling the State Park. And we drove fast. He had a Trans-Am that did 110 and you barely had to turn the ignition on.

And then he started crying. Weeping, really. And so hard that he pulled off the road and I just sat there and watched him and listened to him, not knowing what to do or say.

"I got to tell you something, Spence," he said, Spencer being my last name, and Spence being forever my nickname, "I just want you to take care of her. I want you to be good to her, you understand?"

I nodded.

"She doesn't think much of herself, Spence, which you've probably noticed."

I nodded again. I had noticed that.

"That old man of hers—boy would I like to get him in a fight sometime—he always told her she wasn't worth shit, and now she believes that. She ever tell you how he'd beat her?"

I shook my head. She hadn't told me that.

"She used to come out to the car with black eyes some-times, and once she had a compound fracture from where he'd thrown her into a wall, and another time he cracked her ankle and she was hobbling around almost a week be-fore I got her to go to the doctor's."

It was real strange, the two of us there, talking about the girl we both loved, and him saying that all he cared about was that I loved her true and took gentle care of her.

And then his tears seemed to dry up and he turned more toward me in the seat—the heater pushing out warm air and the radio real low with a Van Morrison song—and he said, "But you don't know the truth yet, do you?"

"The truth?"

"About Cindy?"

I felt a chill. And I shuddered. And I wasn't sure why. Maybe it was just the way he said it there in the dashlight darkness. The Truth.

"I guess I don't."

"She has a friend."

"A friend?"

"Yeah."

"What kind of friend? You mean another boyfriend?"

He shook his head. "Not exactly." He smiled. "You, I could've dealt with. But her friend—"

Then he turned around and put the Trans-Am into gear and we squealed out.

We didn't say a word until we were halfway back to my house.

"Michael?"

"Yeah?"

"You going to tell me any more?"

"About what?"

"About this friend of hers?"

He looked over at me and smiled, but it was a cold and sinister smile and I saw in it his hatred of me. He knew something that I didn't and he was going to enjoy the hell out of me finding out what it was.

When he reached my curb, he reached over and slapped forth a handshake. "Good luck, Spence. You're a lot tougher guy than I am." The quick, chill smile again. "And believe me, with Cindy that'll come in handy."

I went in and said some more Merry Christmas kind of things to my parents and my brother and sister and then I went down to the family room and put in a Robert Mitchum tape, Mitch being my favorite actor, and settled in with a Pepsi and some popcorn.

At the same time I was watching Mitch and Jane Russell try to outfox William Bendix in *Macao*, Michael Henning was up in his bedroom pulling a Hemingway.

Coroner said that the entire back of his head had been blown out and town rumor had it that, try as his parents might over the next few weeks to scrape blood and bone and brains off the wall, they were having no luck at all. Finally, a carpenter came in, cut out that entire section of the wall, and then replastered and repainted it.

Three hundred people came to Michael Henning's funeral. Not wanting to be hypocritical, I stayed home.

I mentioned in the beginning that it took me nineteen dates to seduce Cindy. I am counting only those dates we had after her month-long mourning of Michael Henning, during which time the town had a change of heart about her. Where before she'd been their pride, the poor girl with the drunken father who constantly humiliated her, they now saw her as the whore who'd betrayed her lover and driven him to suicide. Townsfolk knew about me, too, and liked me no better.

We did a lot of driving, mostly to Iowa City and Cedar Rapids, on our dates. Couple town people were so angry about seeing us together, they came right up to us and started arguing that we had no business enjoying ourselves with poor Michael barely cold in his grave. One guy even tried to pick a fight with me but my paratrooper tricks were a little too wily for him. Fat slob ending up on his back, huffing and puffing and panting out dirty words.

The worst, of course, was seeing Michael's parents. We were leaving the Orpheum one night after seeing a Barbra Streisand movie—I guess you can guess which one of us chose that particular picture—and there they were in the lobby, waiting with a small crowd for the next feature to stop. The Mrs. got tears in her eyes and looked away; the Mr. just glared right at me, staring me down. He won. I couldn't look at him very long.

Odd thing was, the night we saw them in the lobby was the night that Cindy let me go all the way, which is how she always referred to it.

Friend of mine had an apartment over a tavern and we went up there because he was out of town on a four-day Army Reserve weekend.

I figured it was going to be the same thing as usual, bringing each other to satisfaction with eager hands and fingers, but this night, she said, "Why don't we do it tonight, Spence? I need to know you love me and you need to know I love you and this is the best way to prove it. Just please let's keep the lights off. You know, my breasts." She really had a hang-up about her breasts. So they were small, I didn't care. But she sure did. A lot of times I'd be petting her or kissing her nipples and she'd push me gently away and say, "That's enough for now, all right, hon?" Michael had been absolutely right. She really was ashamed of herself in a lot of ways.

After that night, we were closer than ever, and a few weeks later I uttered, for the very first time, the word "marriage."

She just looked at me all funny and said, "Spence, you know what your parents think of me."

"It isn't that they don't like you, Cindy, it's just that they worry about me."

"Worry? Why?"

"I told you about Laurie. You know, how screwed up I got and all."

"I'm not like Laurie."

"I know, sweetheart, but they think—well, a young girl doesn't know her mind. We'll announce our engagement and everybody'll start making a fuss and everything—and then you'll feel a lot better."

"That really makes me mad, Spence. I'm not like Laurie at all. I love you. Deeply and maturely. The way a woman loves a man."

How could a guy go wrong with a girl like that?

By spring, I had a better job, this one at a lumber company out on 151. I worked the front desk and handled all the wholesale orders. Salary plus commission. Kept me hopping but I enjoyed it. Nights were all free and only half a day Saturdays.

Couple nights a week we drove up to an old high school haunt of mine, place where kids back in the days of the Bee Gees and Donna Summer liked to make out. It was great because now the high school kids used the state park. Hardly anybody came up here.

One night as I sat there, looking down at the lights of the little prairie town where I'd grown up, Cindy all snug in my arms, she said, "Spence? If I asked you an honest question, would you give me an honest answer?"

"Sure I would."

"Well. . . ."

And right away, I thought of my folks and how smug they'd look when I told them what I feared she was about to say—that she'd been thinking real hard and had decided that maybe I really was just a tad old for her; or that she'd met this senior boy, see, and without wanting to, without planning for it or even wanting it to happen in any way, well she'd gone and fallen in love with somebody else.

"You're trembling," she said.

"I just know this is going to be real bad news."

"Oh, honey, no it's not. Honest. You're so silly."

And then she tickled me the way she always did, and then gave me one of those big, warm, creamy kisses of hers, and then she said, "It's just that I've got this friend I'd like you to meet sometime."

Right away, of course, I remembered what Michael had told me that night in his car. About her friend.

"This is a male friend?"

"Yes, hon, but nothing to be jealous of." She smiled. "When you meet him, you'll see how silly you are. Honest." Then she gave me another one of those creamy kisses.

"How'd you meet him?"

"Let's not talk about him any more tonight, all right? Let's just sit here and look at the stars. I love looking at the stars—and thinking about life in outer space." Pause. "You believe in that?"

"In what?"

"You know, that there is life on other planets."

I made a scary sound and a monster face but she didn't laugh. Didn't even smile.

"I'm serious, Spence. Do you?"

"Guess I haven't thought about it much."

"Well, I do."

"Believe that there's life on other planets?"

"Uh-huh."

I gave her a very long kiss. My crotch started getting real tight. "Well, if you do, I do."

"Believe in life on other planets?"

"Uh-huh."

We had another kiss on it.

Three nights later, Cindy suggested that we drive up by Dubuque which, for a rainy night, was something of a hike, being over one hundred miles away. When I asked her why, she just shrugged and said, "I just like looking at the Mississippi. Makes me feel peaceful. But if you don't want to—"

Makes her feel peaceful. What was I going to say? No, I don't want you to feel peaceful?

We drove up by Dubuque and it was nice, even with the rain. When we reached the Mississippi, I pulled up and parked. In the distance you could see the tugs and barges, and then a fervent, bright gambling boat, and then just the dark river rushing down to New Orleans and the Gulf. We sat there for an hour and then she suggested we head back.

When we were forty miles from Cedar Rapids she spotted a convenience store shining like a mirage on a dark hill. "Could I get you to pull in there?"

"Sure."

"Thanks."

When we got to the drive, she said to just park and she'd run in. "Just need to tinkle," she grinned.

Ten minutes later, we were back on the highway. She kind of scooched up to me the rest of the way home.

Following day, I must've heard the story on the news six, seven times before I finally figured it out. At first, I rejected the whole idea, of course. What a stupid idea it was. That Cindy, good Cindy, could possibly have—

That night, no place better to go, we parked up in the state park and got in the back seat and made love and afterward I said, "I've had this really crazy idea all day."

"Yeah? What kind of crazy idea?"

"You hear the news?"

"News about what?"

But soon as I said it, I felt her slender body tense beneath mine. She hadn't put her bra back on yet and her sweet little breasts were very cold. Usually she would have covered up right away, but soon as I mentioned having this idea, she just kind of froze in place. I could smell her perfume and the cold night air and the jism in the condom I'd set in the rear ashtray.

"You remember when we stopped at that convenience store last night? Coming back from Dubuque?"

"Sure."

"Place got robbed. And the kid working there got killed."

"Oh? Really? I hadn't heard that."

Now she started getting dressed real fast. "You mind if I have a cigarette?"

"Thought you quit."

Smoking was her only bad habit. Winston Lights.

"I just carry one around, hon. Just one. You know that."

"How come you need it all of a sudden?"

She shrugged, twisting her bra cups around so they'd cover her breasts. "Just get jittery sometimes. You know how I get."

"You did it, didn't you?"

"What, hon?"

"Robbing that place, killing that kid. You."

"Well, thank you very fucking much. Isn't that a nice thing to say to the girl you love?"

We didn't talk for a long time. We took our respective places up in the front seat and I got the car all fired up and we drove back into town but we still didn't talk.

When I pulled up in front of her house, I said, "I don't know what came over me, Cindy. God, I really don't. Of course you didn't rob that place or kill that guy. Of course you didn't."

She sat way over against the window in the shadows. I couldn't see her very well but I could sense her warm, full mouth and the gentling warmth between her legs. I wanted to hide in that warmth and never see sunshine again.

"You were right, Spence. I took the money and I killed the kid."

"Bullshit."

"Huh-uh. True. And I've done it before, too."

"Robbed places?"

"Uh-huh."

"And killed guys?"

"Uh-huh."

"Bullshit."

"God, Spence, you think I'd make up something like this?"

I absolutely didn't know what to say.

"He makes me do it."

"Who?"

"My friend."

I thought of poor, dead Michael Henning and the warning he'd given me.

"How does he make you do it?"

"He controls my mind."

I grinned. "Boy, you had me going there, Cindy. I mean, for a minute there I thought you were serious. You were robbin' guys and killin' guys and—"

"You want to meet him?"

"Your friend?"

"Yeah."

"When?"

"Tomorrow night."

"You serious?"

"Yes. But I better warn you, when Michael met him—"

"Yeah."

"Really freaked him out."

"How come?"

"You'll see. Tomorrow night."

"Is this all bullshit, Cindy?"

"None of it's bullshit, Spence, and you know it. You're just afraid to admit it's true."

"If it's true, I should go to the law."

"Then maybe that's what you should do. Lord knows, I couldn't stop you. Big, strapping paratrooper like you."

"But why do you kill them?"

"He makes me." She leaned over to me and now I could see her face in the faint streetlight, see that tears were streaming down her cheeks. "I don't want to do any of it, Spence. But he makes me."

"Nobody has that kind of control over somebody else."

"Nobody human."

"He's not human?"

She kissed me with that luxurious mouth of hers and I have to say that I went a little insane with my senses so full of her—the taste of her mouth, the scent of her skin, the soft warmth of her lips behind the denim covering her crotch . . . I went a little insane.

"Tomorrow night, Spence," she said.

I wanted to say a lot more, of course, but she was gone, her door opening and the dome light coming on, night rushing in like a cold, black tide.

Not human. Those were the two words I thought about all next day. Not human. And around three o'clock, just when the wholesale business was slowing down, I started thinking about two words of my own. Temporarily insane. Sure, why not? A girl who'd grown up without a mother, constantly being beaten by her father? A girl who secretly blamed herself for the death of her boyfriend, as I secretly suspected she did? That could cause her to lose her mind. It happened all the time.

"You not hungry tonight?" my dad said over dinner.

I saw them glance at each other, Mom and Dad. Whenever I did anything they found out of the ordinary, they'd exchange that same kind of glance. The Cindy glance, I called it.

"One of the women at work got a box of birthday candy and she passed it around. Guess I ate too much of it."

Another Cindy glance. They knew that I wasn't much for sweets and that I'd certainly never stuff myself with them. I decided that then would be a good time to tell them.

"I'll be moving out next week."

"Moving out?" Mom said, startled.

I laughed. "Well, I'll be twenty-four this year. Don't you think it's about time?"

"Is—Cindy—moving in with you?" Dad asked. Sometimes they both had a hard time saying her name. Got downright tongue-tied. The way Christians do when they have to say the name Satan.

I nodded to Jeff and Suzie. "These are very young, impressionable children. I don't think we should discuss such matters in front of them." I smiled at Suzie.

"Who would have thought," said fourteen-year-old

Suzie, "my very own brother, shacking up."

Jeff laughed. Mom said, "That'll be enough of that, young lady."

"Is she?" Dad said.

I reached across the table and took their hands, the way we hold hands during Grace on Thanksgiving and Christmas. "She's not moving in with me. And I'm not going to start dealing crack out of my apartment. I'm just going to live there alone, the way any normal red-blooded twenty-four-year-old guy would."

I could tell they weren't happy—I mean, even if Cindy wasn't going to live there, she was obviously going to spend a lot of time there—but at least they let me change the subject. The rest of the meal we talked about some of the new cars I'd been looking at. Last month's bonus at the lumberyard had been pretty darn good.

Funny thing was, that night Cindy went two hours before even bringing up the subject of her friend. We drove to Cedar Rapids to Westdale Mall, where she bought some new clothes. Always before, I'd wondered where Cindy got the money for her seemingly endless supply of fashionable duds. After the robbery the other night, I no longer wondered.

On the way back, radio real low with a Bob Seger tape, windows open to let the warm May breeze bring the scents of new-mown grass and hay into the car, she said, "You know where the old Parkinson cabin is?"

"Sure. Up in the hills."

"That's where he lives."

"Your friend?"

"Uh-huh."

"You want to go up there?"

"Do you?"

"I got to admit," I said, "I'm kinda curious."

"Michael was afraid. He put it off for a real long time." She leaned over and kissed me, making it hard to concentrate on my driving. Like I cared. What better way to die than with Cindy kissing me?

"No," I said, "I'm not afraid." But I was.

Little kids in our town believe that there are two long-haunted places. One is the old red-brick school abandoned back in the fifties. The tale five different generations of boys and girls have told is that there was this really wicked principal, a wilted crone who looked a lot like Miss Grundy in "Archie" comics, who on two occasions took two different first-graders to the basement and beat them so badly that they died. Legend had it that she cracked the concrete floor, buried them beneath it, and then poured fresh concrete. Legend also had it that even today the spirits of those two little kids still haunt the old schoolhouse and that, on certain nights, the ghost of the principal can be seen carrying a blood-dripping ax.

The other legend concerns Parkinson's cabin, a place built in the mid-1800s by a white man who planned to do a lot of business with the Mesquakie Indians. Except something went wrong. The local newspaper—and for the hell of it, I once spent a day in the library confirming the fact that an 1861 paper did run this story—noted that a huge meteor was spotted by many townspeople one night, and that it crashed to earth not far from Trapper Parkinson's crude cabin. Odd thing was, nobody ever saw or talked to Parkinson after the meteor crash. Perfect soil for a legend to grow.

Took us thirty-five minutes to reach the cabin from the road. Bramble and first-growth pine trees made the passage slow. But then we stood on a small hill, the moon big and

round and blanch-white, and looked down on this disinte-
grating lean-to of boards and tarpaper, which a bunch of
hobos had added in the forties when they were trying to fix
the place up with not much luck. An ancient plow, all
blade-rusted and wood-rotted, stood stuck in a stand of
buffalo grass. A silver snake of moon-touched creek ran behind the cabin.

And then Cindy said, "You see it over there? The well?"

Sometime in the early part of this century, when the last
of the Mormons were trekking their way across the country
to Utah, a straggling band stopped here long enough to help
a young couple finish the well they'd started digging. The
Mormons, being decent folks indeed, even built the people
a pit made of native stone and a roof made of birch. And
the well itself hadn't been easy to dig. You started with a
sharp-pointed auger, looking for water, and then you dug
with a shovel when you found it. Sometimes you dug two
hundred feet, sending up buckets of rock and dirt and shale
for days before you were done. It was all tumbledown now,
of course, but you could see in the remnants of the pit how
impressive it must have been when it was new.

We went over to the well. Cindy ducked beneath the
shabby roof and peered straight down into the darkness. I
dropped a rock down there. Echoes rose of its plopping
through the surface. I shone my light down. This was what
they call a dug well, about the only kind a fella could make
back then. Most of the dug wells in this area went down
into clay and shale about fifty feet.

I shone my light down. Dirty black water was still
spiderwebbed from the rock.

"He probably doesn't like the light."

I stood up, clipping off the light. "You going to get mad
if I start laughing?"

"You better not, Spence. This is real serious."

"Your friend lives down in the well?"

"Uh-huh. In the water."

"Nobody could live below the water, Cindy."

"I told you last night. He's not human."

"What is he, then?"

"Some kind of space alien."

"I see."

"You better not laugh."

"Where'd he come from, this space alien?"

"Where do you think, dopey? He was inside the meteor that crashed here that time. Parkinson's meteor."

"And he stays down in the well?"

"Right."

"Because why?"

"Because if humans ever laid their eyes on Him, they'd go insane. Right on the spot."

"And how do you know that?"

"He told me. Or rather, It. It's more of an It than a He, though It's also sort of a He. It told me. But It's also a He."

"So he just stays down there?"

"Uh-huh."

"Doing what?"

"Now how the hell would I know that, Spence?"

"And he tells you to do things?"

"Uh-huh. Once He establishes telepathic contact with you."

"Telepathic. I see."

"Don't be a prick and start laughing, Spence."

"How'd he make contact with you?"

She shrugged. "One night I was real lonely—Michael went to some basketball game with his father—and I didn't know where else to go, so I walked up to the park and then I wandered over here and before I knew it, I saw the old cabin and I just kind of drifted down the hill and—He started talking to me. Inside my mind, I mean."

"Telepathically."

"Exactly, you smart-ass. Telepathically."

"Then you brought Michael up here?"

"Uh-huh."

"And he started talking to Michael?"

"Not right away. Michael and He, well, they didn't like each other much. I always felt kinda sorry for Michael. I had such a good relationship with Him, but Michael—but at least Michael did what He told him."

"Which was?"

"You remember when O'Banyon's trailer burned that night?"

My stomach tightened. Brice O'Banyon was a star baseball pitcher for Consolidated. He lived in a trailer with his folks. One night it burned down and the three of them died.

"Michael did that?"

"He didn't want to. He put up a fight. He even told me he thought about going to the police. But you can imagine what the police would say when Michael told them that some kind of alien being was controlling his mind."

"He do anything else?"

"Oh, yes. Lots of things."

"Like what?"

"We drove up to Minnesota and robbed eleven convenience stores in two nights."

"God."

"Then in Chicago, we set two homeless people on fire. It was kind of weird, watching them all on fire and running down the street screaming for help. Michael shot both of them. In the back."

"While they were on fire?"

"Uh-huh."

I laughed. "Now I know it's bullshit."

"It isn't, Spence. You just want to think it is."

"But setting people on fire—"

"I didn't want to do it, Spence. I really didn't. And neither did Michael. But we kept coming back up here to the well all the time and—"

We didn't talk for a while. We just listened to the dark, soughing night and all the strange little creatures that hop and slither and sidle in the undergrowth. And the wind was trapped in the pines and not far away a windmill sang and then—

She startled me, moving up against me, her hands in my hair, her tongue forcing my mouth open with a ferocity that was one part comic and one part scary—

She pushed me up against the well and deftly got my fly open and fell to her knees and did me. I felt a whole lot of things just then, lust and fear and disbelief and then a kind of shock when I realized that this had been the one thing she'd said she'd never wanted to do, take anybody in her mouth that way, but she kept right on doing it till I spent my seed on the earth surrounding the well.

Then she was in my arms again, her face buried in my neck, and her hands gripping me so tight I felt pain—

And then: "He's talking to me, Spence. Couple minutes, He'll be talking to you, too. You'll be scared at first, hearing Him in your mind this way, but just hold me tight and everything will be all right. I promise."

But I was scared already because I knew now that what I was seeing was the undoing of Cindy Brasher. She probably felt a whole lot guiltier about Michael than she'd realized. And now her guilt was taking its toll. Friend of mine worked at the U of I hospital. He'd be able to help me get her in to see a shrink. I'd call him tonight, soon as I dropped Cindy off.

And then I heard it.

I didn't want to hear it, I pretended not to hear it, but I heard it. This voice, this oddly sexless voice inside my head, saying: *You're just what I've been looking for, Spence. You're a lot tougher than Michael could ever have been.*

And then I saw Cindy's face break into a little girl smile, all radiance and joy, and she said, "He's speaking to you, isn't He?"

I nodded.

And started to tear up and I didn't even know why.

Just standing there in the chill prairie night with this gal I was crazy in love with and this telepathic alien voice in my head—and my eyes just filled up with tears.

Filled way up and started streaming down my cheeks.

And then the alien voice started talking to me again, telling of its plans, and then Cindy was saying, "We're one now, Spence. You, me, and the thing in the well. One being. Do you know what I mean?"

I killed my first man two weeks later.

One rainy night we drove over to Davenport and walked along the river and then started back to Cedar Rapids. Cindy was all snuggled up to me when, through the rain and steam on the windshield, I saw the hitchhiker. He was old and skinny and gray and might have been part Indian. He wore a soaked-through red windbreaker and jeans and this sweat-stained Stetson.

The voice came to me so fast and so strong that I didn't have any time to think about it at all.

"Is He saying the same thing to you?" Cindy said, as the

hitchhiker got bigger in the windshield.

"Yeah."

"You going to do it?"

I gulped. "Yeah."

We pulled over to him. He had a real ancient, weary smile. And real bad, brown teeth. He was going to get his ride.

Cindy rolled down the window.

"Evening, sir," I said.

He looked a mite surprised that we were going to talk to him, rather than just let him hop in.

He put his face in through the window and that's when I shot him. Twice in the forehead. Knocked him back maybe ten, twelve feet. And then he stumbled backwards and disappeared into a ravine.

"Wow," Cindy said.

"Man, I really did it, didn't I?"

"You sure did, Spence. You sure did."

That night we made love with a hunger that was almost painful, the way we hurled ourselves at each other in the darkness of my apartment.

Thing was, I wanted to feel guilty. I wanted to feel that I'd just gone crazy and done something so reprehensible that I'd turn myself in and take my punishment. But I didn't feel anything at all, except this oneness with Cindy. She was right. Ever since the voice had been in my mind, I did feel this spiritual closeness to her. So there was no thought of turning myself in.

Oh, no, the next night we went back to the well and He spoke to us again. Inside our minds. I had a strange thought that maybe what we heard was our own voices inside our respective heads—telling us to do things we'd ordinarily be afraid or unwilling to do. But the voice seemed so real—

In the next week, there were six robberies, two arsons, and a beating. I had never been tough. Never. But one night Cindy and I strolled all fearless into this biker bar and had a couple of beers and of course a couple of the bikers started making remarks about how good-looking Cindy was and what was she doing with a fag like me, things like that, so I picked the toughest one I could see, this really dramatic bastard who had a skull-and-bones tattoo on the left side of his forehead, and rings with tiny spikes sticking up. I gave him a bad concussion, two broken ribs, and a nose he'd never quite be able to breathe out of again. I guess I got carried away. He was all the bullies who'd hurt and humiliated me growing up and in the Army. He was every single one of them in one body—even in the paratroopers, I was afraid of being beaten up. But now those fears were gone. Long gone.

The lovemaking got more and more violent and more and more bedeviling. It was all I could think of. Here I was working a lumberyard front office, not a place that's conducive to daydreaming, what with the front door constantly banging open and closed, open and closed, and the three phone lines always screaming—but all I could do was stare out the window with my secret hard-on in my pants and think about how good it would be that night with Cindy. My boss, Mr. Axminster, he even remarked on it, said I was acting moony as a high school kid. He didn't say it in a very friendly way, either. There was no bonus in my check at the end of that month.

Stopped by a few times to see my folks. They looked sad when they saw me, probably not a whole lot different than they'd look if I'd died in a car accident or something. A real sense of loss, their first and eldest torn away from them and made a stranger. I felt bad for them. I gave them long hugs and told them how much I loved them several times but all they could do was say that I looked different somehow and was I feeling all right and did I ever think of going to old Doc Hemple for a physical.

And of course I went back to the Parkinson cabin and the well. I say "I." While most of the time I went with Cindy, sometimes I went alone. Figured that was all right now that I was with the program. I mean I was one with Cindy and He but I was also still myself.

That's why I was alone when I got the Mex down by the railroad tracks.

He was maybe twenty, a hobo just off a freight, looking for shelter for the night.

I'd been covering the tracks for the past hour, watching the lonesome stars roll down the lonesome sky, waiting for somebody just like him.

The voice this time had suggested a knife. Said there was a great deal of difference in killing a man with a knife and killing a man with a gun. So I drove over to Wal-Mart and got me the best hunting knife I could find. And here I was.

I crouched beneath one of three boxcars sitting dead on the tracks. The Mex walked by, I let him get ten feet ahead of me, then I jumped him.

Got him just under the chin with my forearm and then slashed the knife right across the throat. Man, did he bleed. I just let him sink to the gravel. Blood was everywhere. He was grasping his throat and gasping, dumb brown eyes frantic and looking everywhere. I saw why this was different. And it was real different. With guns, you were at one remove, impersonal. But this was real *real* personal. I watched till I was sure he was dead; then I drove back to my apartment and took a shower.

Twenty-five minutes later, I pulled up to Cindy's place

and she came out. In the dome light, I could see she was
irritated.

"I hope you plan to start by apologizing."

"I'm really sorry, Cindy."

"Almost two hours late."

"I said I'm sorry."

"Where were you?"

So I told her.

"You've been going up to the well alone?"

Somehow I'd sensed that she wouldn't like that. That's
why I hadn't told her about it.

"I don't want you to do that any more."

"Go to the well?"

"Not by yourself, Spence."

"But why?"

"Because—" She looked out the window for a while.
Said nothing. Every few minutes, her drunken old man
would peek out the living room window to see if we were
still sitting at the curb.

"Because why, Cindy?"

She turned and looked at me. "Because He's my friend."

"He's my friend, too."

"Well, He wouldn't be your friend—you wouldn't even
know anything about Him—if I hadn't taken you up there."

Kind of a funny night, that one. We never really got over
our initial mood. Even the lovemaking was off a little.
Sometimes you can feel when a woman is losing interest in
you. Isn't anything they say or do; there's just something in
the air. Laurie had been like that when she'd dropped me
back in high school. I'd gone weeks with this sense that she
found me vaguely distasteful before she actually dumped
me. I was getting the same sense with Cindy. I just prayed
to God I was sensing things wrong.

But next night, things were pretty much back to normal. Drove to an Italian restaurant in Iowa City, little place with candlelight and a chunky guy wandering around with a violin, a kind of make-up dinner. After that, we went straight back to my place and made up for all the great sex we'd missed out on the night previous. Or at least I did. But Cindy—there was a certain vagueness to her sentiments now. No passion in the I-love-you's. No clinging to me after we made love.

Just before I took her home, she said, "Promise me you'll never go to the well again by yourself."

"God, I just don't understand what you're so upset about."

"Just promise me, Spence."

"All right. I promise."

She kissed me with a tenderness that rattled me, that made me think that we really were going to be as tight and true as we'd once been.

Next two visits to the well, we went together. By now, I knew why she always wanted to go there. It was addictive, that voice in your head, the sense that you were an actor in some cosmic drama you couldn't even begin to comprehend. I suppose religious people feel this way when they're contemplating Jesus or Jehovah or Buddha. I needed my fix every few days, and so did Cindy.

Following these two particular visits, we drove to Des Moines and found a darkened building we could climb to the top of. Kind of cold on the fourteenth floor. And it was late May. My knuckles were numb as I assembled the scope rifle. There was a motel and a bar a quarter block away. Must be where the really well-fixed swingers hung out, because the cars ran to BMWs and Porsches. There was even a Maserati.

Cindy crouched right next to me, rubbing my crotch as I sighted the gun. Gray-haired guy came out and started to climb into his Caddy. The dark city sprawled all around him, tattered clouds covering the moon.

"Him?"

"Huh-uh," she said.

Few minutes later, a real drunk lady with a fur wrap came wobbling out.

"Her?"

"Huh-uh."

Then a couple real slick types. Probably in advertising.

"Them?"

"Yeah."

"Both?"

"Uh-huh."

"That'll be tricky."

"You can do it, Spence."

I had to hurry.

Bam.

Guy's head exploded in big, bloody chunks. Man, it was hard to believe that a bullet could—

"Get him!" Cindy cried as the other guy, stunned, looked up at the roof we were firing from.

Knocked him a good clean five yards backwards. Picked him up. Hurled him onto the trunk of a Lincoln Town Car. Even had time to put another bullet in him before he rolled off the trunk and hit the pavement.

And then she was all over me, lashing me and licking me with her tongue, and she kept grinding her crotch against the barrel of the gun and I kept saying, "Cindy, God, listen, we have to get out of here!"

I just about had to drag her.

She wanted to do it right there on the roof.

She seemed crazy. I'd never seen her like this.

She couldn't calm down.

We rolled out of Des Moines about ten minutes later. She had my hand between her legs and her head back and her eyes were all white and dazed-looking. She just kept rubbing against my hand. We must have gone twenty miles that way.

Later, in bed, she said, "We're good again, aren't we, you and me?"

"We sure are."

"I was scared for a few days there."

"So was I."

"I just wouldn't want to live without you, Spence."

"I wouldn't want to live without you, either."

Her craziness had gone. We made gentle love and then I took her home.

And then next day, despite all my promising, I took the afternoon off and went to the well. I wanted to see it in daylight, see if I could see anything I missed at night.

But I couldn't.

I sat on the edge of the pit and watched squirrels and field mice dart in and out of the buffalo grass. And then for awhile I watched a hawk ride the air currents and I thought again, as I had all my boyhood, of how fine and free it would be to be a hawk. There was Indian lore that said that hawks were actually spies from another dimension and that had always intrigued me.

And then the voice filled my head.

I turned around real fast, so I could look down the well and see if the water boiled or bubbled when the voice spoke, but it didn't. Just dirty brackish water. Still. Very still.

But I wasn't still. I was agitated. I said, "No, that's not

right. I won't do that." But the voice wouldn't let go. I tried to walk away, but something stopped me. I tried to shut the voice out, but I couldn't.

I had to listen to His plan. His terrible *terrible* plan.

At dinner that night, a burger and fries with coupons at Hardee's, Cindy said, "I called you after school this afternoon."

"Oh. I should've told you."

"You took off, huh?"

"Yeah."

"Where'd you go?" She wasn't real good at hiding her suspicions.

"Iowa City."

"How come?"

I shrugged. "Check out one of the bookstores."

"Which one?"

"Prairie Lights."

"I guessed that was what you'd say."

"What's that supposed to mean?"

"I figured you'd lie and I figured it would have something to do with Iowa City, so I called some of the places you go. And one of the places I called was Prairie Lights. And guess what?"

"What?"

"They're closed down this week. Doing some kind of remodeling."

"Bullshit."

"Bullshit yourself, Spence. You want to call them? Find out for yourself?"

She leaned back on her side of the booth and crossed her arms over her chest. "You went to the well, didn't you?"

"No."

"You fucker."

She started crying, then, just like that, right there in the middle of Hardee's with all the moms and dads and kiddies watching us, some with great glee, some with embarrassment and a kind of pity.

I put my head down. "I'm sorry, Cindy. I won't ever do it again."

"Oh, right, Spence. You won't ever do it again."

Must have been two hours later before she uttered another syllable.

We were lying in bed and she said, "I need to be honest with you, Spence."

"I was hoping we were done arguing. I said I wouldn't ever go to the well again alone. And I mean it."

"The way you meant it last week?"

"God, Cindy, I—"

"I met somebody, Spence."

"What?"

"A guy. College boy, actually."

"What's that mean, you 'met' him?"

"I met him. That's what it means. Some girls and I went to Cedar Rapids a few days ago, to one of the malls. That's where he works. One of the malls. Anyway, he called me and asked me if I'd go out with him." Pause. "I told him yes, Spence."

"What the fuck are you doing to me, Cindy?"

"I'm not doing anything to you, Spence. I'm just being a nice, normal eighteen-year-old girl who met a nice, normal young man who asked her out."

"We're going to get married."

Pause. "I'm not sure about that now, Spence." Pause. "I'm sorry."

I rolled off the bed, sat on the edge, face in my hands.

She slid her arms around me, kissed me gently on the

back. "Maybe I just need a little break, Spence. Maybe that's all it is."

I took my face from my hands. "You're punishing me, aren't you, Cindy?"

"Punishing you?"

"For going to the well alone."

"God, Spence, that's crazy. I don't play games like that. I really don't."

"We have to get married, Cindy."

She laughed. "Why, are you pregnant?"

"The stuff we've done—"

"We didn't get caught, Spence. Nobody knows. We can just forget about it. Go on with our lives."

"Right. Just forget it. You know how many fucking people we've killed?"

I lost it, then, jumped up off the bed and stalked over to the bureau, and swept it clean with my arm. Brut and my graduation picture and my Army picture and Cindy's picture all smashed against the wall and fell to the floor in a rain of jagged glass.

The funny thing was, I wasn't thinking of Cindy at all, I was thinking of Laurie, and how she'd dumped me back in high school, and how even now I sometimes felt a sudden sharp pain from the memories . . . pain as dangerous as the pieces of glass now scattered all over my floor.

I turned to Cindy. "I'll tell you something, Cindy. If you go out with this guy, I'll kill you."

"God, that's real nice and mature, Spence. Maybe that's why I've lost interest in you. I thought that because you were older, you were an adult but—"

"Don't try and talk around it, Cindy. You heard what I said."

She got up and started putting her clothes on. We hadn't

made love but we'd seemed on the verge of it. Until she'd told me about this guy at the mall.

"If you threaten me one more time, Spence, I'll go to the police. I swear I will."

"Right."

"I will. You wait and see."

I grabbed her. Couldn't control myself. Wanted to smash her face in but settled for throwing her up against the wall and grabbing a bunch of her button-down blouse and holding her several inches off the floor.

"I meant what I said, Cindy. I'll kill you. And that's a promise."

Three hours after she left, the rain started. I lay awake the rest of the night listening to the shutters bang and the wind cry like lost children weeping. How could you hate what you loved so dearly?

I tried not to think what the voice had told me the last time at the well, about killing Cindy. But that's exactly what it said. And that's why I'd threatened Cindy tonight, I realized now. I was only doing the bidding of the voice, acting on its suggestion.

I had been shocked, I had resisted it—but I saw now that He could also see the future. He saw that Cindy would meet a stranger at the mall, just as He saw that Cindy would soon be ready to dump me. That's why he'd suggested I kill her.

I didn't see or hear from Cindy for three days. Things were bad at work. I couldn't concentrate. I sent a wrong shipment to the new co-op they're building out on the edge of the old Galton Farm and my boss did something he'd never done before—started yelling at me right in front of customers. It was pretty embarrassing.

Lonesome, I even thought of going to see my folks but

anything I said would just lead to I-told-you-so's.

Looked up a few buddies, too, but they were like strangers now. Oh, we went through some of the old routines, and made some plans for doing some autumn fishing up at Carter Lake, but I left the tavern that night feeling more isolated than ever.

I wondered what Cindy was doing. I kept seeing her naked and mounting the mall guy the way she sometimes mounted me. I drove and drove and drove, prairie highways leading to more prairie highways, cows and horses restless in the starry, rolling Iowa darkness. Sometimes I merged Cindy and Laurie into one, sometimes I wanted to cry but was unable to. How could you hate what you loved so dearly?

Warm summer arrived like a gift a few days later. People out here always go a little crazy when summer comes. I think they get intoxicated by all the scents of the flowers and the trees and the sweet, sad songs of the birds. I do. Ordinarily, anyway. But this summer was different. I couldn't appreciate any of it. It was as if I'd been entombed in my sorrow over Cindy leaving me. There was no room for anything but her.

I saw them, then. Town square. Around nine o'clock. Walking slowly past the Civil War memorial. Her arm through his. Same way we used to walk. He was handsome, of course. Cindy wouldn't have to settle for anything less.

I stumbled into an alley and was sick. Literally. Took the lid off a reeking garbage can and threw up.

Then I went into a grocery store and bought a pint of Jim Beam and went back to the alley and thought about what I was going to do. How I was going to handle all this.

I'm not much of a drinker. By the time I finished the pint, I was pretty foggy. I was also pretty sleepy. I leaned against the garbage can and slept.

A country-western song woke me a few hours later. Some pore truck-drivin' sumbitch had lost his honey. You know how country songs go. I got up all stiff and chilly and reoriented myself. I took a leak, while never taking my eye from the quarter-moon so brilliant in the midnight sky. I felt homesick; but I also felt as if I had no home to go to. And never would.

Twenty minutes later, I stood out in front of the police station. Town this size, the station is in the old courthouse. Neon sign above the westernmost entrance says: POLICE. There's a lock-up in the basement and a traffic court on second floor. On first floor is where the seven police officers work at various times of day and night.

I was going to do it. I was going to walk right up those stairs, right inside that building, and tell whichever cop was on duty just what Cindy and I had been up to.

"Hey, Spence."

Voice was familiar. I turned to see Donny Newton, whom I'd gone to high school with, walking up the street. He wore the dark uniform of the local gendarmes.

"Hey, Donny. Since when did you become a cop?"

"Took my test last year then went to the Police Academy in Des Moines for three months and voila, here I am. Doesn't pay jack shit for the first couple years but, given all the layoffs we've been having, I'm lucky to have a steady paycheck." Then he ceased being plain Donny Newton and became Officer Donny Newton. Suspicious. "So what're you doing here?"

Maybe Donny could make it easy for me. I'd known him a long time. Maybe he'd let me tell it all my way and not get all self-righteous about it.

My mouth opened. My brain wrote three or four lines of

dialogue for my tongue to speak, just to get things going. But somehow my tongue wouldn't speak them.

"Hey, you all right, man?"

Then I just wanted to get out of there. Fast.

"Little too much to drink."

"You all right to drive?"

I nodded. "Yeah."

"Sure?"

"Positive."

"I'd be happy to run you home."

"Thanks, Donny, but I'll be fine."

But he sure was giving me a funny look. I nodded a goodnight, and took off walking to my car, knowing he was watching me again.

At home I drank four beers and sat in the dark kitchen and listened to an owl who sounded every bit as lonely as I felt. Then I tumbled into bed and began seven hours of troubled and exhausting sleep.

At six I dragged myself from bed for a quick shave and shower. I'd just lathered up when I looked out the bathroom window and saw Donny Newton, still in uniform, doing something to my right rear tire. There's no garage or concrete drive. I just park on the grass on the east side of the house.

I couldn't figure out what the hell he was doing. He was down on one knee, spraying something in the tire tracks I'd made on the grass. Then he took this small, wooden frame and put it over a portion of the tire marks he'd just sprayed.

Only then did I understand what he was doing—getting an impression of my tracks, the way the cops do at a crime scene.

But why the hell was he interested in my tire tracks? Had there been a hit-and-run last night and he suspected me of driving drunk and leaving the scene of the accident?

He left quickly. Probably had no idea I'd seen him. Probably figured I was still asleep.

At noon, I saw him again, Donny. When did he sleep?

He was out in the lumberyard with my boss, Mr. Axminster. Couple times when they were talking, they'd both looked back at the front office where I was. Then he was gone.

The rest of the afternoon, Mr. Axminster acted pretty funny. He was already pissed that I'd been so preoccupied lately, and that I was making a lot of mistakes—but now it wasn't so much that he was mad—more that he wasn't quite sure what to make of me. As if I were some kind of alien being or something.

Just before quitting time, the phone rang. I was checking in some wallpaper kits, so Mr. Axminster had to take it. He talked a few minutes, in a whispery kind of voice, so I figured it was his lady friend. Rumor had it that he was sweet on a waitress named Myrna over at the Chow Down Cafe. I think it was true because she called here sometimes. He was always boasting about how good a Lutheran he was, so his being a family man and having a little strange on the side surprised me.

Then he said, "It's for you, Spence."

He tried to act like everything was just fine and dandy. But he was sweating a lot suddenly and it wasn't hot, and he couldn't look me directly in the eye. He handed me the phone. I said hello.

"Spence?"

"Uh-huh."

"Donny Newton."

I looked at Mr. Axminster, who looked quickly away.

"Wondered if we could get together?"

"When?"

"You're off in fifteen minutes, right?"

"Right."

"How about then?"

"Have a beer somewhere, you mean? Maybe a little bumper pool?" But I knew better, knew what he was really up to.

"Uh . . . well, actually, I was hoping you'd sort of stop over to the station."

"The station? How come?" I played it real dumb.

"Oh, just a couple things came up. Hoping you could help us clear them up a little."

"Well, sure, Donny. If it's important."

"I'd sure appreciate it."

"Sure thing, Donny. About fifteen minutes?"

"Fifteen minutes would be great. That'll give me time to empty the old bladder and grab us a pair of Pepsis."

"See you then, Donny."

Panic. Tried to control it. Closed my eyes. Forced myself to take deep breaths. Gripped the edge of the counter so I'd quit shaking.

Good old Cindy. The only person who could possibly have interested the police in my tire tracks. We'd used my car on all our murders and robberies. If Cindy had decided to blame me and to cooperate with authorities in reeling me in—Cindy would likely avoid jail herself. And she'd have her brand-new beau.

"They asked me about you, Spence. In case you're wondering."

When I opened my eyes, Mr. Axminster was standing there. "You've gotten yourself in some serious trouble, Spence." He shook his head. "When Donny Newton told me, well—" He looked very sad. "I've known your folks all my life, Spence. When they hear about this—"

But I wasn't waiting around for any more of his hand-wringing dramatic presentation.

I ran out to my car, hopped in, tore out of the driveway.

I drove. I have no idea where. Just—around. And fast. Very fast.

When I was aware of things again, it was an hour later and I was racing up a gravel road, leaving a plume of dust in my wake.

Instinctively, I headed for the only place I'd find any wisdom or solace.

I pulled into the surrounding woods, so nobody could see my car from the highway. I waited till dark before finding the trail that led to the well.

Downhill, a crow sat on the rickety remains of the cabin. He was big and shiny in the cool dusk.

The well looked the same as I approached it, the native stone of the pit a dead white in the darkening shadows.

I knelt down next to the well and put my head down inside. I needed to hear Him. Needed His wisdom.

Right away, I started crying. I was going to lose it all. My job. My girl. My freedom.

All I'd done was what the voice in the well had told me to do. And I had no control over that.

You'll feel better soon.

I let those words echo in my mind for a time before asking Him what He meant.

And He told me that I'd soon know what he meant.

And right after that, I heard her laugh.

Cindy. Coming down the path. Then: a second voice. Male. The guy she'd met at the mall.

Everything was dark now. I staggered to my feet and scurried into the woods.

They were holding hands. And laughing. And she was telling him about the well.

"You really love putting me on, don't you?" he said.

"It's not a put-on. Honest."

"There's this voice down the well."

"Not just a voice—an entity."

"Hey—big word. Entity."

"Right," Cindy said.

She slid her arm around him. Kissed him playfully on the chin. I was afraid I was going to be sick again. Real sick.

"It's an alien."

"From outer space?" he said.

"Exactly."

He laughed again. "What a con artist."

He sat on the edge of the well pit and took her to him and then kissed her long and deep and passionately.

And then the knife was in my hand. The knife I'd used on the Mex.

And suddenly I was screaming and running from the woods toward the well and I saw the mall guy looked startled and then terrified and I heard Cindy scream.

But I didn't stop.

I ran straight up to the guy and stabbed him in the chest. Stabbed him again and again and again.

He fell to the ground, all blood and dying gasps now, but I kept right on stabbing him until I heard Cindy's feet slapping up the path as she tried to escape.

But she wasn't going to escape.

No way.

I went after her, grabbed her by the long hair, whipped her back to me until our faces were almost touching.

"I loved you and you didn't give a damn at all."

"I still love you, Spence. It's just that I'm so—confused—

117

please don't—please understand that I love you Spence—
and we can be together again just the way we were and—"

I stabbed her in the chest.

She didn't scream or even cry.

In fact her hands fitted themselves around the hilt of the
knife, as if she wanted to make sure that the blade stayed
deep and true in her heart.

And then she fell into my arms.

And that was the weird thing, you know.

She didn't scream. But I did.

She didn't cry. But I did.

She didn't call for help. But I did.

The way it was later told to me, a farmer looking for a
couple stray head of cattle found me just like that—holding
Cindy lifeless in my arms, and sobbing so hard he was
afraid I was going to suffer some kind of seizure.

Later there were lights and harsh voices and then the
tear-stained faces of my parents.

Oh my God, Spence—

How could you do this, Spence—

Spence, we're going to get you the best lawyer we can afford, but your father's not a rich man, you know.

Mr. Spencer, this is your attorney Dan Myles—

Seven different counts of murder, Mr. Spencer—

Seven different . . .

Same night they put me in jail, they transferred me to a
mental hospital on the outskirts of Iowa City. I was so cold
I ended up with six wool blankets on me before they could
stop me from shuddering. They gave me three different
shots in my hip. Then I seemed to die. There was just—
darkness.

Over the next few weeks, they gave me several tests a
day. I saw medical doctors, psychologists, a priest though

not Roman Catholic, and then a young reporter named Donna Mannering who had just started working for our small-town newspaper.

They let her see me for twenty minutes in a room with an armed guard outside. I had told the M.D. that I wanted to talk to a reporter and he had seen to it that Donna was brought in.

"Doctor Wingate said you were saving something to tell me."

She was blonde and a little bit overweight but very pretty. She was also terrified. I'm sure I was the first killer she'd ever met in person.

"Yeah."

She flipped open her long, skinny reporter's notebook. "I guess I'll just let you do the talking."

"I want to tell you about the well."

"You mean like a wishing well."

I thought a moment. "Yeah, I guess it is kind of like a wishing well. Only you don't make the wishes. The thing in the well does."

"The thing in the well?"

"This alien."

"I see."

Now she looked more frightened than ever. Her blue gaze fled to the door several times. She wanted to be sure she could get away from me if I suddenly went berserk.

"There's an alien in the well."

"Right," I said.

"And it told you to do things?"

"Everything I did. I mean the killing, the robberies, the arson fires."

"The alien?"

"Uh-huh. And you know what?"

"What?"

"I don't mind if you smile. Because I know how crazy it all must sound."

"Well, I guess it does sound a little—" But then she stopped herself. "Did the thing in the well tell you to kill Cindy and her new friend?"

"Yes."

"Would you have done it otherwise?"

"I don't think so." Pause. "I want you to go out there."

"Where?"

"The well." I told her where she'd find it.

"When?"

"Soon as you can. But I want you to go alone."

"Why?"

"Because the thing will be more apt to talk to you, if you're alone."

"Were you alone when you first heard it?"

"No. I was with Cindy but she already knew about the alien, so that was different."

"I see." She glanced at her watch. She was trembling and licking her lips frantically. Her mouth must have been very dry. "Boy, where has the time gone? I need to get out of here. Guard!" She practically shouted.

The guard came in and led her out.

She glanced over her shoulder when she reached the threshold.

I said, "Please go out there, all right?"

She looked anxiously away and followed the guard out the door.

My trial didn't start for seven months. Because we were pleading insanity, there wasn't much I had to do but wait for the trial date.

During this time, I started reading about the strange murders taking place in and around my small hometown.

Old ladies viciously strangled to death with rosary beads.

On the first day of my trial, the day my lawyer spoke aloud my defense, that I had been taking orders from an alien being at the bottom of a well, I saw Donna Mannering sitting with several other reporters near the back of the courtroom. The other reporters were all smirking at the reference to the alien in the well.

But Donna wasn't.

At the end of the day, when I was being led back to county lockup, Donna pushed past the deputies surrounding me and pushed her face into mine. I saw in her eyes that same anger and same madness I'd known when I'd been under the sway of the voice in the well.

"You bastard," she spat at me.

And then she grabbed my right hand and shoved something into it and ran out of the courtroom.

I kept my hand closed all the way back to my cell, for fear that one of the guards would see what she'd given me and confiscate it.

I sat on the edge of my bunk and opened my hand and stared down at the snake-like coil of black rosary beads.

Author's Note

Stephen King has been a big influence on me. Somebody once called him the Thomas Wolfe of popular fiction, but to me he's more the Thomas Hardy. He has Hardy's social eye and his obsession with what time does to us all. And he has Hardy's generosity of spirit, too. The beautiful and forlorn poetry of *Pet Sematary* will tell you all you need to know about King's soul. I like just about everything he does, but I especially like some of the stories nobody seems to mention much: *Christine*, which is one of the great high school novels of our time; "Strawberry Spring," which is one of the best crime stories of the seventies; and "Nola," which I had in mind when I wrote "The Brasher Girl." Some people call this sort of thing homage; others, the more vigilant perhaps, call it theft.

Lover Boy

Ted and I caught the squeal, and it was the kind that makes for good war stories later in cop bars.

"You're not going to believe what happened," he said, laughing.

And when he told me, I laughed, too.

"Captain wants us to interview her," Ted said. "She's skimming back with him, then we'll meet her in the Pentathol room."

I sat there looking at the place, all the dazzling lights out front, all the sexy, throbbing music filling the ears. Places like this were all over the city now, and there were bound to be victims.

Humorous as the situation was, the woman who'd just been arrested had been a victim, for sure. Even knowing the little I knew, I felt kind of sorry for her.

"Name?"

"Vanessa Conway."

"Age?"

"Thirty-six."

"Married?"

"You know I am."

"We have to make it official, ma'am, for the record, I mean."

Sigh. "Yes, married."

"Husband's name?"

"Robert Conway."

"Children?"

"Two."

"Ages?"

"Six and eight."

I looked over at Ted. The Captain likes us to interview certain people because he says we have the common touch. We don't have the kind of handsome faces you see on the cop vids, but we do have the kind of faces most people seem to trust.

"Have you consulted counsel about what happened tonight?"

"Not yet."

"Do you prefer human or android counsel?"

She looked at Ted. She had huge, beautiful eyes. "Human."

"Note that at ten forty-two p.m., suspect was offered counsel."

"The hormones."

"Ma'am?" I said.

"That's when they changed."

"When what changed, ma'am?"

After everything that had happened in the past few hours, I didn't expect her to be completely lucid. She'd had a couple jolts of Pentathol. That can make them fuzzy, too.

"When the parlors changed."

"I see."

"When they started with the hormones."

Ted looked at me.

It was unlikely we'd ever forget the time when the hormones were introduced to the cybersex parlors. Wealthy people can keep their diversions and perversions private in their homes. But for most people who want cybersex, it means going to the bars. And renting the kind of fullbody data suits the wealthy have at home. Then the rich folks dis-

covered that cybersex is even better if you do it in conjunction with hormones that are laced with steroids. These
days, the people who go to the bars don't get hooked just
on the cybersex. They get hooked on the drugs, too.

"Why did you go there tonight, Vanessa?"

"Because I couldn't take it any more."

"Take what, Vanessa?"

"The way he was."

"The way your husband was?"

"Right."

Ted said, "How was he, Vanessa?"

"Cold. Angry. Or indifferent. The indifference was the
hardest thing to take."

"What do you think made him this way?" Ted said.

"What do I think—" She stopped herself. Smiled sadly.
Shook her head. "The cybersex parlors were bad enough. I
mean, he'd come home after spending time there and he'd
want me to perform all these gymnastics. And I couldn't.
And I didn't want to anyway. I mean, I love my husband.
And I want sex to be a part of that love. I don't want sex—"

She paused and looked at me with those gorgeous, lost
eyes of hers. "I want sex to have some meaning for me,
other than a simple orgasm."

"So the parlors got in the way of your home life?" I said.

"Got in the way?" She shook her head again. "He started
spending half our income on the parlors. He also started
spending half his time in the parlors."

She started crying, then. Just that abruptly. Put her
sweet little face in her hands and just started sobbing.

Ted and I looked at each other. Now it was our turn to
shake our heads.

I saw a survey once that said that there were almost as
many women as men addicted to the cybersex parlors. The

image you see on the newsies every night is of some horned-up urban male leaving one of the parlors all bowlegged and dewy-eyed from the incredible sexual experience he's just had.

But every night we checked out the parlors, we saw more than our share of women. And they looked every bit as bowlegged and dewy-eyed as the males.

This was back before the hormones. The hormones sort of tipped the balance. After the hormones, the whole thing got a lot more dangerous. And a lot more male.

"Then we tried a separation."

"When was this, Vanessa?"

"Six months ago."

"How did that go?"

"Well, for a little while, I had a lot of hope. Even to the point where I let him move back with us."

"He gave up the parlors?"

"He said he did. He even convinced the counselor he had."

"Counselor?"

"A head-shrinker."

"I see."

She smiled at Ted. "He was a roid and very good at his job."

Ted smiled back.

"But then one night this old friend of his stopped by our house and started talking about the hormones and—I could see it in his eyes."

"His eyes?"

"My husband's eyes."

"Oh."

"I could see how much he wanted to try it out for himself. His friend kept saying that he'd never had cybersex unless he'd had it with the hormones."

The first couple of times, you needed to take the hormones eight days in advance for them to really work when you got to your cybersex parlor.

But after they'd been in your system for a sufficient time, all you had to do was take a pill when you got to the parlor and you'd be all set.

Shortly after the hormones were introduced, the federal government tried to get them taken off the market, but by then nobody was listening. The FDA had screwed up, but it was too late to put the genie back in the bottle.

The parlors changed, too. The hormones increased cybersex pleasure a thousand times over, according to users, but they also increased the psychotic episodes. And these didn't have to do with bliss. These had to do with rage.

For the first time, the parlors got violent. The users started attacking each other. Murder was not unheard of.

But no matter how dangerous they got, the number of users increased twenty percent a month.

Unfortunately, the users didn't leave their violence at the parlors, either. They brought it home with them.

"I remember the first night he beat me."

"You want to tell us about it?"

"I was asleep and he came in to our bedroom and woke me up. He had just gotten back from the parlor. He wanted to have sex. Very rough sex. I tried to be cooperative, but he was really hurting me. And the less cooperative I got, the more violent he got. He beat me up pretty badly."

"Did you call the police?"

"Not that time. Later on, I did. But the beatings weren't the worst part, anyway."

Ted said, "What was the worst part, Vanessa?"

"When he fell in love with her."

"Her?"

"The woman in the holo at the cybersex parlor."

"The wo—But they're just images," Ted said. "They're not real people."

Ted hadn't been keeping up on his newsies. This was a phenomenon that a lot of head-shrinkers were deeply worried about, the parlor customers starting to prefer the reality of holographic women to the reality of their wives and lovers. Fullbody data suits—and you could jack into a reality far more "real" than the real world.

"He started sending her flowers and wine and little trinkets—having them delivered to the parlor, if you can believe it." Vanessa said. "He even started pretending he was going to leave me for her. One night, he came home and said, 'I've got to be honest with you, honey. I've fallen in love with Angie.' 'Who's Angie?' I said. 'The woman at the parlor. The woman I see all the time.' I couldn't help myself. I laughed. He looked so earnest and pathetic, like this little boy with his head filled with fantasies. And when I laughed—he took me in the bedroom and raped me. And broke my arm in the process."

"Did you move out again?"

"That's what I was in the process of doing tonight," she said. "I skimmed home after work to pick up the kids—but when I got there, the doors were padlocked and the kids were gone. There was a note. He'd taken them to his mother's and didn't want me to bother them. He said he was going to divorce me and get custody. And that Angie was moving in with him over this weekend. And that was when—"

"You went to the parlor tonight?"

"Yes. And walked straight to see Angie—"

She was silent then, staring at the wall.

"Did I really do it?"

"Yes, I'm afraid you did."

"With a scissors?"

"Yes."

"They can . . . re-attach things like that, can't they?"

"He's at the hospital now."

She raised her head. Looked at me. "You know what I did afterward? While he was still lying there bleeding?" Shook her head. "I put the headset on and had a look at Angie for myself. God, she's not even that pretty. She looks kind of cheap, in fact. It must be the hormones."

"Right. The hormones." Then I said: "Vanessa?"

"Yes."

"I've read you your rights. But you've just given us a confession in effect—without counsel being present."

She shrugged. "Oh, I did it. I'm not trying to deny that."

"So you're making this confession voluntarily?"

"Yes, voluntarily. And you know the worst thing?"

"What?"

"I'm not even sorry I did it. Not right now, anyway. I mean, later on maybe I'll be sorry. But not right now."

As we were winding up for the night, Ted said, "I feel sorry for her."

"Yeah, so do I."

"Hard to imagine that a man would prefer a holo to a nice, sweet woman like that."

"Yeah," I said.

We said goodnight as we walked out to our personal skimmers.

"See you tomorrow," Ted said.

I was about halfway home when I watched as my hand

reached for the communicator and punched the "Home" button.

"How's my big, strong policeman doing tonight?" my wife's face said on the tiny screen.

"Fine. But very tired. And they're making me work overtime again."

I saw the disappointment in her face. "But I thought tonight—Well, it's been a while since we've had—oh what did I used to call them?"

"Romantic interludes."

"Oh, right," she laughed. "It's been a while. I even chilled a bottle of wine for us."

"Give me a freaking break, will you?" I shouted at the communicator. "I'm busting my ass off on overtime—and all you can do is whine about it."

I heard the violence in my words and was shocked. Buddy, the guy who got me the hormes, said I had to be careful of sudden temper flare-ups. He wasn't kidding.

"I'm sorry, honey."

"I'll just see you when you get here," she said, and broke communication. She sounded forlorn and confused.

"One-hour ticket," I said to the man at the booth in the front lobby of the parlor.

"And your lady?"

"Alison."

"Alison, it is," he said, and took my credit card and made the necessary arrangements. When he handed it back, he said, "She's a very popular lady."

This was the third night running he'd said that to me. And it was funny, but every time he said it, I felt a strange, hot surge of jealousy.

Then I went in to see my Alison.

Different Kinds of Dead

Around eight that night, snow started drifting on the narrow Nebraska highway Ralph Sheridan was traveling. Already he could feel the rear end of the new Buick begin sliding around on the freezing surface of the asphalt, and could see that he would soon have to pull over and scrape the windshield. Snow was forming into gnarly bumps on the safety glass.

The small-town radio station he was listening to confirmed his worst suspicions: the weather bureau was predicting a genuine March blizzard, with eight to ten inches of snow and drifts up to several feet.

Sheridan sighed. A thirty-seven-year-old bachelor who made his living as a traveling computer salesman—he worked especially hard at getting farmers to buy his wares— he spent most of the year on the road, putting up in the small, shabby plains motels that from a distance always reminded him of doghouses. A brother in Cleveland was all the family he had left; everybody else was dead. The only other people he stayed in touch with were the men he'd been in Vietnam with. There had been women, of course, but somehow it never worked out—this one wasn't his type, that one laughed too loudly, this one didn't have the same interests as he. And while his friends bloomed with mates and children, there was for Sheridan just the road, beers in bars with other salesmen, and nights alone in motel rooms with paper strips across the toilet seats.

The Buick pitched suddenly toward the ditch. An experienced driver and a calm man, Sheridan avoided the common mistake of slamming on the brakes. Instead, he took the steering wheel in both hands and guided the hurtling car along the edge of the ditch. While he had only a foot of earth keeping him from plunging into the gully on his right, he let the car find its own traction. Soon enough, the car was gently heading back onto the asphalt.

It was there, just when the headlights focused on the highway again, that he saw the woman.

At first, he tried sensibly enough to deny she was even there. His first impression was that she was an illusion, a mirage of some sort created by the whirling, whipping snow and the vast, black night.

But no, there really was a beautiful red-haired woman standing in the center of the highway. She wore a trench coat and black high-heeled shoes. She might have been one of the women on the covers of the private-eye paperbacks he'd read back in the sixties.

This time, he did slam on the brakes; otherwise, he would have run over her. He came to a skidding stop less than three feet from her.

His first reaction was gratitude. He dropped his head to the wheel and let out a long sigh. His whole body trembled. She could easily have been dead by now.

He was just raising his head when harsh wind and snow and cold blew into the car. The door on the passenger side had opened.

She got inside, saying nothing, closing the door when she was seated comfortably.

Sheridan looked over at her. Close up, she was even more beautiful. In the yellow glow of the dashboard, her features were so exquisite they had the refined loveliness of sculpture. Her tumbling, radiant hair only enhanced her face.

She turned to him finally and said, in a low, somewhat

breathy voice, "You'd better not sit here in the middle of the highway long. It won't be safe."

He drove again. On either side of the highway he could make out little squares of light—the yellow windows of farmhouses lost in the furious gloom of the blizzard. The car heater warmed them nicely. The radio played some sexy jazz that somehow made the prairie and the snow and the weather alert go away.

All he could think of was those private-eye novels he'd read as a teenager. This was what always happened to the Hammer himself, ending up with a woman like this.

"Do you mind?" she asked.

Before he had time to answer, she already had the long, white cigarette between her full, red lips and was lighting it. Then she tossed her head back and French inhaled. He hadn't seen anybody do that in years.

"Your car get ditched somewhere?" he asked finally, realizing that these were his first words to her.

"Yes," she said, "somewhere."

"So you were walking to the nearest town?"

"Something like that."

"You were walking in the wrong direction." He paused. "And you're traveling alone?"

She glanced over at him again with her dark, lovely gaze. "Yes. Alone." Her voice was as smoky as her cigarette.

He drove some more, careful to keep both hands on the wheel, slowing down whenever the rear of the car started to slide.

He wasn't paying much attention to the music at this point—they were going up a particularly slick and dangerous hill—but then the announcer's voice came on and said, "Looks like the police have really got their hands full tonight. Not only with the blizzard, but now with a murder. Local banker John

T. Sloane was found murdered in his downtown apartment twenty minutes ago. Police report an eyewitness say he heard two gunshots and then saw a beautiful woman leaving Sloane's apartment. The eyewitness reportedly said that the woman strongly resembled Sloane's wife, Carlotta. But police note that that's impossible, given the fact that Carlotta died mysteriously last year in a boating accident. The eyewitness insists that the resemblance between the redheaded woman leaving Sloane's apartment tonight and the late Mrs. Sloane is uncanny. Now back to our musical program for the evening."

A bossa nova came on.

Beautiful. Redheaded. Stranded alone. Looking furtive. He started glancing at her, and she said, "I'll spare you the trouble. It's me. Carlotta Sloane."

"You? But the announcer said—"

She turned to him and smiled. "That I'm dead? Well, so I am."

Not until then did Sheridan realize how far out in the boonies he was. Or how lacerating the storm had become. Or how helpless he felt inside a car with a woman who claimed to be dead.

"Why don't you just relax?"

"Please don't patronize me, Mr. Sheridan."

"I'm not patroniz—Say, how did you know my name?"

"I know a lot of things."

"But I didn't tell you my name and there's no way you could read my registration from there and—"

She French inhaled—then exhaled—and said, "As I said, Mr. Sheridan, I know a lot of things." She shook her head. "I don't know how I got like this."

"Like what?"

"Dead."

"Oh."

"You still don't believe me, do you?"

He sighed. "We've got about eight miles to go. Then we'll be in Porterville. I'll let you out at the Greyhound depot there. Then you can go about your business and I can go about mine."

She touched his temple with long, lovely fingers. "That's why you're such a lonely man, Mr. Sheridan. You never take any chances. You never let yourself get involved with anybody."

He smiled thinly. "Especially with dead people."

"Maybe you're the one who's dead, Mr. Sheridan. Night after night alone in cheap little hotel rooms, listening to the country-western music through the wall, and occasionally hearing people make love. No woman. No children. No real friends. It's not a very good life, is it, Mr. Sheridan?"

He said nothing. Drove.

"We're both dead, Mr. Sheridan. You know that?"

He still said nothing. Drove.

After a time, she said, "Do you want to know how tonight happened, Mr. Sheridan?"

"No."

"I made you mad, didn't I, Mr. Sheridan, when I reminded you of how lonely you are?"

"I don't see where it's any of your business."

Now it was her turn to be quiet. She stared out at the lashing snow. Then she said, "The last thing I could remember before tonight was John T. holding me underwater till I drowned off the side of our boat. By the way, that's what all his friends called him. John T." She lit one cigarette off another. "Then earlier tonight I felt myself rise through darkness and suddenly I realized I was taking form. I was rising from the grave and taking form. And there was just one place I wanted to go. The apartment he kept in

135

town for his so-called business meetings. So I went there to-night and killed him."

"You won't die."

"I beg your pardon?"

"They won't execute you for doing it. You just tell them the same story you told me, and you'll get off with second-degree. Maybe even not guilty by reason of insanity."

She laughed. "Maybe if you weren't so busy watching the road, you'd notice what's happening to me, Mr. Sheridan."

She was disappearing. Right there in his car. Where her left arm had been was now just a smoldering red-tipped cig-arette that seemed to be held up on invisible wires. A part of her face was starting to disappear, too.

"About a quarter-mile down the highway, let me out, if you would."

He laughed. "What's there? A graveyard?"

"As a matter of fact, yes."

By now her legs had started disappearing.

"You don't seem to believe it, Mr. Sheridan, but I'm ac-tually trying to help you. Trying to tell you to go out and live while you're still alive. I wasted my life on my husband, sitting around at home while he ran around with other women, hoping against hope that someday he'd be faithful and we'd have a good life together. It never happened, Mr. Sheridan. I wasted my whole life."

"Sounds like you paid him back tonight. Two gunshots, the radio said."

Her remaining hand raised the cigarette to what was left of her mouth. She inhaled deeply. When she exhaled, the smoke was a lovely gray color. "I was hoping there would be some satisfaction in it. There isn't. I'm as lonely as I ever was."

He wondered if that was a small, dry sob he heard in her voice.

"Right here," she said.

He had been cautiously braking the last minute-and-a-half. He brought the car comfortably over to the side of the road. He put on his emergency flashers in case anybody was behind him.

Up on the hill to his right, he saw it. A graveyard. The tombstones looked like small children, huddled against the whipping snow.

"After I killed him, I just started walking," she said. "Walking. Not even knowing where I was going. Then you came along." She stabbed the cigarette out in the ashtray. "Do something about your life, Mr. Sheridan. Don't waste it the way I have."

She got out of the car and leaned back in. "Goodbye, Mr. Sheridan."

He sat there, watching her disappear deep into the gully, then reappear on the other side and start walking up the slope of the hill.

By the time she was halfway there, she had nearly vanished altogether.

Then, moments later, she was gone utterly.

At the police station, he knew better than to tell the cops about the ghost business. He simply told them he'd seen a woman fitting the same description out on the highway about twenty minutes ago.

Grateful for his stopping in, four cops piled into two different cars and they set out under blood-red flashers into the furious white night.

Mr. Sheridan found a motel—his usual one in this particular burg—and took his usual room. He stripped, as always, to his boxer shorts and T-shirt and got snug in bed beneath the covers and watched a rerun of an old sitcom.

He should have been laughing—at least all the people on the laugh track seemed to be having a good time—but instead he did something he rarely did. He began crying. Oh, not big wailing tears, but hard, tiny, silver ones. Then he shut off both TV and the lights and lay in the solitary darkness, thinking of what she'd said to him.

No woman. No children. No love.

Only much later, when the wind near dawn died and the snow near light subsided, only then did Sheridan sleep, his tears dried out but feeling colder than he ever had. Lonely cold. Dead cold.

Yesterday's Dreams

ONE

1

There was a little boy up here one day, a soft and fertile spring day, and he said to his mother listen to the singing, listen to the singing, and she said that's the wind in the trees, honey, that's not singing. But I agreed silently with the little boy. On this slope of hill, when the wind passes through the trees just right, it really does sound like singing, a sweet, sad song, and sometimes I imagine that it sings the names of those I come here to see, my wife Susan and my daughters Cindy and Anne.

There was no singing today, not a Chicago hot and Chicago humid August day like this one, August 29, to be exact, Anne's twelfth birthday, or would have been if it all hadn't happened, if the three of them hadn't died.

I brought a few garden tools so I could clean everything up around the headstone, and I brought sunflowers, which Anne had always liked especially.

I started out the way I usually do, saying prayers, Hail Marys and Our Fathers, but then just sort of talking to them in my mind, and telling them how it's been going since I took early retirement on my forty-eighth birthday, and how the rest of the family is doing, all the aunts and uncles and cousins who had loved her so much.

I stayed a couple of hours, spending the last twenty minutes or so watching a bright red family of cardinals building a nest on a low-slung branch nearby.

After I left, I drove over by Wrigley Park, where Susan lived when I first started dating her back in the early sixties, past the theaters where we used to see the romance movies she liked so much—you know, with Sandra Dee and Troy Donahue and people like that—and the dance hall where we saw a very young Jimi Hendrix, long before anybody had ever heard of him, or before anybody knew what to make of him, either.

Then I stopped in a bar and had a couple of Lites, me having started to lose that old boyish figure of mine, and then I stopped by a video rental store and picked up three episodes of "Maverick," James Garner being just about my favorite actor. I'd seen this particular batch before, but I never seem to get tired of them.

2

I was supposed to eat dinner at my brother's that night but I canceled because he warned me that his wife Liz had invited one of her church friends along so we could meet. Don't get me wrong. Liz is a nice woman. I like her. But her friends don't appeal to me. They're a lot like Liz, big and purposeful and sure of themselves in ways that aren't always attractive. But then I'm probably not being fair to them. I always end up comparing them to Susan and not many women can stand up to that.

Anyway, I canceled dinner, saying I had a sore throat and headache. Liz sounded irritated, and as if she didn't believe me—and she shouldn't have; hell, I was lying—but she finally forced herself to sound civil and say she hoped I got to feeling better.

So here I was at the microwave when the knock on the door came. I was having the Hungry Man minute-steak dinner. When you eat enough of these jobbies, you get to know how to kill the worst of the taste on each particular dinner. For instance, the chicken dinner can be pretty well covered up with a little mustard on the breast, whereas the beans and franks take a whole lot of ketchup. As yet, I haven't figured out what to do with the fish dinner. No matter what you put on it, and I've tried just about everything, it tastes like it came direct from Lake Erie back when they found all those strange, sad sea creatures floating dead on it.

The knock.

I transferred the dinner from the microwave to the plate I had waiting on the table and then I went to the front door.

Funny thing was, when I got the inside door opened, I didn't see anybody, just a purple dusk through the dusty screened-in-porch.

Then I heard the sniffle.

"I'm real scared, Mr. Flannery."

She was somewhere between six and eight, a raggedy little white girl in scruffy shirt and jeans. She smelled hot and teary. Her mussed blonde hair looked sweaty.

I looked down and said, "What's the matter, honey?"

"People said you was a cop."

"I used to be a cop, honey."

"Somebody kilt my Daddy."

Being a cop is a little like being a doctor. You have to resist panic, not only for your sake but the sake of the others.

"Where is he, sweetheart?"

"Down'n the garage. Somebody shot him. Right here."

She tapped her thin, little chest and started crying again.

"C'mon, honey, we'll go see."

I grabbed the flashlight I keep next to the front door in the little hutch next to the statue of the Virgin Mary Cindy made me when she was in fourth grade. At first I wasn't sure what it was, but she was only too eager to tell me. "It's the Blessed Mother, Dad," sounding as if she had just suspected for the very first time that ole Dad might be a dunce. "Oh, yeah, sure," I said. "That's just what I thought it was." I can still see her smile that day, and how she held her arms out to me.

All these years later, I bent down and picked up a different little girl. But this one wasn't smiling. I held her tight as we went out the door and, just as the screen door slammed, she started crying hot and hard into my neck.

3

In the moonlight and the heat, in the smell of hot car oil and dried dog droppings, the alley was a silver, gravel path past neat rows of garbage cans and plump brown-plastic bags of garbage for the city trucks come Thursday.

"That one?" I'd say, nodding to the girl I was carrying, who was still crying, and she'd just shake her head and say no not that garage.

We ran nearly to the end of the alley to a small, beaten garage that could fit maybe one compact, and she just went hysterical on me, sobbing and kicking her hard little shoes against my legs. "He's in there! He's in there!"

I took her back down two garages and set her on moonlit grass still warm from the afternoon and said you stay there honey, right there, and don't move, all right, and then went back to the little garage at the end of the block and got my flashlight going and found her daddy, who was dead all right, indeed.

I never got used to corpses. In detective stories cops always tell jokes around stiffs because according to the writers this is the only way cops can deal with it all. But I never told jokes and neither did the cops I worked with. If you found kids who were dead, you got mad and wanted to kill somebody right back; but if they were adults you got scared because you saw yourself down there. Like an Irish wake, I guess, the person you're really mourning is yourself.

Whoever shot him must've really hated him.

He had a bullet hole in his trachea, in his shoulder, in his chest, and in his groin, most likely his balls.

He wore a white shirt that was soaked with pinkish blood, and dark slacks that smelled of where his bowels had let go. In life he'd probably been a decent-enough looking blond guy—dishwater blond, I guess they call it, like his daughter—working class probably, like most of the people in the neighborhood, cheap little wedding ring on his left little finger and a messy dragon tattoo of red and blue on his inside right forearm at the base of his dirty rolled-up sleeve.

I didn't touch him. I didn't even go into the garage where he was propped up against the back bumper of one of the old Kaisers that that crazy millionaire had manufactured right after World War II.

I went back to the girl and said, "Honey, what's your name?"

She looked up and said, "He's dead, isn't he?"

"Honey, we'll talk about that later. But now I need to know your name and where you live."

"Somebody killed him."

I bent down and touched her cheek. "Honey, what's your name?"

"Sandy."

"What's your last name?"

"Myles."

"What's your dad's name?"

"David."

"Where do you live?"

She raised a tiny pale arm and pointed. "Over there." She pointed to a house across the alley and two doors down.

"See that house behind us?"

She turned and looked. "Uh-huh."

"I'm going to run in there and call the police and then I'll come right back out. I'll take you in with me if you want to."

"He's dead," she said, and started crying again.

I reached down and scooped her up and carried her up to the house. An old and frightened Polish woman came to the door and opened up only after I told her six different times that I really was Nick Flannery, the ex-cop from down the street, and I really did need to use her phone.

4

A male-female team of uniforms showed up first. I didn't recognize them and vice-versa. They were very young, probably no more than a year out of the academy.

They reached the garage before I did. Sandy had started crying so hard that she'd thrown up. I'd stayed with her to get her washed and give her a couple of sips of the strawberry pop the old widow offered her.

I left Sandy inside and went out to the alley, and when I got to the garage I saw the female inside with her flashlight and the male standing out on the gravel looking at me.

"You're Mr. Flannery?"

"Right."

"You called in about the murdered man?"

"Yes."

"Dispatcher said the body was in the garage."

"Right. It is."

He gave me a quizzical cop look—the same kind of look I'd given hundreds of drunks, fakers, and lunatics during my own career—and said, "Maybe you'd like to show us where the body is, then."

"It's not in the garage?"

"Not that we can see."

I took my flashlight and walked into the garage. Several old tires hung on the wall, laced up with silver cobwebbing. You could smell rain and sweet rot in the old wood.

The female officer had stacked three crates on top of each other and was exploring an attic-like shelf made from plywood sheeting.

"Nothing," she said. And then sneezed from the dust.

Heavy tires popped gravel outside. Car doors opened and slammed. I heard the young cop say, "Nothing here. No body we can find."

A familiar voice said, "Like we don't have enough to do already."

I went out and let him see me and he was just as surprised as I figured he'd be.

"Hey," he said, "what're you doing here?"

"I called it in."

"The dead guy?"

"Yeah."

"Then where is he?"

"I don't know."

Hodiak and I had started out as rookies together. I spent my nights with my kids and Hodiak, unmarried, spent his at night school. He got his B.A., then his Master's in Criminology. He made detective about seven years before I retired. I hadn't seen him in a while, not since his hair had turned white. "Let's go in and talk to the little girl," I said.

5

Hodiak spent fifteen minutes with Sandy in the kitchen. By this time, the old woman had fixed her up with more strawberry pop and a small dish of ice cream, at least half of which was white and sticky on her face and pink little hands.

She said that she and her daddy had been walking home from the grocery store, taking the alley as they usually did, when this man appeared and started arguing with her daddy, saying he owed him money and everything, and then the guy got real mad and took out a gun and shot her daddy several times, and then the guy took off running. She cried and cried but she couldn't get her daddy to wake up. He'd managed to crawl into the garage but now he wasn't moving. And that's when she remembered that a cop named Flannery lived down the street—people always told her to run to my place if she ever got in any trouble—and that's how we met.

Hodiak left her in the kitchen and walked me back outside. He took his own flashlight and we went over the garage again.

"There's a lot of blood."

"There sure is," I said.

"So we know he was at least wounded pretty bad."

146

"He was more than wounded. He was dead."

"Then if he was dead—and believe me, a cop like you, he'd know a dead guy when he saw one—but if he was dead, then where the hell is he?"

I shook my head again.

"No offense, Flannery, but if he was dead, then he'd still be here."

"Somebody moved him."

"Who?"

"I don't know."

"And why?"

"I don't know that, either."

The uniformed cop came up. His female counterpart was sitting with her car door open, filling out a couple forms. "I canceled everything. The ambulance and all."

"Thanks," Hodiak said. "You two start by checking that house over there, where the little girl lives. Then start looking around the neighborhood. He couldn't have gone very far if he was shot up so bad."

The male cop nodded, then walked back to the car to tell his partner their instructions.

"No body," Hodiak said. He sounded tired. "It never ends."

I'd been thinking the same thing. "No, it doesn't."

Hodiak shrugged. "Well, there are eight million stories in the Naked City, *compadre*, and this has been one of them." He clapped me on the back. "You get my note about the funeral?"

"Yeah. Appreciated it."

"Sorry I couldn't make it. Some police convention in Arizona."

"Sounds like tough duty."

He smiled sadly. "Sorry about what happened, Flannery.

You had one hell of a nice family. They ever nail anybody yet?"

"Not so far."

I walked him back to his car. The temperature had started to fall suddenly. You could see silver dew on the grass. There was a hint of fall in the air. September and its fiery leaves and harvest moons would be here soon enough.

"You doing all right with your leave and all, Flannery?"

"Pretty good. I do a little security work now and then. Gives me something to do."

He got in his car, started it, rolled the window down. His radio squawked with raspy dispatcher sounds. "I still get out to that old bowling alley a couple times a month, see some of the old guys. You know. You should stop out there sometime."

"Maybe I will."

He nodded. "I'll keep you posted on all this. If we hear anything, I mean."

I smiled. "Yeah, if a dead guy checks himself into a hospital, be sure and let me know."

6

Over the next week, I walked back up the alley at least twice a day. Disappearing bodies were the stuff of mystery novels, not reality. The odd thing was, the blood tracks didn't leave the garage. He bled a lot while he was propped up against the Kaiser but when he left the garage—

All I could think of was that somebody had wrapped him up in a tarpaulin and stashed him in a car trunk.

I suppose I enjoyed it, playing detective. Sure beat flat-footing it all over a busy Saturday afternoon mall in rubber-soled shoes and a uniform designed to look like a cop's. I went to Sandy's house several times, each time her neighbor telling me that Sandy was at her aunt's house, but she didn't know the aunt's name or address. Poor little kid, I wondered how she was doing.

Gradually, I gave it up. Hodiak phoned a few times to tell me that they'd had absolutely no leads, and to invite me out to the bowling alley again. And after skipping a few days, I walked to the garage again but found nothing helpful whatsoever.

Autumn came nine days following Sandy knocking on my door. You know how it is in the Midwest. The seasons rarely give warning. They sneak up on you and pounce. I drove to one of the piers and looked at Lake Michigan. When the sky is gray and the temperature face-numbing, there's a kind of bleak majesty to the big international freighters set against the line of the horizon. At home, I turned on the heat and put the Lipton iced tea away and hauled out the Ovaltine.

On Tuesday of the following week, just at dusk, I saw Sandy. Or thought I did.

I was on my way back from the grocery store, making the six-block afternoon walk, when I saw a little girl at the far end of the block. I called out to her and waved but, instead of waving back, she seemed to recognize me and then took off running.

After dinner, I went back up the alley with my flashlight. Checked out the garage. Noted where the blood trail ended. And then raised my eyes and looked at the back of Sandy's house, where a light shone in a small, upstairs window, be-hind heavy drapes drawn tight.

I went over and knocked on the front door. The wind was up, a November wind in mid-September, and you

could hear leaves scraping the sidewalk like a witch's fingernails on a blackboard, and hear the lone neighborhood owl
cry out, lonely in the chilly gloom. No answer. I looked at
the curb. A red Honda sat there. I hadn't noticed it on my
previous trips over here. I went out to the curb and opened
the driver's door and rooted around until I found the registration. No help. Car belonged to one Jessica Williams.
Sandy's last name was Myles, her father's name David.

I went around back and tried that. No answer there, either. I tried the doorknob. Locked.

I took a few steps back, so I could get a better look up at
the window where the light had shone. There was no light
now. Somebody had turned it off. I sensed somebody
watching me from upstairs.

I trained my light on the upstairs window. The curtains
fluttered slightly.

Hide and seek. But whoever was up there sure wasn't
about to come down. I stood there staring up at the window
for a while, wondering who Jessica Williams might be, and
where Sandy was and if she was all right.

After a while I went home and made myself some
Ovaltine and found a Randolph Scott Western on one of
the cable stations and went to bed around midnight. I
didn't sleep well. I was too excited about the coming day.

7

I was up at 5:30. I made some instant coffee in the microwave and took it out the door with me. It was overcast and
cold enough for frost.

At 5:45 I parked six spaces down the street from Sandy's
house. The red Honda was still there. A yellow rental trailer

had been added. Sandy, a woman of about thirty, and David Myles, the same man I'd seen dead in the garage, were carrying overloaded cardboard boxes from house to trailer.

I picked up my Smith and Wesson, the one I'd kept from my days in uniform, and got out of the car and walked up to the trailer. Sandy and the woman were inside. Myles was rearranging boxes in one corner of the trailer.

"I'd like to talk to you, Mr. Myles."

He jerked around as if he were going to clip my jaw with his elbow. He wore a short-sleeved shirt. His splotchy red and blue dragon tattoo was easy to see.

"Who the hell are you?"

"You want to talk out here or you want to go inside?"

"You didn't answer my question."

He came at me but he wasn't much good at violence. I grabbed him by the shoulder, turned him around, and wrenched his tattooed arm into a hammerlock.

"You leave my daddy alone."

Sandy was back, scared. She pounded my hip with her tiny fists.

"I don't want to hurt him, honey. I just want to talk to him." I put more pressure on his arm. "Tell her, Myles."

He spoke through gritted teeth. "It'll be all right, sweetheart. You and Jessie just wait inside."

"Jessie's scared, Daddy."

"Tell her I'm fine."

I let go of him. "We're just going to talk, honey. See?"

She looked sleepy as she glanced from her father to me. "You won't hurt him no more?"

"I won't, honey. I promise."

"Jessie, she's got a gun, Mr. Flannery, and she could shoot you."

I smiled. "Then I'll be sure to be real careful."

She watched us a little while longer, thinking things she didn't express, or maybe didn't know how to express, and then turned and ran fast back up the walk and steps and inside the house where she called, "Jessie! Jessie!"

"You've got a nice daughter."

"Cut the crap. What's this all about?"

He had the sullen, dumb good looks of half the grifters you see in prison. "I want to know how you came back from the dead."

"Back from the dead? Gimme a break."

The street was awakening. Cars and trucks and motorcycles rumbled past on the ancient brick streets, and bass speakers announced the day. A boxy white milk truck, the kind you don't see very often any more, stopped on the far corner and a woman in a white uniform jumped down to the street, walking fast to an apartment house.

"The last time I saw you, Myles, you had four gunshot wounds."

"You're crazy."

"Sandy said she saw a man shoot you."

"Kids make things up."

"Am I making it up about seeing you with four bullet holes?"

"You got the wrong guy, mister. Do I look like somebody who's been shot four times recently?"

Not much I could say to that. I had no idea what I was dealing with here.

Jessie and Sandy came down the walk, both carrying boxes. Jessie slammed the door behind her. They got the boxes in the trailer, then stood watching us. Jessie was pretty in a weary way.

"Who is he?" Jessie said to Myles.

"He's Mr. Flannery," Sandy said. "A cop."

Myles said, "You know what he's trying to tell me?"

"Huh-uh," Jessie said.

"He's trying to tell me that somebody shot me four times a couple of weeks ago."

I bent down to Sandy. "You saw somebody shoot your dad, didn't you, sweetie?"

Sandy glanced up at Jessica, then at Myles. She shook her head. "No."

Myles said, "You and Jessie get in the car now, honey."

He was leaving. I'd never find out what happened. As the ladies went around and got in the car, I grabbed Myles and said, "I've got your license number. I can get an APB put on you in five minutes."

"What the hell is your problem, man? I'm not hurting nobody. My girlfriend and I got jobs in another city and so we're moving. What's the big deal?"

"You coming back from the dead, that's the big problem. And I wasn't bluffing about that APB."

"Just walk away from him, David," Jessie called. "Just walk back here and get in the car and we'll drive away."

Myles looked confused and exasperated now. "I knew I couldn't get away clean from this."

He did kind of a James Dean thing, where he hung his head and kind of muttered to himself. "I told her this'd happen."

"Told who?"

He looked up. Leaned closer. "I gave her my word."

"I still don't know who 'her' is."

"The blind girl: 3117. That pink stucco apartment building halfway down the block."

"What's she got to do with all this?"

"What's she got to do with all this? Who do you think healed me?"

"So you were shot four times?"

He nodded. "Yeah, you got the right guy." He made a face. "It sounds crazy but it's the truth. This guy shot me point-blank—I owed him a little bit of money—and then all of a sudden I can feel myself dying and then all of a sudden—Well, I woke up and there was this really pretty blind girl, probably eighteen, nineteen, somethin' like that, leaning over me and helping me to my feet."

"What about your wounds?"

He shrugged. "I know how it sounds, but they were all gone. I mean I still had blood all over me but the wounds were all healed. You couldn't even see any scarring. It was just like I'd never been shot."

"And this blind girl did it?"

He nodded. "I guess. I mean, I don't know who else it would've been. She made me promise not to tell anybody and I really feel bad, you know, even telling you. But I guess I didn't have much choice, huh?"

"No, you didn't."

He glanced back at his car. "We've got to get going. Our jobs start tomorrow and we'll be driving all night as it is. Plus I don't want this guy to find out I didn't die. He'd kill me again."

"You know I don't believe you."

He grinned. "That's what I told her, the blind girl. I said, even if I did tell anybody, who'd believe it? Just like you, man. You don't believe it."

He walked back to his car, started it up, the muffler needing some immediate repairs, and took off.

Without quite knowing why, I walked down the block to 3117, the pink stucco apartment house. A bald man in a blue work shirt and tan work pants came whistling out the front door. He swung his black lunch pail in time to a tune I couldn't hear.

I wanted to go over to him and ask him if there was a blind girl in the apartment house who could heal people the way Jesus used to. But I figured the guy would probably think I was just some drunk rambling past.

TWO

1

That day, I called Hodiak three times but he wasn't in and I left no message. In the afternoon, I raked leaves in the backyard and then cleaned out the west side of the garage. Every once in a while, I'd look over at the back of 3117, the rusty fire stairs that climbed four floors, and all the flower pots people had setting in their rear windows.

In the evening I drove over and parked several spaces away from 3117. I sat there until around 8:00 and then I gave it up and went home and had a Hungry Man I needed both catsup and mustard for. It was a new model and I hadn't figured out how to deal with it yet.

In the morning it rained, and I went back to my post at 3117. I spent three hours there, mostly listening to callers on a talk show arguing about all the new taxes.

I spent the first half of the afternoon at the library, checking out more books on Chicago history. These days the past is a lot more restful to contemplate. Chicago was just as violent then as it is now, but even the atrocities of yesteryear have a glow about them. Even killers look kinder when you set them back a hundred years or so.

This time I was there twenty minutes when the blind girl came down the steps, her white cane leading the way. She was slender and pretty in a summery blue dress with a blue sweater over her shoulders. She moved with the jerky speed of blind people making their way through a dark universe filled with land mines and booby traps, the white cane her flicking antenna. When she reached the sidewalk, she turned right.

In the next half-hour, a strange time when the sun would make an appearance in three-minute segments, then disappear behind rolling black thunderheads, she went three places—the corner grocery store where she bought a small sack of groceries, the corner pharmacy where she bought something that fit into her grocery sack, and a large stone Catholic church built back in the early part of this century. She stayed in church fifteen minutes, then walked back home.

I parked and got out of the car and was within ten feet of her when a man in his thirties came out of the apartment house door and said, "I wondered where you went. You should've told me you were going somewhere." He had paint daubs all over his T-shirt and there were a few yellow streaks on his jeans. In his hand he held, with surprising delicacy, a paint brush. The kind Degas used; not the sort the Acme House Painting Co. prefers.

He met her halfway down the walk, took her in his arms, and then, for the first time, became aware of me. He had good instincts. I could tell right away he was suspicious. He glared at me, then turned away and walked the blind girl inside.

When I got back to my car, I noticed something curious. Four spaces back from where I'd parked was another car, a blue Saab. A man with a dress hat sat inside. He was pulling surveillance and I figured I knew which house he was watching. He caught me looking right away and pulled a paperback up over his face.

Apparently, I wasn't the only one who'd heard about the blind girl.

2

"You saw this man yourself?"

"Yes, Father, I did."

"And he was dead?"

"Definitely."

"You couldn't have made a mistake?"

"He'd been shot four times. Including a shot right here." I tapped my throat.

"And then you saw him a few weeks later?"

"Yes."

"And he was alive?"

I nodded.

"And there was no evidence of any wounds?"

"All I could see was his throat but it was clear. No sign of a wound at all."

"This is pretty strange, I sure have to say that."

He was a young priest, thirty-five at most, with the face of an earnest young altar boy who was suddenly old, sitting in a dusty den in a dusty rectory next to the same dusty church where my girls had been baptized and from which, too few years later, they'd been buried. I recalled the first time I'd ever been inside a rectory, how disillusioning it was. In my Catholic boy's mind I'd imagined that priests spent all their time praying and discussing urgent theological matters. But when I came inside that day, I must have been twelve, I saw a Cubs game on TV being watched by the Monsignor himself. He wore a T-shirt and smoked a cigar and had a can of Pabst Blue Ribbon balanced in his lap. This was a long way from Jesus and the twelve apostles.

"And the girl?"

"The blind girl," I said.

"You don't know anything about her?"

"No, nothing."

"But the man—Myles—he said she was the one who healed him?"

"That's what he said."

The priest thought for a long moment. "I guess you're asking me if it's possible?"

"Right. I mean, have you ever heard of this before, of healing like this?"

"Oh, sure, I've heard of it. But I've never witnessed it, if that's what you mean. And I have to say, Rome is very skeptical of things like this. Especially these days." He smiled sadly. "Between pedophile priests and the church going broke, we don't need to play a role in a hoax."

"Is that what you think this is?"

"I think it's a possibility."

"With four bullet wounds in him?"

"There have been hoaxes a lot more complex than something like this." The sad smile again. "I'm not being much help, am I?"

"I appreciate your being honest."

"Maybe it's better to just let this go."

"You mean forget it?"

The priest nodded. "You strike me as a man who needs to relax and forget about things for a while. I mean, it wasn't that long ago that your family—Well, you know what I mean."

I stood up, laughed. "I thought you'd call Rome and tell them that you had another Miracle of Fatima on your hands."

He stood up, shook his head. "There are people who say that was a hoax, too."

"Fatima? But hundreds of people said that they saw the Virgin."

"Mass hypnosis. It happens. Look at Hitler."

He walked me to the door. "You ever think of going on a vacation?"

"I've thought about it."

He grinned. "Well, think some more about it, all right?"

3

Twice that night I drove past 3117. The blue Saab was there both times. He might not be a master of disguise but he sure was dogged.

Later on, sleeping, I got all wound up in the covers and woke myself up. The girls were with me, and their mother, present in the dark room somehow. I had tears in my eyes and I was scared but I wasn't sure of what, and I was so lonely that I needed to be held like a child or a small, scared animal. I got up and straightened the covers and laid back down. I slept, but when I woke I wasn't rested at all.

At nine that morning, I sat at the kitchen window watching the bright autumn leaves in the gray autumn rain, and saw a tiny wren drenched on the sill, and then I got up, put on my fedora and my rain coat, and walked up the soggy alley to the corner, where I turned right and walked to the end of the next block.

The blue Saab sat just about where it had been last night. He had the engine running. Probably using his heater. It was cold enough.

I walked back to the alley, then cut in the yard behind

3117. There was a rear door leading down five concrete steps to a laundry room. The air smelled of detergent and heat from the drier.

At the far end of the laundry were five more steps, these leading up to the apartment house proper. I checked the row of twelve mail boxes in the lobby. Everybody was Mr. and Mrs. Somebody, except for a Vic McRea and Jenny Conners. They lived on the third floor, to the back.

I was starting up the stairs when I heard a male voice two floors above me. "Jenny, you think I like going out in the rain? You think I'd go if I didn't have to?"

The girl said something, but she spoke so softly I couldn't pick it up.

I hurried back to the basement, where I stood in the shadows waiting for Vic to pass by.

His steps were heavy on the stairs. Halfway down, he paused. I heard the snick of a match head being struck. The heavy footsteps picked up again.

When he passed me, I saw he was the same young guy who'd given me the big glower yesterday afternoon.

He turned the collar up on his London Fog and went out into the rain.

I waited ten minutes and then I went upstairs and knocked on the door where the blonde girl lived.

"Yes?" she said from behind the closed door. The hallway carpet was worn to wood in places, and everything smelled of dust.

"There's been an accident, ma'am."

"What?" Panic fluted her voice already.

"A man named Vic McRea. Do you know him?"

"Know him? Why—"

Chains were unchained, locks unlocked.

She was much prettier close up, long blonde hair to her

shoulders framing a face both lovely and eager, a child hoping to please. She had dark blue eyes and only when you studied them carefully did they reveal their blindness. She wore a white blouse and blue cardigan sweater, big enough that I suspected it was Vic's, and a pair of jeans that fit her well.

When I got inside the door, I said, "I'm sorry I had to do that to you."

"But you said Vic—"

"I was lying. I'm sorry."

She started to say something but then stopped herself. Then, "You're here to rob me, aren't you? Vic said someday somebody would trick me into opening that door."

"I'm not going to rob you, I just want to talk to you."

"About what?"

"About how you can heal people."

She waited a long time before she spoke again. "That's ridiculous, healing people, I mean. Nobody can heal people except God."

"How about if we sit down?"

"Who are you? You scare me."

"My name's Nick Flannery. I used to be a Chicago cop. There's no reason to be afraid of me."

She sighed. "I really have a headache. And anyway, I don't know anything about healing people."

"Please," I said. "Let's sit down."

We sat. She navigated the room quickly, moving over to a green couch as worn as the runner in the hallway.

I took a vinyl recliner that had a cigarette burn in the left arm and several cuts on the right one. The place had the personality of a decent motel that had been allowed to deteriorate badly. The air was filled with a kind of weary history. You could hear WW II couples in this room dancing to Glen

Miller, and their eager, bright offspring, long years later, toking up a joint and listening to Jefferson Airplane.

Jenny was too nervous to sit back. She stayed right on the edge of the couch, her fingers tearing at the edges of a magazine as she spoke. "Why did you come here?"

"I told you."

"The healing thing? But that's crazy."

"I know a man named David Myles. He said you healed him."

"I've never heard of him before."

"I can understand why you wouldn't want people to find out about you."

"I'm just a plain, ordinary person. I'm blind, as you can see, but that's the only difference between me and everybody else."

She tore the magazine edges with quiet fury.

"What happens? People find out about you and you have to run away?"

"What would they find out?"

I sighed. "Jenny, I'm not going to hurt you; I'm not even going to tell anybody about you. But I did see David Myles the night somebody shot him—and then I saw him several days later. There weren't even any scars. It was as if he was never shot."

"Do you really think that somebody could do that—heal somebody that way?"

"Well, somebody did. And the man who was healed said that you were the one who did it."

For the first time she sat back on the couch, as if she were exhausted. She dropped her head slightly and put her hands together in her lap.

After a long silence, I said, "Jenny."

"I wish you'd just leave."

"I want to know the truth, Jenny."

She raised her head. Her beautiful but blind eyes seemed to be looking directly at me. "Why is it so important to you?"

"I—I'm not sure I could explain it so that it'd make any sense."

She said nothing. Just stared.

"A while back, my wife and two daughters were murdered in a robbery. One of those wrong time, wrong place situations. They happened to be in this store buying some school clothes when this guy came in all coked up. He killed six people in the store." I snuffled up tears. "She was my partner, my wife I mean. I'd never had a partner before. And I really miss her."

"I'm sorry for you—and them. But I still don't see—"

"I'm not sure there's a higher power, Jenny. God, or whatever you want to call it. I want to believe but I can't—not most of the time anyway. I kneel down and I close my eyes and I pray as hard as I can but—But then I get self-conscious and I hear my own prayers echo back at me and I think, Hell, I'm just repeating a bunch of mumbo-jumbo I heard when I was a kid. None of it's true. You're born and you die—that's all there is. And that's what I believe, most of the time."

Softly, she said, "That's not all there is. I know it's not, Mr. Flannery."

"That's what I mean, Jenny. Maybe if I could believe in you—well, maybe then I could believe in some kind of higher power—and believe that someday I'll see my wife and daughters again."

"Would you get me a Diet Pepsi?"

"Sure," I said, standing up.

"In the kitchen. In the fridge. And—take your time."

"All right."

"I need some silence. Silence is good for people."

"Yeah—yeah it is."

I took my time getting her the Diet Pepsi, finding a glass and dropping three cubes in it, and then stopping in the bathroom before returning to the living room.

I set the glass and can on the coffee table in front of her and filled the glass with fizzing cola.

I went over and sat down. I was careful not to speak.

"I really can't talk to you without Vic being here, Mr. Flannery."

"Who is Vic exactly, anyway?"

"My fiancé."

"I see."

"The way you say that, I take it you don't approve of him."

"It's just that he doesn't look like the kind of guy you'd be with."

She smiled. "That's one thing you learn from being blind, Mr. Flannery. You have to learn to see inside because you can't see outside. I don't mean that I'm any kind of mind-reader or anything—but Vic isn't as rough as he seems. Not inside, anyway."

"He knows about your—ability?"

"He knows everything about me that matters, Mr. Flannery, including any special talents I might have." She brought her glass to her lips and sipped cola. "You seem like a very decent man, Mr. Flannery."

"Thank you."

"But I had a very different impression of you when you lied to me at the door," she said. "Vic isn't a bad man."

I laughed. "All right, Vic's an angel. You've convinced me."

"Hardly an angel. He's made mistakes—one very, very

164

bad one, in fact. It almost broke us up."

"Can you talk about it?"

She shrugged. "He doesn't have much money. He saw a way to make what he thought was a fortune and he took it." She shrugged again. "There was a man who had a very sick wife and Vic decided to—" She shook her head. "Vic wasn't a very honorable man in that situation."

"He wanted to charge the man money for what you do?"

"It doesn't matter any more. Vic learned his lesson. He's changed completely now."

"What time will he be back?"

"Probably around three."

"Why don't I call you around four, then? All I want is to talk to you. Learn some things about you. It'll help me, I know it will."

I got up and went over to the couch and lifted her hand and held it in mine. "This is very important to me, Jenny."

"I know it is, Mr. Flannery, and I think if I approach Vic in the right way, he'll let me do it."

She brought her other hand over and covered mine. "I'll be waiting for your call."

4

But I wasn't the one who called.

Two hours later, my phone rang and I picked up and a harsh, whiskey voice said, "You stay goddamn away from her, you understand?"

"Who is this?"

"Who is this my ass. You know who it is."

As, of course, I did.

"You understand me, jerk-off?"

"Yeah," I said. "I understand."

"You'd better," he said, and slammed the phone.

5

That night, I watched a couple more "Mavericks" and had a Hungry Man that took a whole lot of mustard. But I was distracted. I just kept thinking about her sweet, dignified little face and the great, wise peace I felt within her. I wanted to go back and see her some more, ask her more questions about life beyond this one, but there would be Vic, and with Vic there would be a fight, and I would likely hurt him and then she'd never talk to me again, not the way she loved Vic she wouldn't.

A knock came at the door about the time the second "Maverick" ended. I went and opened the door and there she was.

She wore a transparent plastic rain scarf and a white raincoat that looked soaked. The rain had been pounding down for the past three hours. In her right hand she clutched an umbrella, in her left her white cane.

"I decided to go for a walk," she said, and shrugged. "I just wanted to stop by and apologize for the way Vic talked to you." She started to say something else and then abruptly started crying. "He's got somebody on the side again—and I just needed to talk to somebody."

"C'mon in," I said, and took her around the shoulder and led her into the living room.

In the next fifteen minutes, I hung up her coat to dry, set her wet shoes in front of the small crackling fireplace, got us some Ovaltine, and then listened to the problems she was having with Vic. She smelled of rain and perfume, and that made me sentimental.

She told me about Vic.

Seems every city they moved to, Vic found himself a new girlfriend. The pattern was pretty much the same. At first it would be just a kind of dalliance. But then gradually it would get more and more serious. Vic would start staying out later and later. Eventually, he'd start staying out all night. He always had the same excuse: poker. But she'd never been aware of him winning or losing any appreciable amount, so she had no reason to believe his story.

"But he always comes back to you?"

"In his way, I suppose."

"I'm not sure what you mean."

"He comes back and makes all kinds of promises but I don't think he means to keep them. He's just biding his time till his next girl."

"I'm sure you don't want to hear this, but maybe you'd be better off without him."

"I love him."

"Trust is a big part of love. For me, anyway. And it sure doesn't sound like you can trust him."

"He's only twenty-nine. Maybe he'll change someday. That's what I keep hoping anyway."

"How's the Ovaltine?"

She smiled. "I haven't had this since I was a little girl at the convent."

"The convent?"

"Well, actually, it was an orphanage but a very small one. There were more nuns than kids. So we always called it the convent."

"Your folks put you there?"

She shook her head, staring into the fireplace. I had to keep reminding myself that she was blind. "I don't know anything about my folks. Nothing at all. I was left with the nuns when I was six days old. That's why—well, that's why I don't know anything about my . . . gift. I just have it. I don't know how I got it or where it came from. It's just always been there. And maybe it'll go away some day."

"Have you ever talked to a doctor about it?"

"Right after I got out of high school, this was when I was living in New Mexico with a foster family, I went to visit a parapsychologist at the state university. He told me that there's a tradition of psychic healing in nearly every culture, dating back to earliest man and the shaman and the Babas of Africa. He told me there's a man named Dawson in Montana who can 'influence' the course of somebody's illness, if not exactly 'heal' it. He also said that most of psychic healing is a fraud and that if I ever went public, the press would attack me and discredit me—and that if I ever demonstrated that God used me to heal others—well, I'd be a freak all my life and I'd never be left alone.

"The thing we talked about this afternoon, when Vic tried to 'rent' me to the rich man with the sick wife?"

"Right."

"That proved just what the parapsychologist told me. How they'd never let me alone. When I found out that Vic was asking the rich man for money, I got furious and told the rich man that I would try and help his wife but that I didn't want any money at all. Then Vic got curious."

"You helped her?"

She shook her head. "She was so sick. I just couldn't believe that Vic would do anything like that. I was able to help her. I thanked God I could do it. But it didn't end there. The rich man saw a way to get even richer. What if I worked for him and he sold my services to the highest bidder? That's what he wanted to do. Vic and I ran away.

That was four months ago. The rich man probably has people looking for us. I just wanted to hide out when we got here. But six weeks ago, I saw a boy hit by a car and I went out and helped mend his leg. And his mother knew what I was doing. She started telling people around the neighborhood. The mother ran up here and told me about David Myles being shot."

"So what's next?"

A sad smile. "I guess I just wait for Vic to get over his latest crush."

There was no point in my railing about Vic again. She'd just get defensive. "How's the Ovaltine?"

"The Ovaltine's fine. But I sense that you're not."

"I'm all right."

"You mentioned your wife and daughters were killed."

"Yes."

"Why don't you come over and sit next to me?" This time the smile was bright. "I promise I won't make a pass at you."

"That wouldn't be the worst thing in the world, you know."

I went over and sat next to her on the couch. And I told her about my wife and kids, not their dying but their living. How Susan had gone back and gotten her degree in English at night and had planned to get her teaching certificate; how we bought a horse for Cindy on her eighth birthday and kept "Lady" out in a stable in the farmlands; how Anne was a very gifted ballet dancer, and how her teachers talked of her going to New York to study when she reached ninth grade. And a lot of other things, too, the odds and ends that make up family life: the birthday parties when daddy dresses up in silly hats, the puppy who poops everywhere, the vacation to Yellowstone, the terrifying weekend when

Susan found a lump on her breast but it proved to be nothing serious, the times when I found myself falling in love all over again with my wife, the life we planned for when the girls grew up and left home.

I must have talked for an hour. She spoke only rarely, and then little more than a word or two to indicate that she was still paying full attention. At first I tried to stop myself from crying but somehow with her I wasn't ashamed, and so when I was overcome by my terrible loss and the great sorrow that had followed, I cried, full and open.

During this time, we never touched, no consoling hands, no reassuring pats.

When I was done, I was exhausted. I put my head back and closed my eyes and she said, "Just stay like that. I want to help you."

I wasn't sure what she was talking about. No broken bones, no illness that I knew of, where I was concerned.

Out of the corner of my eye, I watched her situate herself pretty much as I had, leaning her head against the back of the couch, closing her eyes.

She felt around the open space between us until she found my hand.

"This will probably scare you a little bit at first but just give in to it, all right? Close your eyes now."

I closed my eyes.

There was a minute or two of absolute self-conscious silence. I felt the way I did when I prayed sometimes, that I was performing a charade, hurling pathetic words into the cosmic and uncaring darkness.

And then I felt it.

A few years ago, I had a hospital exam where the doctor gave me a shot of Valium. I couldn't even count backwards from ten before a great roaring sense of well-being overcame me. The nervous, anxious person I was too often was gone, replaced by this beatific man of inner peace.

I felt this now, though a hundred times more, as I sat on the couch next to Jenny, and when I saw Susan and the kids I cried, yes, but they were tears of joy, celebrating all the sunny days and gentle nights and faithful love we'd shared for so many years.

I don't know how long it was before I felt Jenny's hand leave me; I just knew that I never wanted to come back to reality. I wanted to be in college again with Susan, and in the delivery room when Anne came along, and watching Cindy wobble down the block on her bike the day we took the training wheels off. So much to remember. . . .

"I'm sorry," Jenny said. "I need to get back in case Vic gets home early."

"I don't know what you did there, on the couch I mean, but—"

She touched my cheek, her blind eyes seeming to search my face. "You're a decent man. You should take comfort from that."

I stood up, helped her up. "I'm walking you back. And no arguments. This isn't the neighborhood it used to be. It's not real safe."

6

This late at night, ten o'clock, lights were out in most houses, and the night air smelled of cold rain.

For a time we walked without saying anything. Then I said, "How'd you learn to do that?"

"To make you feel better?"

"Uh-huh."

171

She wasn't using her cane. She had her arm tucked through mine. It felt good.

"A few years ago, I visited this friend of mine in the hospital. Down the hall from her was this man dying of cancer. He was very angry and very frightened. And he was very abusive to the nurses. When I passed by his door one day, I heard him weeping. I'd never heard anybody cry like that before. I went in to his room and went over and took his hand and I felt this—energy; I don't know how else to describe it—this great, warm feeling in me that I was able to transfer to him simply by holding his hand. I didn't help him with his disease at all—he was in his early nineties and it was his time to go, I suppose—but I did comfort him. He died peacefully a few weeks later."

"And since then—?"

"Since then, when I sense that somebody's in great pain, I try to help them."

"You're quite a woman."

She laughed. "Oh, yes, I'm a regular role model. I'm blind and I'm broke and I have a fiancé who keeps stepping out on me."

"But your gift. You—"

"Not 'my' gift. God's gift. You asked me if I believed there was some plane of reality beyond ours. Yes, I believe there is. I mean, I'm not sure it's 'God' as we think of him but there's something out there, a place where we survive what we think of as death. And whatever that force is, it's chosen to use me as one of its tools. I'm sure there are a lot more people like me in the world, all hiding out, all afraid of any exposure because they don't want to be treated like freaks."

We reached her corner.

"It smells so clean. The wind and the rain," she said.

I saw the blue Saab parked a few spaces from her apartment house. I thought of what she told me about the rich man trying to find her.

I took her arm a little tighter.

"Is everything all right? You seem tense all of a sudden."

"I just don't want you to get blown away in this wind."

The man in the Saab shrank down some.

We reached her apartment house. By now I knew what I needed to do.

I walked her to the door.

"This is sort of like a date, isn't it? Walking me to the door, saying goodnight." She leaned forward and kissed me on the chin. She smiled. "I meant to kiss you on the cheek. Bad aim."

"I really want to thank you for—"

"I'm the one who should be grateful. I had a very nice time tonight."

She turned and opened the door. "Goodnight."

"Goodnight," I said.

I watched through the glass door as she climbed the steps, her white cane leading the way.

7

Ten minutes later I slid my car into the last space on Jenny's block. The blue Saab was still there. I wanted to see where he went after leaving here.

Thirty-five minutes later, his headlights came on and he drove away. I let him get to the corner and then I went after him, staying a half-block away. With so little traffic at night, following him was not easy.

He took the Dan Ryan. If he was aware of me, he didn't let on. Fifteen minutes later, he took the exit he'd been looking for, and drove over to a motel that sat on the east edge of a grim little strip mall.

He pulled up to his room and went inside. The lights were already on. He stayed twenty minutes. When he came out, another man accompanied him. The man carried a small black-leather doctor's bag.

I gave them ten minutes before I went up to the door and put some of my old burglary knowledge to work. A cop picks up a lot of skills in the course of his career.

The room smelled of stale cigarette smoke and the moist walls of the shower stall. I used a flashlight to go through three different suitcases and a bureau full of drawers. The red eye of the answering machine blinked, signaling a message had been left. It must have come in between the time they left the room and I entered.

I went over and picked up the receiver and dialed the operator. "Yes?"

"There's a message for you, Mr. Banyon."

"Yes."

"From a man named Vic. He said things won't be ready till eleven. That's all he said."

"I appreciate that." According to my watch, it was 10:30. I had a terrible feeling that I knew what was going on here. I just hoped I wasn't too late.

8

Twenty-five minutes later, I pulled into the same space I'd used earlier that night.

The blue Saab was in place.

I saw Vic helping Jenny out the door.

She didn't know that anything was wrong. She loved Vic

and trusted him, and if he suggested that they go for a late-night stroll, or maybe plant themselves in the Chicago-style pizzeria around the block, why that would be just fine with her.

Vic led her to the sidewalk just as the two men were leaving the Saab. The second man had lost his black leather bag but he seemed to be carrying something with great delicacy in his black-gloved fingers.

I had to move fast to reach them just as they reached Jenny and Vic. Cold mist whipped my face in the dark windy night.

When I reached them, I saw what the man held in his hand. A hypodermic needle. He was going to drug Jenny.

"Jenny!" I said.

They had been so intent on what they were doing that they didn't notice me until now.

"Who is this?" the man with the needle said. He spoke in a European accent, German maybe. Then, "Quickly, give me her arm!" he said to Vic.

Vic pushed Jenny forward.

I had my Smith and Wesson in hand and I said, "Stop right there. I mean everybody."

The man with the needle held Jenny's arm. He could easily jab her with the needle and accomplish his task. I put the gun barrel inside his ear.

"Drop the needle."

"You have no business here," said the other man, in an identical accent.

Both men looked at Vic.

"Who is this?" the man with the needle asked.

"Some clown, some ex-cop. He's nobody."

"Perhaps you haven't noticed, my friend," said the other man, "but he has a gun."

"He's no friend of yours, Jenny," Vic said. "You have to

trust me. These men are going to help us."

"It's the rich man, isn't it? That's who they're working for."

"We just got off to a bad start, Jenny. With him, I mean. He wants to help us, put us in a nice new home and have some doctors study you—but privately, so nobody else will know."

Silently, she raised his hand, felt through the darkness for his face. When she found his cheek, she said, "They paid you to help them, didn't they, Vic?"

"I never claimed I was an angel, Jenny."

"No. But you did claim you loved me."

I was caught up enough in their words that I didn't hear the driver take two steps to my right and then bring down a black jack with considerable force on the back of my head.

I heard Jenny scream, and somebody clamp his hand over her mouth, and feet scuffle on the rainy sidewalk. I smelled autumn and cold and night; and then I just smelled darkness.

I didn't go all the way down, just to my knees, and I quickly started reviving myself, forcing myself to take deep breaths, forcing my eyes to focus. There was blood on the back of my neck, but not much and not serious.

Car doors opened and slammed; the Saab, I knew. They'd left the motor running and when the doors opened I heard a Frank Sinatra song. Briefly.

Then they were gone.

9

I was starting the long and painful process of standing up when I heard somebody nearby moaning.

Vic was propped up against a tree. They must have hit him very hard in the seconds when I was unconscious. Blood streamed down his face from a wound on top of his skull.

I stood up and wobbled over to him.

"Where did they take her?"

"Can't you see I'm bleeding, man? Maybe I have a concussion or something."

I kicked him in the ribs, and a lot harder than was necessary, I suppose.

This time he didn't moan, he cried. "Shit, man, I just wanted a little money and the whole goddamned thing went wrong." He looked up at me with puppy dog eyes. I wanted to kick him even harder. "They didn't even pay me, man. They didn't even keep their word."

I reached down and yanked him to his feet. It took me five good shoves to get him to my car. He started crying again when I opened the door and pushed him inside.

I got behind the wheel. "Where're we going?"

"You think I'm gonna tell you? They'll kill me, man."

"Yeah, well, I'll kill you first, so you'd better keep that in mind."

I gave him a hard slap directly across the mouth to make my point.

He started crying again. Only now did I realize he was all coked up. Everything was probably very crazy to him, fast and spooky. "You probably don't think I care about her, do you?"

"Vic, I want to know where they took her."

"I was gonna give her half the money. I really was. I mean, I really like Jenny. She's marriage material, man. It's just that right now I'm not ready—"

This slap cut his mouth so that blood trickled out. He put his head down and sobbed.

I didn't want to feel sorry for him but I couldn't help myself. "Vic, just tell me where they took her. This may come as a surprise, but I really don't enjoy slapping you."

He tilted his head in my direction and laughed. "You could've fooled me."

I laughed, too. "Vic, you're out of your league, don't you understand that?"

He shrugged, daubing at the blood in the corner of his mouth. "That's what Jenny always says. That I'm out of my league." He shook his head. "What a miserable bastard I am."

"Right now I wouldn't disagree."

He sighed. "They're taking her to their Lear jet. We'd better hurry."

I knew the airport he named.

10

On the way, he said, "Maybe she's an angel."

"What?"

I was driving fast, but allowing for the wet streets.

"An angel. From heaven, you know. I mean, maybe that's what Jenny is. Maybe that's why she can heal people."

"Maybe," I said, having no idea what else to say, and being embarrassed by talking about angels.

The airport was toward Waukegan. The rain had started again and the dark, rolling Midwestern night made the few lights on seem distant and frail, like desperate prayers no one hears.

"Or a Martian," Vic said. He had a handkerchief and he kept daubing his lips.

"A Martian?"

"Yeah, I don't mean from Mars necessarily but from outer space, anyway. I saw this 'Star Trek' deal once where they found this girl who could heal people. I think she was a Klingon."

"I thought Klingons were the bad guys," I said. "At least that's what my two daughters used to tell me."

"Yeah? Well, maybe there were some good Klingons they didn't know about."

What could I say?

In the rain and the gloom, the small airport had the look of a concentration camp about it. The cyclone fencing, the mercury vapor lights, the signs indicating that attack dogs were on the prowl—nice, friendly place.

I pulled up to the gate and flashed the badge I knew I shouldn't be carrying.

"Some problem?" the uniformed guard said.

"Not sure yet."

"You'd better check in with the office before you do anything."

"Fine."

He nodded and waved me through.

I didn't check with the office. I drove straight out to the landing strip.

"There," he said.

The Lear jet was fired up and just getting ready to go. The passenger door was still open. Apparently not everybody was aboard.

I swung the car wide, so that we came around from behind the graceful white plane.

I pulled around to the front, parking in front of the wheels, and got out. Vic was a few minutes behind me.

"I don't want to get in anything with guns 'n' shit, man. I mean, that's not my style."

"I just want to get Jenny away from them."

"They're bad dudes, man. They really are."

I saw the man with the doctor's bag walking across the

tarmac to the Lear jet. We were hiding behind the car. I didn't think he saw us.

I moved fast, running toward him so that there was no chance for him to get away.

He tried, of course, turning around and running in a bulky way back toward the office.

I got him by the collar and spun him around. He smelled of expensive cologne.

"Let's go get Jenny."

"There are six people aboard that plane," he said in his European accent. "The odds aren't very good in your favor." He glared at Vic and shook his head. "And certainly this lounge lizard will be no help to you."

"Let's go," I said, putting the gun into his ribs.

The three of us walked to the plane.

We climbed the stairs and went inside, where two men in black turtlenecks and black Levis held Mausers on us.

"I want Jenny," I said.

"Not going to happen, babe," said Mauser number one. "Hand over the doc and we'll let you go."

Vic said, "They got us, man. Just let them have the doc."

"Where's Jenny?" I said.

"Here," she said, and appeared in the doorway behind the Mauser twins.

"Are you all right?" I said.

"So far."

They hadn't drugged her, probably deciding they didn't need to. Her clothes were wrinkled and her hair was mussed. Her mouth was drawn tight. She was scared.

The doc made his move, then, and it was a bad move. He tried to jerk free of me and when he did, the Mauser twins, who had been trained for split-second action, opened fire, no doubt figuring they would hit me instead of him.

But they hit the doc, and several times, and right in the chest.

Vic dove left, I dove right.

After the first burst, the Mauser twins quit firing so they could assess the damage.

"Oh, God, babe," said one Mauser twin to the other, "we shot the doc."

"The old man is going to kill us," the second Mauser twin said.

By then, the shooting over, the pilot and co-pilot had drifted up to the front of the plane. So did the stake-out driver.

They all stood around and looked down at the doc. He was dying. He was already an ashen color, his breathing in tattered gasps.

"Man," said one Mauser twin to the other. "You really got our tit in the wringer."

"Me? Listen, babe, that was your bullet, not mine."

Jenny stepped forward, saying, "I would appreciate it if everybody would leave this plane."

"What's that supposed to mean?" said the first Mauser twin.

The stake-out driver said, "It means just what she said." With the doc down, he was apparently the man in charge. "I want everybody off this plane."

11

Took twenty minutes, during which all of us stood on the tarmac in the mist and fog. The Mauser Twins went and got coffee for everybody from a vending machine.

Vic, pacing around in little circles to stay warm, said,

181

"She could make a lot of money."

"I thought you said she was an angel."

"Angels can't make money?"

I just shook my head.

The stake-out driver came over. He looked sad. "The doc, he's my cousin." He spoke with his cousin's accent.

"I see," I said.

"The girl," he said, "if she saves him, I'm going to let her go."

"That's the right thing to do."

"Do you understand any of this, the way she heals people?"

"Not a bit."

"I still say she's an angel," Vic said. "Or a Martian."

Just as he started to scowl at Vic, Jenny appeared in the passenger door. "You may come back now."

Five minutes later, we were feeding the doc some of the tepid vending machine coffee we'd had earlier.

I can't say he looked great—he was still very shaky and pale—but he was awake and talking.

He sat in one of the passenger seats, Jenny next to him.

"I wish you would let me learn about you," the doc said.

She sat there so pretty and sad and said, "I just accept it, Doctor. It's a gift and you don't question gifts."

I went over and said, "You look tired, Jenny. How about if I take you back?"

12

The three of us sat in the front seat. Vic had his arm around Jenny. I wanted my arm to be around Jenny. I wanted Vic to be on the other side of the world.

"We really owe you for this, man," Vic was saying. "I mean, you really came through for us."

"He's right," Jenny said gently, speaking above the hot blast of the car heater. "We really are very grateful."

"I'm gonna change, man. I really am. I'm taking this pledge right now. Vic McRea is a brand-new man. And I mean that, babe."

My God, I thought, is she really going to buy into this bilge?

When we reached their apartment house, I pulled over to the curb. I felt great sorrow and rage. I was losing her.

"Jenny, I—" I started to say.

But Vic already had the door open and was climbing out.

Jenny quickly took my hand and leaned over and kissed me on the cheek. "You're really a remarkable man. I hope you know that."

"C'mon, babe," Vic said from outside. "I'm freezing my tush."

And then they were gone.

13

I didn't sleep well. I had all the old bad dreams and then I had a new bad dream, that Jenny and Vic were on an airplane and flying away and I was standing on the tarmac, feeling an icy emptiness and a kind of animal panic.

And then somebody was knocking at my door and I was looking at the sunlight in my bedroom window.

I got my robe on and answered the knock and there she was.

"I heard you were looking for a new partner," she said, "so I thought I'd apply for the job."

I kept my lips pressed tight so nothing of my morning mouth would escape and then I took her in my arms and held her right there in the doorway.

Inside, she said, "I told Vic goodbye this morning. He took it a lot better than I thought he would. Especially after I gave him my last five hundred dollars."

"Good old Vic," I said.

"Yes, good old Vic," she said. "Now how about some coffee?"

The Broker

Every six months or so Rick Marner puts his ass on a plane and flies out to Vegas. Not that he doesn't like Chicago. Just he needs some fresh every once in a while. Fresh pussy. Fresh faces around the poker table. Fresh dinners on the menus.

Marner is one of those guys you always see in the supper clubs of rich and important people. The Marners never quite look as if they belong. Not even Armani suits can disguise them. Not even proper English can disguise them. Not even all the courtesy and polish in the world can disguise them. They weren't born to this life and it will always show. Like a nasty facial scar or the wrong color skin.

They're in these places, the Marners of the world, because the wealthy and affluent people need them to get certain things for them, merchandise of all kinds. The Marners never approach the important people.

The important people have to approach the Marners before any kind of conversation is struck. These are the rules, and the Marners of the world better damn well understand them or the wealthy will just go and get themselves new Marners.

Tonight, Marner is feeling pretty good about himself as he sits at the bar of a pricey Loop restaurant and watches himself in the mirror running behind the cash register. When he was a little kid, he never had any trouble recognizing himself. He was always Marner and life was uncomplicated. Now he doesn't know who he is any more. The body a mite fleshy. The hair a mite gray. The handsomeness soft, no longer weapon-sharp. The eyes are what's most distressing. They aren't his eyes. They really aren't. They don't even look like his color any more. This is a masquerade of some kind. It really isn't Marner at all. Someday, he's going to tear this middle-aging mask off his face and find the boy inside him again.

This morning, he sent his seventeen-year-old daughter a birthday present and he feels good about it. The good parent and all that. She lives with her mother in San Diego. Marner hasn't seen her in six years. He doesn't really want to see her. She'd put on a lot of weight the last time he'd visited. He'd been embarrassed about walking down the street with her. She was that fat. Marner tries always to put on a sleek and knowing front. This English teacher he was balling one summer (she liked dangerous men), she taught him proper grammar. She also taught him a little bit about literature. He listened to *The Great Gatsby* on audiotape. He identifies with Jay Gatsby. She also took him to the art museum. Now when books are brought up at a high-tone dinner table, he talks about Gatsby. Or, if the subject is art, Modigliani. So, you have a guy in Armani who knows about Scott Fitzgerald and modern art, do you really want to see him walking down the street with some wallowing, fat kid? No. It just doesn't reflect well. It doesn't mean he doesn't love Doris (though he's never been crazy about her name) or that he isn't proud of the fact that she's an A student. It's just that a guy has a certain image of himself—and the people who should be around him—and Doris just doesn't fit.

He senses somebody near him. He has this kind of radar. Somebody near him he doesn't want near him. And he turns. And there's this guy and at first he doesn't recognize him.

"You sonofabitch," the guy says. And when he says this, the bartender, who is maybe ten feet away, looks up.

Dawson, the guy's name is. Peter Dawson. But my God. That was forty pounds ago. The deep raccoon-black circles under the eyes. The uncertain gait. The vampire-pale skin. Even the once-glossy black hair is now a dirty white.

"You want to talk to me," Marner says, "we'll go get a table." He tells the bartender to bring them two scotches straight up.

Dawson looks as if he's going to collapse before he makes it to the table. He moves jerkily, a bad imitation of a Romero zombie. When he sits down, he sighs deeply, as if he's just climbed a mountain. Marner thinks back, not all that long ago, when Dawson had been a jaunty, arrogant man bored with his wife and his girlfriends. He was all yacht club and country club and Gold Coast condo, all cold, hard demand. Not that long ago. Now, he is emaciated and very drunk.

The table sits in a shadowy corner. A jungle of trendy ferns form a partial wall around them, making the section even more private. Dawson starts to talk but Marner says, "Shut up."

"What?"

"Wait till he gets our drinks."

The bartender brings two things: drinks and a very suspicious gaze. He sets the liquor down and leaves. But his gaze lingers. Marner knows he's lost a couple of points with this bartender tonight. Doesn't do you any good to have people who look like Dawson come in and walk up to you. It sure doesn't.

Dawson says, "You sonofabitch, you didn't tell me what I was getting into."

"Yes, I did. I told you there might be a downside."

"Might be—" Dawson shakes his head. "I've been to every doctor in this town. I even spent a week at the Mayo Clinic. They've run every test they can. And they can't find anything. Nothing." His eyes suddenly glisten with tears. "But I'm dying. They give me three months at the outside. And I've got a family, a wife and two kids. Do you understand that, you sonofabitch? I've got a family!"

"Maybe you should've thought of that."

Dawson is done with theatrics, at least for now. His breath is coming in small gasps. He seems to be getting paler right before Marner's eyes. "You should've told me what she was."

For a moment, Marner allows himself a moment of sentiment. "I'm sorry it happened, pal. I really am. But I did warn you. Two or three times, I said that there could be a downside to this babe. But you weren't listening. You'd just heard all the stories about her and wanted some of it for your own. 'The Wildest Fuck in the Windy City.' That's what you said about her, remember, after you'd been with her a couple of times. You didn't have any complaints then."

"No, not back then. But after a couple of months—"

Marner takes a drink. "I told you that, too, if you think back. I said, you should move on to something else because if you don't, there can be trouble if you're with her too many times. But you didn't listen to that, either." Marner is practiced at this kind of situation, however uncomfortable it makes him sometimes, his customers complaining about the merchandise he's obtained for them. Rich people are like anybody else; they don't like to spend any more money than they absolutely have to. How Marner obtains his merchandise is something they don't want to know. That's his business. He's brokered items as various as a Mercedes-Benz limousine, a summer cottage, mink coats, expensive watches, and even famous pieces of jewelry. For a price, no questions asked. And sometimes he handles women, too. Not your everyday hookers, God forbid. Not even the undernourished beauties who model during the day and put out for big bucks at night. No, he went for the exotic. The extremely special ones.

"You've got to help me," Dawson says, sounding sick again.

"I can't. If I could, I would."

"Who is she?"

"I don't know."

"What the hell does that mean?"

"She just appeared one night. In this bar."

"She just appeared? Just walked up to you?"

"Right. I was sort of preoccupied, and she walked up to me told me her name was Nadia."

"Nadia what?"

"Nadia nothing. She's never given me a last name."

"And what'd she say?"

"She told me about herself. That she was special. And that she understood that maybe I could help her and that we could both make some money."

"Money, of course. It's always money."

"I wasn't born wealthy, the way you were. I have to make a living."

The sick man looks embarrassed. "I'm sorry. Go on."

"So I set her up in the penthouse and things have gone well ever since." He is understating; Nadia is the single most-profitable item he has ever offered his clientele.

"Oh, yes, very well. Look at me, Marner. I'm dying and the doctors can't even tell me why. I'd turn you both in, if it wouldn't cause my family a scandal."

Marner stares at him a moment. "This has only happened a few times. The way you got sick and everything. Whatever she does . . . it only affects a few people."

"And one of them, unfortunately, is me." He puts his elbow on the table and his head in his hand. He begins quietly crying.

Marner glances around, seeing if anybody is watching. "This isn't the place," he says. A man in his position, a man who brokers things the way he does, a man like him can't afford to cause scenes.

"Then just where the fuck is the place, Mr. Marner?"

This time, no doubt, half the restaurant hears Dawson. Marner freezes in place, so many people staring.

They will think that Marner has himself a very unhappy customer, which can't be a good advertisement for his business.

"Then just where is the place, Marner?"

"We're going now, Mr. Dawson."

"You put a hand on me, I'll kill you. And you'd better understand that."

"You're going to walk out of here quietly, Mr. Dawson, or I'm going right to that phone and call your wife and tell her everything."

"You would, wouldn't you, you bastard?"

"Yes, I would."

"You sonofabitch."

"You need to get some new insults, Mr. Dawson. You've called me that several times already tonight."

"You don't give a shit that I'm dying, do you?"

"I'm sorry you're dying, Mr. Dawson. But I warned you about the risk of going back and back and back."

"But she addicts you, don't you understand that?"

"Just a few people is all, the ones she addicts. Just a few."

It takes Marner twenty minutes to get Dawson out of the place. By then, Marner knows that he can never again come in here. If he doubts that, all he has to do is look at the bartender, at that cold, superior sneer on his face.

Marner spills Dawson into his Bentley and then walks away. Even when he gets to the other end of the parking lot, he can hear Dawson in his car, weeping.

Seven months ago, after he realized just how much money Nadia was going to make him, just how many men wanted to spend time with her, Marner laid out the bread for a beautiful condo just off Lake Shore Drive. An A location. Underground parking garage. Smiling, uniformed doorman at the front door. The swiftest of elevators to the ninth floor. Room 907. Marner has the key, of course. And lets himself in.

Darkness. The only light is in the full window, where a quarter moon and stars look down upon the city. This is Thursday night, collection night. Nadia never keeps any of the money. She puts it in an envelope for him on the coffee table in the well-appointed living room.

Thursday is her down night. He never makes any appointments for her on Thursday. She says she needs her rest. One time, and only one time, he opened her bedroom door and peeked in. And still wishes he hadn't. Even in the briefest of glances, she is ghastly, a squid-like thing on the bed, the pus-bag center section rising and falling with each breath, the noise a frantic rasping. The stench is even worse. He clamped his hand over his mouth and quickly closed the door.

How something like this could turn itself into beautiful Nadia, The Wildest Fuck in the Windy City, he doesn't know. And doesn't want to know. All he wants is what he has now, his envelope with all that lovely money in it.

As the elevator falls quickly and certainly to the ground level, he finds himself thinking about his daughter again. God, he wishes she'd lose some weight. It'd be so nice to have a good-looking young daughter on his arm to show off to people. It would be so damn nice.

Second Most Popular

The girl behind him went "sssttt" and tapped him on the shoulder. Before turning around, Sully Driscoll first checked out Sister Mary Philomena. She was a bitch and had forty-one eyes. Presently not one of them seemed to be watching him, so he twisted his body half-backwards.

"Note," the girl whispered.

If he had shown such speed in sports, the coach would have overlooked Sully's habits of smoking cigarettes and sneaking beers. For in less time than it took Sister Mary Philomena to crack you across the mouth with her big, mannish hand, Sully had turned around, taken the note, and turned frontward again.

After reading it, he wondered if it had been worth risking the nun's wrath. For worse than hurting you physically, she could cower and embarrass you, as if you were a girl or something. And that should not happen to an eleventh-grade boy, particularly one who was generally considered to be the second most popular and third most tough boy in the entire class. The note just didn't justify such danger. It said only, "I want to see you," and it was signed, "Louise."

Louise Malloy, of course. She was the second most popular girl in the class and, for Sully, the first best looking. Opinion was divided on the subject—some of his buddies preferred Linda Carmody who had extraordinary breasts but, Sully felt, a face merely "cute." Where Louise Malloy's face was more classic and nearly beautiful.

Louise and Sully had been going steadily for two

months, and it was assumed by those who cared—generally homely or fat girls who did not have boyfriends of their own and who followed the love lives of others with the same passion they read movie magazines—it was assumed that the two would soon be going steady.

Which Sully absolutely wanted to do but Louise did not. Not yet. Not, she said, until she felt she could "trust" Sully and that meant only one thing. That Sully keep absolutely secret the privileges Louise granted him with her body. As she told Sully, she'd heard how the other boys discussed their girls and she did not want to be reduced to that. As if the boys were in some sort of competition with each other to "get the most" and "go the farthest." If Sully told no one what they did and, as she always pointed out, they did not do that much, then someday, and probably it would be soon, then someday soon she would consent to go steady with him and their affair would be in the eyes of everyone who mattered, especially Tim Moore, whom Sully considered his chief rival for her heart and her proclivity to French kissing; then everyone would know, the world itself would know, how serious they were.

Complying with her single demand was not easy. And Sully wasn't always faithful to it—not exactly. He had devised ways of letting what they did be known without using specific words. For instance. When another boy was relating how the night before he'd had his girl so hot a football team couldn't have handled her, Sully would start laughing very loudly and maybe even slapping his knee like some old sourdough in a cowboy movie and say, "I know what you mean" or "I sure know what that's like." And that way they'd all be jealous.

For only Jim Murrin, who had access to the wiles of Linda Carmody, only Jim Murrin was doing things to anybody as socially prominent as Louise Malloy. The rest of the boys were spending their time with plain or even homely girls and getting things off them was not, when you really thought about it, much of a big deal at all.

The second most popular boy and the exclusive boy-friend of the first best looking girl was nobody to mess with. Especially when they were one and the same person and that person happened to be Mr. Sully Driscoll himself, Esquire and bad ass.

"Sully."

He looked up from the note he held in his hands and stared directly at Sister Mary Philomena. Christ, he must have dozed off or something. He had one of those scary, inexplicable feelings of having just been dropped off here on this planet and not knowing a word of the native tongue. After a long time, in which his heart against his chest felt like a hardball being tossed into a glove with increasing ferocity, he finally said, "Yes, Sister?"

"Who was Victor Hugo?"

"A writer."

"And he wrote what?"

"Books."

The class laughed and giggled, delighted.

Sully felt blood as warm as fever flood his neck and face. He did not like to appear stupid nor did he wish to have Sister Mary Philomena, who after all could do much worse than hurt you physically, he didn't want her thinking he was being a smartass.

"He wrote *The Hunchback of Notre Dame*," Sully said quickly.

Thankfully, she seemed impressed and asked somebody else another question.

He waited several minutes at Louise's locker before, with

her friend Dottie who, because she was plain ugly sometimes treated Louise with sickening obeisance, before Louise, looking peculiar and maybe even perturbed, arrived. "Bye for now," she said to Dottie, who left immediately, pushing her glasses up her nose with an ink-stained finger.

"What's up?" Sully asked, and all of a sudden he was afraid. All of a sudden he could sense something in her manner and in the abrupt way she'd dismissed Dottie. All of a sudden he was scared.

She looked at him and he could see that her lips were white. White. And her eyes were a fierce and angry blue. "I hear I'm a lot of fun."

"What?"

"Janice Farraday told me that Don said I was a lot of fun."

"You know how Don talks. He lies through his teeth."

She grabbed his wrist suddenly and there were tears in her eyes and she stood so close to him and whispered so ferociously that she sprayed spittle all over him. "You broke your word to me and I'll never trust you again!"

He could sense their eyes and their whirring little minds, all his classmates who clogged the hall watching him, for it was his turn to act. The boys would be wondering if he'd lose face and get punked off by a girl. The girls would be wondering if he'd crumble, too, for most of them did not think he was quite good enough for her.

And in a second he figured out what to do, it was his only hope; he'd light a votive candle for that sonofabitch Robert Mitchum, the patron saint of studs and tough guys.

He leaned quickly forward and kissed her on the forehead and said in his deepest voice, so that everybody could hear, "I'll call you as soon as you grow up."

Just like in the Robert Mitchum movie.

Which would have been so fine and so cool and worth so many retellings, except that before he could walk away and out of the school and over to the little hamburger joint where they smoked and played pinball, before he could really enjoy his moment of glory, he glanced at her eyes and he goddamned near burst into tears, because it was right there gazing up at him with the innocence and vulnerability of a child, right there he saw how much he'd hurt and betrayed her, and then he didn't give a damn at all what anybody thought, not the bragging boys or the jealous girls or even the busybody nuns.

He moved toward her now. There were tears in his eyes but he didn't care. He was going to say it in front of everybody, no matter, how much he loved her and how much he was sorry because he hadn't kept his promise, he had broken his word and it had been the only word she'd asked him to give. And with all this pushing up in him and about to erupt, just exactly then, he saw the blur on the right side of his head but he wasn't sure of what it was, he didn't at the moment give a damn what it was.

And then it landed and it was as strong and hurting as any he'd ever had from a boy. He could hear them gasp. He still hadn't quite realized what it was. And then Louise was walking away and he could only stand there.

He had been slapped, slapped so hard he could not quite believe it even yet.

"Hey, Driscoll," somebody said, "you got a date for the dance tonight?"

Their laughter did not make him feel any better.

He would be more honest, more truthful with her than he'd ever been with anyone. Than he'd ever been in confession. He'd tell her his insecurities, all of them, and then she would see and understand, then she'd take him in her arms and she'd cry—no, they'd both cry—and then things would be as they'd been before.

At least that was his plan as he walked up the front steps to her house that night.

She was on the porch, on the same swing where they'd spent half the nights of the summer. Since it was October and mildly chilly, she wore a sweater over her school blouse. And she wore jeans. She looked so good in jeans. So sexy. His lust annoyed him. This was no time.

He sat beside her and started to say something and she said, "Be quiet." Not harshly, just purposefully.

They swung, then, and he got to like the way the squeaking sounded in the clear night and the way the leaves smoldered in the gutter and the way the smoke from them haunted the air like a melancholy song.

Every few minutes he would move a bit closer to her. If he tried to move too much too quickly, he was afraid she would bolt. He had to treat her like some shy animal, like a little kitten or a doe, something precious and skittish like that.

Even with a few feet between them he could feel how rigid her body was. Oh, he'd screwed it up and screwed it up so badly.

Finally, when his right leg was only an inch from touching her left leg, and when her body felt a little less stiff, finally, and with a great deal of fear, he said, "You know how much I love you, don't you?"

She said nothing.

"You do know, don't you?"

"I know," she said.

"Then you should also know how sorry I am."

"I know you're sorry. And I know why you came here and I know what you're going to say and I believe you. It's just that—well, it doesn't make any difference any more."

Hearing her say that, and the way she said it, he got dizzy, as if someone had smacked him on the side of the face again. He couldn't recall anybody's words ever having such impact on him before.

Now he was afraid to say anything, scared that she had said what she'd wanted to and would go into the house. But they went back to swinging. Sometimes cars went by and sometimes they honked, but neither Sully nor Louise looked to the street. They just continued swinging, one full inch between their bodies, the squeaking loud and the night air rich with the smoke from the leaves.

This time she spoke first. "Why did you have to tell them?"

"I'm going to tell you the truth. Will it help if I tell you the truth?"

"I don't think so."

"I'm not very tough."

"You act tough."

She looked at him then. "I didn't think you were tough. I don't know why. Maybe because you tried to act so tough."

"And I'm not very popular."

"As far as I know, you are."

"Not when you really ask people about me."

"Why aren't you popular?"

"Because I'm not tough and I'm not good-looking."

"You're cute."

"Not very cute. Not really cute. Not like Murrin or Delaney." He sighed. "Or not like Tim Moore."

"Tim Moore."

"He's popular."

"Not with me," she said.

"Well, anyway."

"You still told everybody, Sully. You still broke your word."

"That's what I'm trying to tell you. Why I told."

"It doesn't make any difference. Not to me. Not now."

"I told because people would think I was popular if they believed we did things."

"Oh, Sully, that's crazy."

"No, it's not. You know Fred Quinn in twelfth grade? He came up to me one day and said, 'You go with Louise Malloy?' And I said yes and he said, 'She's really fine, you lucky bastard.' And ever since he always makes a point of saying hello to me. He never spoke to me before he found out I went with you."

"Fred Quinn. I could care."

"And not just him. Myrna. She flirts with me all the time now."

"Myrna's an idiot."

"She never paid any attention to me until I started going out with you."

"I'm happy your social life's improving. You still broke your word. You were the one boy I trusted and look what's happened. Look what's happened, Sully."

"But I don't give a damn about anything but you any-more, that's what I want you to understand."

"It's too late, Sully."

He put his arm around her shoulder and he almost winced, afraid she would slap him or jump up and scream or run inside. But she did none of these things. First she sighed and then she shuddered and then she moved over against him and then she found his face and kissed him.

"I knew you didn't mean what you said," Sully said.

"I did mean it, Sully. I was just saying goodbye."

And then she did stand up and then she did go inside.

And Sully just stood there. There was really nothing else to do. At least for now.

The breeze stirred then and that helped some, the way the smoke from the leaves made the night air so rich and romantic-smelling.

He thought of farmfields and scarecrows and jack-o'-lanterns.

He thought of everything but Louise because that would be too painful.

The porch light came on. Mr. Malloy pushed his big, Irish face past the partly-opened door and said something that Sully didn't hear.

He left then and he was thankful for the smoke that waited for him like wraiths along the curb. Because he could hide in the smoke. Inside the smoke he did not have to think about being second most popular or third most tough or any of it.

It seemed safe inside the smoke.

And he could blame his tears and his empty feeling on the smoke, the way it whirled around him and blinded him and suffused his senses.

He could blame the smoke.

Junior

The first thing my Pa did when we came to this town was kill a man. Actually, two men, if you're of a mind to count Indians.

Two years ago, it was.

This happened over at the livery stable, and it happened the way it always did with Pa—fast and pretty much unexpected. It was that temper of Pa's that always did it.

The livery man overcharged my Pa for some smithing work. Or my Pa said he did, anyway. He and Ma had been drinking some of that liquor my uncle puts up, and well Pa's kind of mean even when he ain't drunk so when he's got a snootful . . . The livery man and his Indian friend started arguing with my Pa and, being that they were both armed, my Pa saw no reason not to kill them. There were witnesses who testified to the Sheriff that it was all fair and legal, the way it always was when Pa killed people, at least most of the time.

What the livery man and the Indian didn't know is that they had just gone up against Earle C. Kenton, Sr.

But the town knew who they'd gone up against.

By the time our wagon drew up in front of the small house my Pa had bought along the creek, as many as twenty townspeople stood in our yard, bringing us all kinds of good gifts, everything from smoked meat to wine to tobacco. A lot of them stood under the big shade tree that Ma liked so much.

Earle C. Kenton, Sr., probably the most feared man in

the entire Territory, was somebody you wanted to keep happy. Real happy. Even the Sheriff was there that day with some fresh cut flowers for Ma and a pint of sour mash for Pa, which, unfortunately, Ma snatched up before Pa could drink it. She likes to pour whiskey on boils. Her other favorite thing is to squeeze blackheads. She likes to make it hurt when she's squeezing. I got a lot of them on my back and she always says, "You're just like a little girl, you sissy," whenever I complain about her hurting me.

And so we became citizens of Alberne, Wyoming, population 2,104, every single one of them living in terror of displeasing my Pa, Earle C. Kenton, Sr.

This was in hot, ripe September—September 4, 1886, if you want the exact date—right when school started.

My first morning there, nobody was especially friendly to me. I admit I've always been a little bit plump, and my eyeglasses are pretty darn thick when you come right down to it, and I always had had a certain problem with gas, but once the teacher introduced me—"Boys and girls, this is Earle C. Kenton, Jr."—they all looked at me in a whole new way.

They didn't have much choice.

Their daddies were afraid of my Pa, and so they were smart enough to be afraid of me.

I guess right here I should tell you some of the things that I did not do over the past two years of living here.

I did not set fire to the Lutheran church.

I did not stampede the Bar2's horses the night they trampled that Mex family that had been sleeping outdoors near the line shack.

I did not hang all six of Widow Barker's cats by their tails on the clothesline, and then set them on fire.

Now, I admit that I have sometimes abused my position

in this town. But tongues got so wild that they had me doing everything terrible that was ever done in the whole Territory.

I did set fire to that blind girl's braids that time and the fire did get sort-of out of control.

I did make Tom Wyman dive off the bridge but I didn't have any idea he'd strike his head on a rock and be paralyzed the rest of his life.

And I did switch tracks on that engine but I didn't have any idea that it would run into that other engine. And anyway, nobody was hurt all that bad, except for a couple of them.

Oh, and one other thing: I did do a little bit of fibbing that day when I told my Pa that my teacher Mr. O'Neill got mad at me and slapped me across the face. Actually, he didn't slap me, he just said, "Everybody else may be afraid of you, Earle, Jr., but I'm not. And if you don't have your homework in tomorrow, I'm going to give you an F." True, Mr. O'Neill was unarmed when my Pa killed him, but I quick-like slipped a gun into his hand so that when the Sheriff saw him lying there, he looked up at Pa and said, "Sure looks like it was a fair fight to me, Mr. Kenton, sir."

I was sleeping when Ma got home last night. She'd gone with Pa to the next county to look at some land.

The liquor from the Silver Dollar had me sleeping pretty good. Technically, they aren't supposed to serve me because of me being only sixteen and all but they aren't about to argue. I didn't even hear Ma come in, or light the kerosene lantern, or pull the chair up to my bed. From what she said, I didn't even feel her shake me at first.

"Earle, Jr., you gotta wake up. It's terrible, it's terrible."

I didn't really want to wake up but I couldn't get back to sleep without knowing what she meant by "it's terrible," so

I sat up on the edge of the bed and started rubbing sleep from my eyes. I stank of perfume and I knew it. I always cadge a free gal or two couple nights a week at Emma's red-light house out on the edge of town. Emma doesn't really want to give her gals away for free but I always just kind of hint that my Pa, Earle, Sr., wouldn't be very happy if he knew she was hurting my feelings that way, and then she gives me pick of the litter.

"What's wrong?" I said.

The only light was moonlight; the only sound my Ma's cursing.

"You know what the dumb idiot did?"

She didn't really expect me to answer.

She just went right on.

"He seen this rattler by the side of the road and Pa was dead-ass drunk and he took his gun out and tried to kill the snake and then guess what?"

It was another one of those questions she liked to ask. Rhetorical is what I think that sissy teacher Mr. O'Neill called them. Any time I ever answered one of them, she slapped me. So I knew to be quiet.

"The darned bullet hit a rock and ricocheted up and hit him right in the head."

"Hit Pa in the head?"

She slapped me hard across the mouth. "You stupid moron, that's what I said, ain't it? Hit him right in the head. Now you come out and help me get him out of the wagon."

He was worse than she said.

I couldn't see his face, there was so much blood.

I got his shoulders and she got his legs and we carried him inside and laid him out on the bed.

She got a lantern lit and then stared down at his face and said, "I sure hope he don't die."

I nodded. "I sure hope so, too."

She looked up at me sharply. "He dies, this whole town's gonna turn on us, you know that, boy?"

"I know."

"No more free meat from the butcher for me," she said.

"And no more free cigars for me at Swenson's."

"And no more gettin' all the bustles and bonnets I want from Freida's Lady's Shop."

"And no more shootin' free pool over at Spitzer's."

"And no more pickin' out free furniture down at Sondrol's."

"And no more gettin' free Ned Buntlines over at Nicholson's."

We both looked down at him at the same time and said the same mournful thing. "Doggone it, Pa, you miserable sonofagun, you can't die. You just can't!"

But he was worse in the morning. He wasn't even moaning much.

"You gonna get Doc over here?" I said.

"Junior, you always will be a damned idiot, won't you?"

"Huh?"

"If I get Doc over here," Ma said, "then he'll tell everybody in town that Pa is dyin'—and then they won't be afraid of us no more."

"Oh, right, guess I didn't think of that."

She leaned over the bed and checked him out. The blood was all crusted in his hair and down the side of his face. He was paler than the white sheet he laid on.

"He's just about gone," she said. "So we got to get started."

"Get started?"

She sighed one of those deep sighs of hers, then slapped me a good one right across the face.

"Figure it out, boy. We got to get out of this town before people figure out Pa is dead, right?"

"Right."

"But we got somethin' else to do before we leave here, don't we?"

"We do?"

Another deep sigh. But at least this time she didn't slap me.

"We got to get everything we've been wantin' to get, and do it in a real hurry—get it while we can still get it free."

I finally figured out what Ma was talking about.

Of course.

Nobody was gonna give us anything free, once they knew that Pa was dead.

"I been wantin' that saddle," I said.

"And I been wantin' that real purty emerald ring."

"And I been wantin' that Remington rifle."

"And I been wantin' that high-necked blouse."

"And I been wantin' that lariat like the fella throws in the Wild West Show."

"And I been wantin' a prairie wolf robe like I seen in the Sears catalog."

"And I been wantin'—"

"Junior, we got to get busy and get all the stuff we want and bring it back here and load up the wagon and git out of town before they find him."

We took another look down at Pa, who looked sorrowful weak now. He could barely even moan.

"We got to get busy," Ma said.

In case you're interested, the saddle I wanted was a Texas style, with Mexican hide on the seat and on the horn and cantle as well. And the fenders was extra-wide.

Mr. Bulow, the saddlemaker, was just handing it over

when Sheriff Lacy walked in.

"Morning," he said to both of us, standing in the sunlight streaming through the front window.

We both morninged him back.

"That's a right smart saddle," Sheriff Lacy said.

"Best one I got," Mr. Bulow said, and you could see in his eyes he wasn't too happy about giving it to me for free.

"Puttin' it on the 'account,' huh?" the Sheriff said.

Bulow nodded, still looking unhappy.

"Oh, one more thing to put on the account, Mr. Bulow," I said. "You had a rawhide lariat in here the other day. I'd sure like to take that one home to Pa. He tole me just last night how much he'd like to have it."

Mr. Bulow frowned and said, "I sold the one you're talkin' about. I'll have to see if I've got another one back in the stock room. You can stop by a little later."

"I'll do that, Mr. Bulow," I said, and walked outside carrying my saddle.

"You're havin' a busy morning," Sheriff Lacy said, walking along the board sidewalk, him nodding good morning to ladies in sunbonnets and men in Stetsons. "Every store I stop in, they tell me you just been there and put something on the account."

"Well, there was a whole bunch of stuff Pa told me to get for him today, so I guess I have been kind of busy."

Just then, Mr. Houseman from the general store opened his door and pushed a wheelbarrow full of stuff in front of us on the sidewalk.

"Here's all the things you wanted, Junior," he said. He sounded even unhappier than Mr. Bulow had when he'd handed me the saddle. I told Mr. Houseman to throw in a wheelbarrow so I'd have some way to get all the stuff home.

"That sure is a mighty impressive mountain of merchandise there," Sheriff Lacy said.

There were fancy shirts and leather boots and a couple of Colts and some ammunition and some Ned Buntlines and two gold railroad watches and a Remington breech load and some duck calls for hunting next fall and a nice new fireman's lantern and then on top of it all—the brand new saddle.

Sheriff Lacy looked at the merchandise and then looked at Mr. Houseman and said, "Sure wish I could afford all this stuff."

"Sure wish I could, too," Mr. Houseman said, still mighty unhappy as he wiped his hands on his denim store apron.

"Well," I said, just to remind them of why I was getting all this merchandise free of charge, "I'd better get this on home to Pa. We sure wouldn't want to get him in a bad mood, now, would we?"

I said a good morning real nice and polite, and then relieved Mr. Houseman of the wheelbarrow.

When I got home, Ma was loading the wagon. It was damned near three-quarters full and none of the stuff was old, either. She was only taking the items she'd gotten that morning. There were dresses and fancy lamps and huge picture hats and parasols and high-button shoes and leather traveling bags and two trunks and a steroscopic camera and even the stove she'd always fancied down at Semple's.

"How'd you get all this home?" I said.

"Oh, they helped me, Junior. I just told them that Pa was on a drinkin' jag and in a real terrible mood." She grinned. "They always help me real nice and polite whenever I tell 'em that."

After we loaded everything up, we went inside to pay our last respects.

Pa was dead.

Ma slapped him a lot and I kicked him three times in the ribs and he didn't make even a peep so we knew for sure he was dead. Pa would've killed us for abusing him that way if he hadn't been dead.

Ma glanced around the house and said, "We had a nice good life here, Junior. But now it's time to skedaddle."

Just as she said that, I heard heavy footsteps on the front porch, and then the door was flung inward and there stood Sheriff Lacy with his badge and his carbine.

"I don't want neither of you to move," he said.

Behind him, out on the lawn, I could see a whole crowd of people, maybe thirty or forty. A lot of them were the merchants we'd been visiting this morning.

"He's gonna kill you for bargin' in here like that," Ma said. "Kill you right in your tracks."

"Where is he?" Sheriff Lacy said.

"He's sleepin' off a drunk," Ma said.

When Sheriff Lacy walked past us, two men took his place in the doorway: Mr. Houseman from the general store and Mr. Semple from the hardware store where Ma got the stove.

They both had carbines.

I looked at Ma and she looked at me.

She had one of those expressions where I knew she wanted to slap somebody and slap him real hard and for a real long time.

Sheriff Lacy came back and said to Mr. Houseman and Mr. Semple, "Just what we suspected, gentlemen. They were piling up the merchandise before they got out of town. Earle C. Kenton, Sr. is in there, dead."

Mr. Houseman turned in the doorway and shouted to the crowd. "Earle Kenton, Sr.'s dead! Did you hear that everybody? Earle Kenton, Sr.'s dead!"

Not even at a baseball game where the home team just hit a home run had I ever heard such cheering.

Sheriff Lacy pointed his carbine at us and said, "Outside, you two. And now."

I guess I expected them to be cursing at us, or maybe even throwing stuff at us, but all that crowd did was stand in a semicircle under the big shade tree and watch us.

And then one man stepped from the crowd and it was Mr. Bulow the saddlemaker and he stepped up to me and said, "You know that rawhide lariat you wanted, Junior? Well, here it is."

They hanged Ma first, and then it was my turn.

Emma Baxter's Boy

The night rain didn't slow them down any. Sheriff Dan Gray had his lantern, and his breed deputy had his own lantern, too.

They had gone through the house, and now they were searching the outbuildings: barn, silo, chicken house. In the barn, you could hear the restless horses above the hiss of cold November rain.

Joel Baxter and his wife Emma stood on the porch of the farmhouse, just beneath the dripping overhang, watching the lawmen set about their work.

Joel was a scrawny man in his late twenties. He shaved only once a week, which left him with a heavy growth of dark, gristly stubble. He had guilty, frightened blue eyes and more of a tic than a smile. He wore bibs and a flannel shirt, and a corncob pipe was stuck in the corner of his mouth.

Emma was twenty-five. She'd been pretty but went early to fat. Her prettiness was hidden now in her fleshy cheeks. She wore a gingham dress, a soiled apron, and a red woolen shawl. The temperature could be no more than thirty. When they talked, their breath was silver.

The Baxter farm was on the outskirts of Dade Township, which was a small community of merchants that served the surrounding agricultural areas. The sheriff and the breed worked out of there.

Joel watched as the sheriff and the breed came together in front of the silo. They were talking, their words lost in

212

the sibilance of the rain. There being no moonlight, their expressions were hard to read. They both wore ponchos heavily oiled for just such a downpour, ponchos and wide-brimmed Texas hats.

Emma said, "Maybe they'll want to search the house again."

"It'll be all right."

"But what if they do?"

"They won't, Emma. Don't get all excited now." Emma had a tendency to do that, to get all excited whenever the root cellar was threatened. Nobody knew about the root cellar but her and her husband. She meant to keep it that way. She had lost two babies to miscarriage. She didn't plan to lose this one to anything.

The sheriff and the breed came over and stood below them on the ground.

"You wouldn't have any coffee, would you, Emma?" the sheriff said.

Joel looked at her. He knew what she was thinking. Let them in for coffee, they just might start searching the house again. This time, they might just find the trapdoor to the root cellar.

"Sure we do," Joel said. It would look funny, turning the sheriff down.

A few minutes later, the three men sat at the kitchen table, the large kerosene lamp casting off smoky illumination. On the counter beneath the three-shelved cupboard, a large piece of pork soaked in brine. Also on the counter was a bottle of New England rum, which Joel had bought for Emma in town earlier that day. She used it to wash her hair with, which kept it clean and free of prairie mites. The pride she'd once had in her face and body, she now had in her auburn tresses.

She brought them steaming hot coffee.

The breed said, "Thank you very much, ma'am." The breed was always polite. The priests had educated him. He was clean, too, and never looked insolent the way most breeds did.

She went into the bedroom to sew. Women were not welcome when men were talking. She kept the door open, though, so she could hear them.

"There's a child out here, somewhere," the sheriff said. "I don't see no reason to keep bullshittin' us about it, Joel. You've got a kid of some kind on these premises." The sheriff was a fleshy white-haired man whose white beard was stained a chestnut color around the mouth from chewing tobacco. He had a bad pair of store-boughts that clicked and clattered when he talked too fast, so he made a point of speaking slowly and distinctly, which strangers mistook for him being wise and deliberate in his words.

"Mrs. Calherne drove by up on the hill in her buggy the other day," the sheriff went on, "and she seen Emma and a kid playin' in the yard here. She was too far away to see what the kid looked like. But it was a kid, all right."

"She must have bad eyesight, Sheriff, that's all I can figure."

"Bad eyesight?" the lawman said. The breed never talked except to say thank you. "Then we must have a lot of people around Dade Township with bad eyesight, because this is about the tenth, eleventh party to see a kid in your yard."

Emma had to be more careful about where she takes the kid out. He'd have to remind her of that again.

"One of the other ones who saw the kid, saw him a couple of times, matter of fact," the sheriff said, "was my deputy, Frank Sullivan. He was real curious about why somebody would want to keep their kid hidden the way you folks do."

The sheriff looked over at the breed. "Then one day Sullivan, he told me he was going to come out here and look around when he knew you folks was in town. Well, he did that, Joel, two weeks ago it was, and nobody's seen him since. He come out here and then he disappeared. Now what the hell's that all about, and why are you keepin' this kid of yours a secret, anyway?"

Joel said, "I don't know what happened to your deputy, Sheriff."

The sheriff looked at the breed again, then back at Joel. "Where's the kid, Joel?"

"What kid?"

"You know what kid. The kid a whole lot of people have seen from a distance, but you won't admit to."

"There isn't any kid," Emma said, as she entered the kitchen.

She stood next to the stove, watching the men. "I don't know what those folks think they're seeing but it isn't a kid. I guess I'd know if I had a kid or not, wouldn't I?"

The sheriff sighed. "He's here somewhere. I'm sure of it."

"You looked everywhere," Joel said.

"Maybe not everywhere," the sheriff said. "Maybe you've got a secret place, something like that."

"No secret place," Joel said. "Where would there be a secret place?"

Thunder rattled the farmhouse windows. In the lightning that followed, Sheriff Gray's face looked lined, old, dead.

"Guess we have searched it pretty good," he said. He sounded too tired to move. He sighed. "Maybe we'll push on back to town," he said to the breed. The breed nodded. "I appreciate the coffee, Emma."

"Yes, thank you," the breed said. The priests on the reservation had done a good job of educating him. He sounded a lot whiter than most white men.

They stood up and shrugged into their ponchos and shoved their hats down heavy on their heads and said a few more goodnights, and then pushed on into the cold, slashing rain.

When they were sixty seconds gone, Emma said softly, "My heart was in my throat. The breed, he kept looking over there by the stove."

"I think you're imagining things, Emma. I didn't see him looking over there once."

Her reaction was immediate, angry. "You don't give a damn about your own son, do you? You want them to find him, don't you? You know what they'd do to him, don't you? They'd kill him. They'd take one look at him and then they'd kill him, and you wouldn't give a damn, would you, Joel? Your own son and you wouldn't give a damn at all."

"They're not gonna quit lookin' for their deputy," he said quietly. "They're gonna come back here, and they're gonna keep comin' back."

"That all you got to say?"

"That's all I got to say."

"I don't suppose you're gonna go down there with me and say goodnight to him and say his goodnight prayers with me. That'd be askin' too much, wouldn't it?"

"Yes," he said. "Yes, it would."

She took the lamp and walked over by the stove and lifted up the small hooked rug and bent down and lifted the metal ring on the trapdoor.

The root cellar stank of dirt and cold. They'd kept vegetables fresh down there, but the coldness muted all the other odors. His grave would smell like that, Joel knew, dirt and cold. This was the smell of eternity. Darkness, rot, nothingness.

She went down the steps quickly, pulling the trapdoor closed behind her.

Joel stood there, listening to the noises the child in the cellar always made. He had never heard anything like these noises, a very low keening followed by a kind of sucking sound.

Without the lamp, the house was dark now, a lonely, empty dark.

Joel went into the bedroom and stripped to his long johns and lay down and listened to the rain thrum on the roof. He wished he could pray. He wished he still believed. He didn't know what they were going to do about the root cellar.

He rolled over and went to sleep. There was no sense waiting up for her. Sometimes, she stayed down there till dawn.

Sound woke him.

What kind of sound?

He sat up, listened, reaching for the Navy Colt on the floor next to the bed.

Kitchen. Table. Somebody bumping against it.

Hiss of rain.

It could be Emma, but instinct told him otherwise.

He eased himself out of bed, tiptoed to the bedroom doorway that looked out upon the one large room that was both living space and kitchen. He glanced out the window. A lone horse was ground-tied by the silo.

The trapdoor. Somebody crouching there. Opening the door six inches to peer into the dank darkness below, the keening sound louder suddenly, agitated. Lamplight flickering up from the cellar.

"Joel?" Emma said from the root cellar. "Is that you up there?"

The crouching man heard him then. Started to turn, started to stand.

"Better come up here, Emma," Joel said.

"What's wrong?" Emma called.

"The breed came back."

"The breed? I tole you, Joel. I tole you."

The keening sound became mournful then, the way it always did when Emma left the root cellar and came back upstairs, mournful and frightened and impossibly lonely.

She came up, bringing light in the form of the lamp.

The breed stood next to the stove.

"You saw it, didn't you, when you were looking down there, in the lamplight I mean," Joel said.

"I didn't see anything," the breed said in his perfect English. His poncho and his hat stank of rain.

"Maybe he didn't see, Joel," Emma said hopefully.

"Oh, he saw, all right," Joel said. "He saw all right." Then, "Where's the sheriff?"

"He's outside waiting for me. I don't come out pretty soon, he'll come in here."

"Oh, my Lord," Emma said. "What're we gonna do, Joel?" In Emma's voice, he could hear her fears: now her third child would be taken from her, too. Emma Baxter, it seemed, was never to be blessed with a child she could keep.

"You're lying," Joel said. "The sheriff ain't out there."

"Oh? And how would you know that?"

"Because there's only one horse out there."

"That doesn't prove anything."

"It proves it to me," Joel said. Then, "Come over here."

"What?"

"Step away from the wall."

"Why would I want to do that?"

"Because I told you to."

"I only take orders from the sheriff."

Joel decided to get it over with. He crossed the floor in three steps and brought the barrel of his gun down hard on the breed's right temple.

The breed looked startled for a moment. Then he sank to the floor, unconscious.

"Oh, my God, Joel, what're we gonna do?" Emma said. "What're we gonna do?"

But Joel didn't say anything. He just got the rope and tied the breed up, wrists and ankles, then dragged him over to the corner.

"We got to put him down there," Emma said twenty minutes later.

The trapdoor was shut. She had poured them both coffee. The breed was still unconscious.

"Emma," Joel said, "you know what we got to do?" He sounded as sad as Emma looked.

"Oh, no, Joel, oh, no. You don't do that to our son. He's your own flesh and blood."

"Part of him is my flesh and blood," Joel said. "Part of him is somethin' else."

He still recalled the night it happened, a steamy August night, him waking to find the bed empty, Emma gone off somewhere. Him scared. Where had she gone? And then her coming back, telling him she'd heard this strange sound in the sky, and then seen this explosion over the hills in the woods, something falling from the sky. And then her going out there to see what it was. And finding the fire and next to the fire the odd bubbling muck—like quicksand, she kept saying, like quicksand—and then her stumbling and falling into it, and grasping and gasping to be free of it, the thing boiling and bubbling and sucking her down, sucking her down, and her free finally, finally free.

She'd vomited several times that night. And run a fever so hot Joel was sure she was going to die right there in their wedding bed. But in the morning, she was not only alive, she rolled over when the rooster crowed and shook him gently and whispered, "I'm going to have a baby again, Joel. I'm going to have a baby again."

Her fever was gone, and no more vomiting.

Joel himself went over the hill to the woods that morning. He could see where a fire had burned an area of the forest, a scorched black circle as if a fiery disk had fallen from the sky, but there was no evidence of the bubbling hole she'd described, no evidence at all, though on her dress he could see strange mauve stains, and knew she was telling the truth.

Winter came, and the child was born, and when the midwife delivered it, she screamed and tried to run from the room. But it was too late. Joel buried what was left of her, her flesh so shredded and torn, up in the hills by the deep stand of hardwoods. She was the first person to die because of what had been birthed between Emma's legs. If they killed the breed, he would be the fourth.

"I got to, Emma," he said. "I got to. We just can't go on killing people this way. They'll figure it out and they'll hang us. They'll hang us right down in Tompkins Square the way they did those two breeds last spring."

"He's our son."

"No he ain't, Emma," Joel said gently, "and I think deep down you know that."

"He come from my womb."

"Yeah, but it wasn't me that put him there, and you know it."

She looked at him. He'd expected tears, argument. All she said was, "Then I'll do it, the breed I mean."

He shook his head. "Emma, listen, the breed wakes up, I'm gonna take him into town, and we're gonna talk to the sheriff, and I'm gonna explain everything, how none of this was our fault, and how we want to stop it now before it gets any worse. That's the only thing we can do, Emma. The only thing."

No reaction this time either. She just watched him. She didn't even look angry any more. Just watched him.

The breed moaned. He was coming around.

"I love you, Emma," Joel said. "I want a good life for us. It wasn't our fault what happened. I think Sheriff Gray'll understand that. He seems to be a good man."

"What is that thing, anyway?" the breed said. You could hear pain in his voice. Joel had cracked him pretty darned good on the side of the head.

"You shut up, breed," Emma said. "That's our son is what that thing is. And we're proud he's our son. Very proud."

Now she was crying, crying hard. "You don't call him a 'thing,' either, you understand that?" Emma said.

"C'mon, Emma," Joel said gently, touching her hand. "I'm gonna let the breed go and then we'll ride into town, all right?"

But all she did was weep. Weep.

Joel, more tired suddenly than he'd ever been in his life, stood up and walked over to Emma on the other side of the table and kissed the top of her head, the way he'd do with a child. "It'll be better once we tell the sheriff, Emma. It really will."

Then he went over and crouched down and started

undoing the ropes binding the breed.

And that was when the breed shouted, "Watch out, Joel!"

All Joel had time to see was the carving knife coming down in an arc, the huge and terrible blade gleaming in the lamplight, coming down, down, down. And then the pain in his shoulder, then the pain all over the upper part of his body.

When she was all finished with the knife, Emma dragged Joel over to the trapdoor and pushed him down into the root cellar. His body made a big noise when it collided with the dirt floor.

She did the breed the same way. He was even bloodier than Joel had been. She'd gotten the breed to admit that he'd been lying. He'd come back here after riding back to town with the sheriff.

She gave the breed an extra hard push through the opening.

Then she closed the trapdoor and left her son to his business.

An hour later, Emma hefted the large metal trunk on to the back of the buckboard. Her son would be safe and dry in there, especially after she threw the blanket over it and fastened it down with rope.

Then she climbed aboard and took the reins and set off. The roads were muddy, but at least the rain had let up. She wasn't quite sure where she was going. She just needed to get to another part of the Territory as fast as possible.

She thought about Joel, and that first spring she'd met him, and how he'd courted her with his big, wide, country-boy grin. He'd been so nice back then, nice all the time right up to the night when their son was born. And then he hadn't been nice at all. Then he'd changed so much he wasn't like Joel at all.

By sunrise, they had reached the stage road. The rain hadn't been so bad over here. The going was easier, much easier.

Deathman

The night before he killed a man, Hawes always followed the same ritual.

He arrived in town late afternoon—in this case, a chill shadowy autumn afternoon—found the best hotel, checked in, took a hot bath in a big metal tub, put on a fresh suit so dark it hinted at the ministerial, buffed his black boots till they shone, and then went down to the lobby in search of the best steak in town.

Because this was a town he'd worked many times before, he knew just which restaurant to choose. A place called "Ma's Gaslight Inn." Ma had died last year of a venereal disease (crazed as hell, her friends said, in her last weeks, talking to dead people and drawing crude pictures of her tombstone again and again on the wall next to her death bed).

Dusk and chill rain sent townspeople scurrying for home, the clatter of wagons joining the clop of horses in retreat from the small, prosperous mountain town.

Hawes strode the boardwalk alone, a short and burly man, handsome except for his acne-pitted cheeks. Even in his early forties, his boyhood taint was obvious.

Rain dripped in fat, silver beads from the overhangs as he walked down the boardwalk toward the restaurant. He liked to look in the shop windows when they were closed this way, look at the female things—a lace shawl, a music box with a ballerina dancing atop, a ruby necklace so elegant it looked as if it had been plucked from the fat, white neck of a duchess only moments ago.

Without his quite wanting them to, all these things reminded him of Sara. Three years they'd been married until
she'd learned his secret, and then she'd been so repelled she
invented a reason to visit her mother back in Ohio, and
never again returned. He was sure she had remarried—he'd
received divorce papers several years ago—and probably
even had children by now. Children—and a house with a
creek in back—had been her most devout wish.

He quit looking in the shop windows. He now looked
straight ahead. His boot heels were loud against the wet
boards. The air smelled cold and clean enough to put life in
the lungs of the dead.

The player piano grew louder the closer to the restaurant
he got; and then laughter and the clink of glasses.

Standing there, outside it all, he felt a great loneliness,
and now when he thought of Sara he was almost happy.
Having even sad memories was better than no memories at
all.

He walked quickly to the restaurant door, pushed it
open, and went inside.

He needed to be with people tonight.

He was halfway through his steak dinner (fat pats of
butter dripping golden down the thick sides of the meat and
potatoes sliced and fried in tasty grease) when the tall man
in the gray suit came over.

At this time the restaurant was full, low-hanging Roch-
ester lamps casting small pools of light into the ocean of
darkness. Tobacco smoke lay a haze over everything,
seeming to muffle conversations. An old Negro stood next
to the double doors of the kitchen, filling water glasses and
handing them to the big-hipped waitresses hurrying in and
out the doors. The rest of the house was packed with the

sort of people you saw in mining towns—wealthy miners and wealthy men who managed the mines for eastern bosses; and hard, scrubbed-clean working men with their hard, scrubbed-clean wives out celebrating a birthday or an anniversary at the place where the rich folks dine.

"Excuse me?"

Hawes looked up. "Yes?"

"I was wondering if you remembered me."

Hawes looked him over. "I guess."

"Good. Then you mind if I sit down?"

"You're damn right I do. I'm eating."

"But last time you promised that—"

Hawes dismissed the man with a wave of a pudgy hand. "Didn't you hear me? I'm eating. And I don't want to be interrupted."

"Then after you're finished eating—?"

Hawes shrugged. "We'll see. Now get out of here and leave me alone."

The man was very young, little more than a kid—twenty-one, twenty-two at most—and now he seemed to wither under the assault of Hawes' intentional and practiced rudeness.

"I'll make sure you're done eating before I bother you again." Hawes said nothing. His head was bent to the task of cutting himself another piece of succulent steak.

The tall man went away.

"It's me again. Richard Sloane."

"So I see."

The tall man looked awkward. "You're smoking a cigar."

"So I am."

"So I take it you're finished eating?"

Hawes almost had to laugh, the sonofabitch looked so young and nervous. They weren't making them tough, the way they'd been in the frontier days. "I suppose I am."

"Then may I sit down?"

Hawes pointed a finger at an empty chair. The young man sat down.

"You know what I want?" He took out a pad and pencil the way any good journalist would.

"Same thing you people always want."

"How it feels after you do it."

Hawes smiled. "You mean do I feel guilty? Do I have nightmares?"

The young man looked uncomfortable with Hawes' playful tone. "I guess that's what I mean, yes."

Hawes stared at the young man.

"You ever seen one, son?"

The youngster looked as if he was going to object to "son" but then changed his mind. "Two. One when I was a little boy with my uncle and one last year."

"Did you like it?"

"I hated it. It scared me the way people acted, it made me sick. They were—celebrating. It was like a party."

"Yes, some of them get that way sometimes."

Hawes had made a study of it all, so he considered telling Sloane here about Tom Galvin, an Irishman of the sixteenth century who had personally hanged more than one thousand six hundred men. Galvin believed in giving the crowd a show, especially with men accused of treason. These he not only hanged but oftentimes dismembered, throwing arms and legs to the crazed onlookers. Some reports had it that some of the crowds actually ate of the bloodied limbs tossed to them.

"You ever hang two at once?"

"The way they did in Nevada last year?" Hawes smirked and shook his head. "Not me, son. I'm not there to put on a show. I'm there to kill a man." He took a drag on his cigar. "I don't want to give my profession a bad name."

God knew that executioners, as a group, were unreliable. In seventeenth-century England, the executioner himself was put in a jail cell for eight days preceding the hanging—so officials would know he'd show up on time and sober.

"Will you sleep well tonight?"

"Very well, I hope."

"You won't think about tomorrow?"

"Not very seriously."

"How the man will look?"

"No."

"Or how the trap will sound when it opens?"

"No."

"Or how his eyes will bulge and his tongue will bloat?"

Hawes shook his head. "I know what you want, son. You want a speech about the terrible burden of being an executioner." He tapped his chest. "But I don't have it in me."

"Then it isn't a burden?"

"No, son, it isn't. It's just what I do. The way some men milk cows and other men fix buggies—I hang people. It's just that simple."

The young man looked disappointed. They always did when Hawes told them this. They wanted melodrama—they wanted regret and remorse and a tortured soul.

Hawes decided to give him the story about the woman. It wasn't the whole story, of course, but the part he always told was just what frontier newspapermen were looking for.

"There was a blonde woman once."

"Blonde?"

"So blonde it almost hurt your eyes to look at her hair in the sunlight. It was spun gold."

"Spun gold; God."

"And it was my duty to hang her."

"Oh, shit."

"The mayor of the town said I'd be hanging a woman but I never dreamt she'd be so beautiful."

"Did you hang her anyway?"

"I had to, son. It's my job."

"Did she cry?"

"She was strong; she didn't cry and her legs didn't give out when she was climbing the scaffold stairs. You know, I've seen big, strapping men just collapse on those stairs and have to be carried all the way up. And some of them foul their pants. I can smell the stench when I'm pulling the white hood over their eyes."

"But she was strong?"

"Very strong. She walked right over to the trapdoor and stood on top of it and folded her hands very primly in front of her. And then she just waited for me to come over there."

"What was she guilty of?"

"She'd taken a lover that spring, and when her husband found out he tried to kill her. But instead she killed him. The jury convicted her of first-degree murder."

"It doesn't sound like first-degree to me."

"Me either, son. But I'm the hangman; I'm not the judge."

"And so you hanged her?"

"I did."

"Didn't you want to call it off?"

"A part of me did."

"Did she scream when the door dropped away?"

"She didn't say anything."

"And her neck snapped right away?"

"I made sure of that, son. I didn't want her to dangle there and strangle the way they sometimes do. So I cinched the knot extra tight. She crossed over right away. You could hear her neck break."

"This was how many years ago?"

"Ten."

"And obviously you still think about her."

It was clear now the angle the young journalist would be taking. Hangman kills beautiful woman; can't get her out of his mind these long years later. His readers would love it.

"Oh, yes, son; yes, I still think about her."

The excitement was plain on the man's young face. Hangman kills beautiful woman, can't forget her. This may just have been the best story he'd ever had.

He flipped the cover of his pad closed. "I really appreciate this."

Hawes nodded.

The young man got up, snatched his derby from the edge of the table, and walked to the rear where the press of people and smoke and clatter were overwhelming.

Hawes took the time for another two drinks and half a Cuban cigar and then went out into the rain.

The house was three blocks away, in the opposite direction of the gallows, for which Hawes was grateful. A superstitious man, he believed that looking at a gallows the night before would bring bad luck. The man would not die clean, the trap would not open, the rope would mysteriously snap—something. And so he didn't glimpse the gallows until the morning of the execution.

Hawes came this way often. This town was in the exact center of the five-hundred-mile radius he traveled as an executioner. So he came to this town three or four times a month, not just when he had somebody to hang here.

And he always came to Maude's.

Maude was the plump, giggling madam who ran the

town's only whorehouse. She had an agreement with the sheriff that if she kept her house a quarter mile away from town, and if she ran her place clean, meaning no black whores or no black customers, then the sheriff would leave her alone, meaning of course he would keep at bay the zealous German Lutherans who mostly made up the town. Maude gave the lawman money but not much, and every once in awhile he'd sneak up on the back porch where one of the runaway farm girls she employed would offer the sheriff her wet, glistening lips.

He could hear the player piano now, Hawes could, lonely on the rainy prairie night. He wished he hadn't told that pipsqueak journalist about the blonde woman, because now Hawes was thinking about her again, and what had really happened that morning.

The house was a white two-story frame. In front, two horses were tied to a post, and down a ways a buggy dun stood ground-tied.

Hawes went up to the door and knocked.

Maude herself opened it. "Well, for shit's sake, girls, look who's here."

Downstairs there was a parlor, which was where the player piano was, and the girls sat on a couch and you chose them the way you did cattle at a livestock auction.

Hawes always asked for the same one. He looked at the five girls sitting there watching him. They were about what you'd expect for a Midwestern prairie whorehouse, young girls quickly losing their bloom. They drank too much and laughed too loud and weren't always good about keeping themselves clean.

That was why he always asked for Lucy.

"She here, Maude?"

Maude winked at him. "Just taking a bath."

"I see."

"Won't be long." She knew his tastes, knew he didn't want to stay downstairs with the girls and the piano and the two cowboys who were giggling about which girls they'd pick. "You know the end room on the hall?"

"Right."

"Why don't you go up there and wait for her?"

"Good idea."

"You'll find some bourbon in the drawer."

"Appreciate it."

She winked at him again. "Hear you're hanging the Parsons boy in the morning."

"I never know their names."

"Well, take it from me, sweetie, when he used to come here he didn't tip worth a damn. Anything he gets from you, he's got coming." And then she whooped a laugh and slapped him on the back and said, "You just go right up those stairs, sweetie."

He nodded, mumbling a thank you, and turned away from her before he had to look directly at the small brown stubs of her teeth. The sight and stench of her mouth had always sickened him.

He wondered how many men had lain in this dark room. He wondered how many men had felt his loneliness. He wondered how many men had heard a woman's footsteps coming down the hall, and felt fear and shame.

Lucy opened the door. She was silhouetted in the flickering hall light. "You want me to get a lantern?"

"That's all right."

She laughed. "Never known a man who likes the dark the way you do."

She came in, closed the door behind her. She smelled of

soapy bath water and jasmine. She wasn't pretty but she kept herself clean and he appreciated it.

"Should've just left my clothes off, I guess," she said. "After my bath, I mean."

He could tell she was nervous. The darkness always made her like this.

Wind and rain spattered against the window. The fingers of a dead branch scraped the glass, a curious kind of music.

She came over to the bed and stood above him. She took his hand and pressed it lightly against her sex. She was dry and warm.

"You going to move over?"

He rolled over so there was room for her. He lay on his back and stared at the ceiling.

As usual when they lay there, Lucy smoked a cigarette. She always hand-rolled two or three before coming to see Hawes, because many times the night consisted of talk and nothing more.

"You want a drag?"

"No, thanks."

"How you doing?"

"All right, I guess."

"Hear you're going to hang a man tomorrow."

"Yes."

Next to him, she shuddered, her whole naked, skinny body. "Forgive me for saying so, Hawes, but I just don't know how you can do it."

"You've said that before."

She laughed again. "Yes, I guess I have."

They lay there silent for a time, just the wind and the rain pattering the roof, just the occasional glow of her cigarette as she dragged on it, just his own breathing.

And the darkness; oh, yes, the darkness.

"You ever read anything by Louisa May Alcott?" Lucy asked.

"No."

"I'm reading this book by her now. It's real good, Hawes, you should read it sometime."

"Maybe I will."

That was another thing he liked about Lucy. Where most of the girls were ignorant, Lucy had gone through fourth grade before running away, and had learned to read. Hawes could carry on a good conversation with her and he appreciated that. Of course, she was older too, twenty-five or so, and that also made a difference.

They fell into silence again.

After awhile he rolled over and kissed her.

She said, "Just a minute."

She stubbed her cigarette out and then rolled back to him and then they got down to it seriously.

The fear was there as always—could he actually do it and do it right without humiliating himself—but tonight he had no trouble.

He was good and hard and he got into her with no trouble and she responded as if she really gave a damn about him, and then he climaxed and collapsed next to her, his breath heaving in the darkness, feeling pretty damn good about himself as a man again.

She didn't say anything for a long time there in the wind and rain and darkness, smoking a cigarette again, and then she said, "That's why she left you, isn't it?"

"Huh?"

"Your wife. Why she left you."

"I'm not following you." But he was in fact following her and he sensed that she was going to say something he didn't want to hear.

"That time you got drunk up here in the room."

"Yeah? What about it?"

"You told me about your wife leaving you."

"So?"

"But you wouldn't tell me why she left you. You just kept saying 'She had a good reason, I guess.' Well, I finally figured out what that reason is."

He was silent for a time again, and so was she.

Obviously she could sense that she'd spooked him and now she was feeling bad about it. "I shouldn't have said anything, Hawes. I'm sorry."

"It's all right."

He was feeling the loneliness again. He wanted to cry but he wasn't a man given to tears.

"Me and my big mouth." Lucy said, lighting another cigarette.

In the flash of flame, he could see her face. Soft, freckled; eyes the blue of a spring sky.

They lay in silence a long time.

She said, "You angry at me, Hawes?"

"No."

"I'm sorry I said anything."

"I know."

"I mean, it doesn't bother me. The way you are."

"I know."

"It's kind of funny, even."

"It isn't funny to me."

And it hadn't been funny to his wife, Sara, either. Once she figured out the pattern, she'd left him immediately.

"How'd you figure it out?" he asked.

"I just started keeping track."

"Oh."

"But I won't tell anybody. I mean, if that's what's bothering you."

"I appreciate it. You keeping it to yourself, I mean."

"You can't help the way you are."

"No; no, I guess I can't."

He thought of how angry and disgusted his wife Sara had been when she'd finally understood that he was impotent all the time, except for the night before a hanging. Only then could he become fully a man.

The snap of the trapdoor, the snap of the neck. And then extinction. Blackness: utter, eternal blackness. And Hawes controlling it all.

In the wind and darkness, she said, "You ever think about how it'll be for you personally?"

"How what'll be?"

"Death."

"Yeah, I guess so."

"You think there're angels?"

"No."

"You think there's a heaven?"

"No."

"You think there's a God?"

"No."

She took a long drag on her cigarette. "Neither do I, Hawes. But I sure wish I did."

From down the hall, Hawes could hear a man laughing, then a woman joining in. The player piano downstairs was going again.

"Would you just hold me?" Hawes said.

"What?"

"Just hold me in your arms."

"Sure."

"Real tight."

"All right."

She stubbed out her cigarette and then rolled back to him. She took him in her arms with surprising tenderness, and held him to her, her soft breasts warm against his chest, and then she said, "Sometimes, I think you're my little boy, Hawes. You know that?"

But Hawes wasn't paying attention; he was listening to the chill rain on the dark wind, and the lonely, frantic laughter down the hall.

The wind grew louder then, and Lucy fell silent, just holding him tighter, tighter.

Author's Note

I wanted this to read like a suicide note, and from the mail it got, I succeeded. Many of the readers were angry that the editor had ever agreed to publish a story this dark and perverse. Actually, I, too, sort of wondered why the editor agreed to publish it.

Masque

From a police report:

I found the nude body of Janice Hollister in a deep ravine. Some children who'd been playing in the neighborhood told me that they'd seen a dog with what appeared to be blood on his coat. The dog led me back to her. The first thing I noticed about the Hollister woman was the incredible way her body had been cut up. Her entire right breast had been ripped away.

"I've listed it as a car accident," Doctor Temple says.

They are in a room of white tiles and green walls and white cabinets and stainless steel sinks. The room smells of antiseptic and the white tile floor sparkles with hot September sunlight.

Doctor Temple is in his mid-fifties, balding, a lean jogger in a white medical smock. He has very blue eyes and very pink skin. He is an old family friend.

"You've taken care of the records, then?" Mrs. Garth asks. She is sixty-eight and regal in a cold way, given to Dior suits and facelifts.

"Yes."

"There'll be no problem?"

"None. The record will show that he was transferred here two weeks ago, following a car accident."

"A car accident?"

"That will account for the bandages. So many lacera-

237

tions and contusions, we had to cover his entire body." He makes a grim line of his mouth. "Very dramatic and very convincing to the eye. Almost theatrical."

"I see. Very good. I appreciate it."

"And we appreciate all you've done for the hospital, Ruth. Without your generosity, there'd be no cancer clinic."

She stands up and offers her delicate hand in such a way that the doctor fears for a terrified moment she actually expects him to kiss it.

From a police report:

> *I thought the dog might have attacked her after the killer fled. But then I saw that her anus and vagina had been torn up just the way the rest of her had, and then I knew that it had to be him. The perpetrator, I mean. I checked the immediate vicinity for footprints and anything that might have fallen from his pockets. I found nothing that looked useful.*

A new elevator, one more necessity her money has bought this hospital, takes her to the ninth floor.

She walks down a sunny corridor being polished by a dumpy middle-aged black woman who has permitted her hose to bag about her knees. The woman, Mrs. Garth thinks, should have more respect for herself.

Mrs. Garth finds 909 and enters.

She takes no more than ten steps inside, around the edge of the bathroom, when she stops and looks in horror at him.

All she can think of are those silly movies about Egyptian mummies brought back to life.

Here sits Steve, his entire head and both arms swathed entirely in white bandages. All she can see of him are his face, his eyes, and his mouth.

"My Lord," she moans.

She edges closer to his hospital bed. The room is white and clean and lazy in the sunlight. Above, the TV set mounted to the wall plays a game show with two fat contestants jumping up and down on either side of the handsome host who cannot quite rid his eyes of boredom.

"Aren't you awfully hot inside there?" she asks.

He says nothing, but then at such times he never does.

She pulls up a chair and sits down.

"I am Zoser, founder of the third Dynasty," he says.

"Oh, you," she says. "Now's no time to joke. Anyway, I can barely understand you with all those bandages over your face."

"I am Senferu, the Warrior King."

"Oh, you," she says.

From a police report:

> Her neck appears to have been broken. At least that was my first impression. The killer's strength must be incredible. To say nothing of how much he must hate women.

An hour after she arrives in the hospital room, she says, "An old man saw you."

Inside the mummy head, the blue eyes show panic.

"Don't worry," she continues. "He has vision trouble, so he's not a very credible witness. But he did describe you pretty accurately to the press. Fortunately, I told Doctor Temple that some drug dealers were looking for you. He seemed to accept my story."

She pats him on the arm. "Didn't that medication Doctor Gilroy gave you help? I had such high hopes for it.

He said you wouldn't any longer want to . . . You know what I'm trying to say."

But now that he knows he's going to be safe, the panic dies in his blue eyes and he says, "I am King Tut."

"Oh, pooh. Can't you be serious?"

"I'm not serious. I'm King Tut."

She clucks.

They sit back and watch the Bugs Bunny cartoon he has on. He says, through his bandages, "I wish they'd show Porky."

"Porky?"

"Porky Pig."

"Oh, I see." My God, he's forty-six years old. She says, "In case there's any trouble, Doctor Temple is going to tell the police that you've been here two weeks and that the old man couldn't possibly identify you, because even if you were out and about, you'd have been wearing bandages."

"They won't arrest Senferu, the Warrior King, mother. They'd be afraid to."

"I thought after that trouble in Chicago you told me about—"

"There's Sylvester!" he exclaims.

And so there is: Sylvester the cat.

She lets him watch a long minute, the exasperated cat lisping and spitting and spraying. "You were very savage with this one," she says. "Very savage."

"I've seen this one before. This is where Tweety really gives it to Sylvester. Watch!"

She watches, and when she can endure it no more, she says, "Perhaps I made some mistakes with you."

"Oh, God, Sylvester—watch out for Tweety!"

"Perhaps, after your father died, I took certain liberties with you I shouldn't have." Pause. "Letting you sleep in my bed . . . Things happened and I don't suppose either one of us is to blame, but nonetheless—"

"Great! Porky's coming on! Look, Mother, it's Porky!"

From a police report:

Down near the creek bed, we found her breast. At first I wasn't sure what it was, but as I stared at it I started getting sick. By this time, the first backup was arriving. They had to take over for me a few minutes. I wasn't feeling very well.

In the hospital room, sitting there in his mummy bandages, his mother at his side, Steve stares up at the TV set. There's a commercial on now. He hates commercials.

"Maybe Daffy Duck will be on next, Mother. God, wouldn't that be great?"

Now it's her turn for silence. She thinks of the girls in Chicago and Kansas City and Akron. So savage with them; so savage. She will never again believe him that everything's fine and that his medication has gotten him calmed down once and for all and that she should let him take a trip.

But of course this time he didn't even go anywhere. Most dangerous of all, he did it here at home.

Right here at home.

"Wouldn't it be great, Mother?" he asks, wanting her to share his enthusiasm. He loves those occasions when they share things.

She says, "I'm sorry, darling, my mind just wandered. Wouldn't what be great, dear?"

"If it was Daffy on next."

"Daffy?"

"Daffy Duck," he says from inside his mummy head.

And then he does a Daffy Duck imitation right on the spot.

Not even the bandages can spoil it, she thinks. He's so clever. "Oh, yes, dear. That would be great if Daffy came on next."

He reaches over and touches her with his bandaged hand and for a horrible moment she almost believes he's been injured.

But then she sees the laughter in his blue blue eyes inside the mummy head.

She pats his bandaged hand. "You'll get a nice rest here for a few weeks and then we'll go home again, dear, and everything will be fine."

He lays his head back and sighs. "Fine." He repeats the word almost as if he doesn't know what it means. "Fiiiine." He seems to be staring at the ceiling. She hopes it's not another depression. They emerge so quickly and last so long.

But then abruptly he's sitting up again and clapping his bandaged hands together and staring up at the TV screen.

"It is Daffy, Mother. It is Daffy!"

"Yes, dear," she says. "It is Daffy, isn't it?"

The Long Sunset

The afternoon it all started, Sean and I were playing basketball. Or rather, Sean was playing basketball, and I was trying to keep up with him. Sean was the star athlete of Woodrow Wilson High. I was the basketball team manager, thanks to his influence. I played like a team manager, too.

It was just after the season had ended. There were still patches of dirty, April snow on the playground asphalt. The wind was warm and hinted of apple blossoms and the first sputtering sounds of lawn mowers and Saturday afternoons, of little kids with their wobbly kites and adults with their Frisbees and happy dogs. Just a few weeks away now.

Ken Michaels pulled his red Kawasaki motorcycle right up to where we were playing and whipped off his helmet. "Hey, you hear about Jenna?"

"Jenna?" I said, knowing instantly that something terrible had happened to her.

"Downtown," Ken said. "A car hit her."

"Oh, God," I said.

"Is she alive?" Sean asked.

"Yeah. But she's in pretty bad shape."

A minute later Sean and I jumped on his motorcycle and headed for St. Mary's Hospital. Jenna, Sean, and I had grown up in the poor section of our little town of Black River Falls, Iowa. The Knolls they call it, up in the hills above where the great factories used to roar before all the manufacturing went first down South, and then to Mexico. We were inseparable friends. We were bright and ambitious, too, and determined not to stay in the Knolls (or Black River Falls, for that matter) any longer than we had to. There was only one problem. Jenna was in love with Sean, and I was in love with Jenna. And Sean was in love with the princess of Woodrow Wilson High, Kim Westcott.

The good news was that Jenna wasn't as death-threatened as Ken Michaels had led us to believe. The bad news was that her right leg was so badly smashed by the car—the driver a local guy with two previous drunk-driving arrests—that the doctor told her folks that she would probably always limp. They hadn't mentioned any of this to Jenna. This wasn't the time.

I stayed until they kicked me out around seven o'clock. Jenna, pale, pretty, scared, was obviously happy I was there. But she was even happier that Sean was. But after four o'clock, which was when he left to get ready for his date with Kim, Jenna didn't look so happy again. She chit-chatted with her folks, and then chit-chatted with me while they were down in the cafeteria having dinner. But she kept staring longingly at the empty doorway, as if she thought Sean might magically reappear for her.

She stayed in the hospital almost three weeks. The tests and examinations were intense. They told her about the limp. She took it so badly, they put her on one of those psychoactive drugs for depression.

She made it back to school just in time for graduation. Sean wasn't around much, spending every possible moment with Kim and her friends. Knolls people like Jenna and I weren't invited.

The first time I ever saw her drunk was graduation night. She'd asked if she could ride to the ceremony with me. When I went to pick her up, her mother came to the door and whispered, "Jenna went somewhere this afternoon and got drunk. You weren't with her, were you?" I assured her I wasn't. "We've been pouring coffee into her for the last couple of hours."

Her father brought her down. She looked sweet in her cap and gown. She made it about halfway across the tiny living room and dropped straight down, unconscious. No graduation ceremony for Jenna.

"She was afraid of walking across the stage to get her diploma," her father said, "everybody staring at her. You know, her crutches and cast and everything."

"But she's so pretty," I said. "Nobody cares about that."

"She cares," her mother said. "And that's all that matters."

The first time she was arrested for driving while intoxicated, I was the one the Chief of Police called. Jenna's parents were out of town visiting relatives. He wanted $350 in bail money. I had about $3,000 in the bank, my savings toward college. Iowa City was less than an hour away. I was taking three classes a semester and working at a supermarket the rest of the time. I'd been planning to go full-time, but then there was a downturn in the agricultural market. Since my father sold big-ticket farm implements, we didn't have much money.

This was two years after graduating high school. Jenna hadn't gone to college at all. The problem wasn't money. It was alcohol. Jenna had become a serious alcoholic very quickly. A lot of public scenes, slapping people in bars, drunken crying jags at parties, a couple of half-assed suicide attempts. She worked at the mall sometimes. The job had been regular at first. But then her uncle, who had a caramel-corn concession out there, just let her come in when she wanted to. He was her godfather and didn't know what else to do.

The first time I bailed her out wasn't so bad. She was contrite and full of resolve never to take a drink again. We ended up sitting in my car in her darkened driveway for almost three hours. She cried a lot. She even let me kiss her a few times. It was heady, and I'm not kidding. This girl I'd loved since I was a little kid . . . at last in my arms.

Over the next year, I bailed her out twice more. One time she was belligerent. Fucking cops. Fucking stupid laws. She'd been walking, for God's sake. Not driving. And since when could fucking stupid cops pick you up for fucking walking. Public intoxication, I said gently. Oh, you're so fucking full of shit, I can't believe it, she said, and slammed out of the car.

The next time she was really sick. She opened the door and threw up twice before I even got her home.

I guess it was around this time—to be honest, I didn't have any reason to pay this kind of thing any particular attention—that a few farmers started calling the local radio station and newspaper with stories of spaceships hovering over their houses late at night. And not long after that, some of the same people started talking about being abducted by creatures from those very same spaceships, little aliens with tear-shaped heads and glowing emerald-colored eyes. At the time I remember thinking, sure, whatever.

Sean didn't get back to town until he was twenty-eight. By then, he'd spent three years as an All-American at Ohio State and four years as the star quarterback of the Bears, his career ending when his throwing hand was crushed in a riding mower accident. He'd invested his enormous salary, though, and was rich.

He came back to town with his high school princess and three gorgeous blonde daughters in tow. He built a house that cost almost as much as our library had six years earlier, and bought a horse ranch that provided the stud services for two thoroughbreds that had come very close to winning the Derby. He drove around town in a big Mercedes-Benz convertible the color of a misty dawn.

As for the princess, she took over the Junior League, the country club, all the charities that could get her on TV, and the major party scene, such as it was. Fluttering about her at all times was a group of smirking empty-headed gossips whose husbands were this generation's city fathers. Giggle giggle giggle; whisper whisper whisper.

Jenna and I watched him and his life the way you would a movie. Parts made us laugh, parts made us mad, parts made us sad. He hadn't forgotten us entirely. Jenna and I hung out at a tavern called Dudley Do-Right's. Every so often Sean's Mercedes would sweep into a parking lot filled with Harleys and pickup trucks, and he would come inside and have a few beers with us. The men inside tended to fawn over him when he walked in. They always asked for the inside scoop on this player or that coach, and he gave them enough tidbits to make him forever popular there.

One rainy August night, the rain hotter than the day itself had been, he came in late. Jenna had already gone home. She was working her way back to detox. Her pattern was always the same. A month or so after detox, she'd start hanging around Dudley's again. She'd start out with just Diet Pepsi. A week later, it was beer. Alcoholics will always argue that beer doesn't really count. A week after that, she'd be back on the hard stuff. Then it was a matter of five, six months. She'd lose another job, have another lousy affair, sleep with Dudley a few times so he'd forgive her bar tab, and then start calling me in the middle of the night to cry over Sean. She was still in love with him; she would always be in love with him.

Not that my own life was any better. A two-year marriage gone bust. A job out at the mall hawking computers. Watching my parents slowly fade and die. I was long over loving Jenna. But instead of relief, all I felt was emptiness.

I was always eager to see Sean because he represented a life I'd never have. Not just the big car or the horse ranch or the investments, but the wife and daughters. Unlike my life or Jenna's, his had a definable and discernible meaning.

Or so I thought till that rainy August night.

He said, "I envy your life, Randy."

He said, "Man, it was so fucking wonderful on Sunday afternoons. All those fans screaming and shouting and applauding. And my life'll never be like that again. Not ever again."

He said, "You know how many women I've slept with in the last year? Over fifty. And you know what? I didn't come with any of them. I can't have an orgasm anymore. I used to think it'd be so great, to be able to go all night, literally all night if you wanted to. But it's a curse, man. Believe me, it's a curse. And the fucking doctors can't seem to find any way to help me."

He said, "You know what I've been thinking lately? I've been thinking maybe I married the wrong woman. Maybe I should've married Jenna. Maybe I've been in love with Jenna all along and didn't know it. All that society bullshit my wife is into. I hate it. Jenna isn't like that at all."

He didn't say all these things in sequence, of course. He said them over the course of several hours, both of us getting drunker and drunker. In between, we talked a little town gossip, a little local politics, a little nostalgia. He was once again the Sean I'd grown up with.

But he was going to destroy Jenna. He wanted an easy answer to what he saw as the torpor of his life, and he was going to try anything that was at hand. He didn't care if an affair was good for Jenna. All he knew was that it would be good for him. At least temporarily. He disagreed, of course, when I brought it up.

"You didn't hear what I said, Randy. I said I think I love her. Not just that I want to hop in the sack with her. That I love her." He brought his fist down on the booth table so hard that everybody looked in our direction.

I knew then that there was nothing I could do to stop it. Jenna was finally going to have that love affair with Sean she'd wanted since we were all little kids, growing up poor and sad in the Knolls.

Jenna bloomed. She even cut her drinking way back. Sean was able to provide what the detox clinics hadn't been able to. She went to work regularly and bought herself a lot of new clothes. Her drab apartment became festive with new paint, new curtains, a new couch. On the nights when Sean couldn't make it over, and I didn't have a sex date with one of my waitresses or mall clerks (a bad marriage can scare you off romance for a long time), Jenna'd have me over so she could tell me all about how wonderful it was to be in love with Sean, and to have Sean in love with her. He'd leave his wife, and they'd be married. They'd build a new house, a huge masterpiece of a house, out on the edge of Hartson Woods, where they'd raise themselves some gleaming children.

Sean was just as taken with Jenna. I'd never seen him vulnerable to anybody before. It made him human in a way he'd never quite been. He'd grin like a kid when he talked about her; and stare off with great, grave melancholy when he recalled certain tender things they'd said to each other. Even the swagger vanished. He was just a simple man in simple love.

It lasted longer than I thought it would. Four-and-a-half months. I've never been sure exactly how he met Kristin, but suddenly she was there—she'd moved here from Cedar Rapids to take over a small real estate firm—and suddenly Jenna was in my apartment sobbing and frantically throwing back straight scotches.

I slept with her. I knew I was taking advantage, but I didn't care. I no longer loved her, not romantically anyway, but I'd always been curious about sex with her. The first time, she was so drunk she had to excuse herself in the middle of it to hurry into the bathroom and throw up. The second time, she was so drunk she passed out beneath me. But the third time . . . she was sweet and sad and tender and it was the best sex I'd ever had, her hair fragrant as flowers, her voice gentle and even poignant at times, and her slender body a marvel of surprising richness. The only time she got spooked was when she was naked in any kind of light. The limp. The crushed leg. She was so ashamed of it. For a while I was afraid I was going to fall in love with her again. But it didn't happen, and a part of me was sad about it. It had been a long time since I'd burned with that searing fever that takes over your whole life. And I wanted it again. But she was gone from me now, we truly were just friends now, and so the best I could do for her—or for myself—was hold her when she wept, and make timid, cautionary remarks about how her drinking was getting out of hand again. I knew I was wasting my time. She was drinking harder than she ever had.

There were scenes. She drove drunkenly out to his horse ranch and slapped him and started sobbing. And then she accosted him in a bar one night and spat in Kristin's face. And then she called Sean's wife and they commiserated on what a shit he was and (at least according to Jenna's drunken retelling) they became friends for life on the basis of that single phone call.

I didn't see Sean for a while. He had his shiny New One to spend time with. The night I did run into him in one of the local pubs, I was drunk enough to follow him out the door—he and the bartender were sick of me telling him what an asshole he was—and hit him hard in the mouth. Hard enough to split his lip. It felt great. Then he hit me three or four times and not only bloodied my lip but my nose as well.

He went back in and got a six-pack and we sat in his Benz convertible polishing off the beers and listening to blue Miles Davis jazz low on the CD player and talking about the old days in the Knoll and how he was sorry he'd hurt Jenna and would do anything he could to help her, including picking up the tab for this special detox clinic he'd heard of just outside St. Paul. We used the alley as our chamber pot. We sat there two hours and in the course of it I was able to gauge just how much he'd changed. Or maybe he'd always been like this and I just hadn't been observant enough to understand it. The kindness, the concern, was there to make him palatable to his fellow humans. He was a good actor. But he didn't really give a shit about Jenna or his wife or his kids or me. He was even waffling on Kristin, her no longer being "quite as interesting" as she'd once seemed. There was a new New One, it seemed. . . .

When I got home, Jenna was asleep in my bed. I slipped in beside her. In the morning we made quick love and then took a shower together. She said she'd make some breakfast while I got ready for work. The breakfast was Cheerios and orange juice out of a can. And, for Jenna, a generous glass of my whiskey. . . .

I guess it was about four or five weeks later that she

called me and asked me to come over. She sounded strange—distracted and distant—and I wondered if she was thinking about suicide or something. The tone of her voice made me nervous as hell.

She was sober. That was the first thing I noticed. And she had this velvet painting of a forlorn Jesus sitting on her dining room table, a dinner candle burning in front of it like a votive candle in a Catholic church. Jenna was a Methodist.

She was better kept than I'd seen her in a long time. Scrubbed, short dark hair combed forward to flatter the elegant bones of her small face, white blouse, and designer jeans clean and freshly pressed.

"Pepsi all right?"

"Fine," I said.

"I haven't had a drink in three weeks."

"Great. I'm proud of you. AA again?"

Shook her head. "On my own."

"Wow."

She disappeared into the kitchen, returned with glasses heavy with ice and dark with Pepsi. "Diet was all I had."

"No problem. I prefer it, actually."

She sat on the couch, pulled her legs up under her wonderful buttocks. She made me horny and sad at the same time. She said, "You're the first one I'm telling."

"All right."

"And I know you're going to be skeptical. And think that this happened when I was drunk. And that it was just a dream or something. That's why I mentioned the drinking. The first time, I was drunk, and I'll admit it. But that's why I mentioned about not having a drink for three weeks."

"I see."

"I want to tell you, but I'm afraid to tell you."

"All right."

"Just please don't laugh, Randy."

"I promise."

"Or smirk."

"Scout's Honor."

"Or ask me to see a shrink or anything like that."

I smiled. "You ever going to tell me what it is?"

She hesitated. "All these people who say they were abducted by aliens?"

"Uh-huh."

"They're telling the truth. At least, the majority of them are."

No laughing. No smirking. No asking her to see a shrink. Those were the groundrules. My body did tighten up, though. Nothing I could do about that.

"All right."

"Is that a smirk?"

"Nope."

"You know what I'm going to tell you, don't you?"

"That you were abducted?"

"That's right. I was. Three times, in fact."

"Two of them sober."

"Two of them sober." She hesitated again. "So what do you think?"

"I guess I take your word for it."

"It happened. It really did."

"And I believe you believe that."

She laughed, but there was more sadness than joy in the sound. "That's what most people around here'll say when they hear it. Stuff like that. I don't think they hate me, actually. They just feel sorry for me. The booze and all. And this'll be one more step up to the mental hospital door. Permanent residence, this time. Die in there at the ripe old age of one hundred and three."

"Maybe you shouldn't tell anybody."

"In other words, you don't believe me."

"No," I said. "Not that at all. It's just that I know how people respond to things like this."

"Come over here."

"Over there?"

"Yes. The couch. Next to me."

"You sure?"

"I'm sure."

"I thought we agreed not to—"

"I don't want sex. I just want you to hold me."

"I charge by the hour."

"How much?"

"A nickel."

"I think I can swing that."

We ended up in bed, of course. Slow, sweet love. I couldn't ever recall sex being so tender or innocent. And she must have found it the same way because after we were done, we lay next to each other holding hands and talking about when we were little kids up in the Knolls: the good stuff, not the bad stuff, the good, sweet, innocent times, kittens and puppies and TV shows and movies we loved and funny things happening at school and how much we'd loved our now-dead folks, a sweet sadness coming on with that, and when it was time to go, I realized that something had crept up on me: happiness. Usually, I spent my time looking back at all the bad things that had happened to me. But being with Jenna this snowy afternoon—I was so exultant, I left my car and walked home. I stopped and helped a little girl build her snowman, giving her my brand-new fedora for the snowman's hat; I got in a friendly snowball fight with some high school kids; and I stopped in a Catholic church and said a few Presbyterian prayers; and at the comic book shop, I bought thirty dollars' worth of *Batman* and *Daredevil* comics from the late seventies and early eighties and took them home and had a great, grand night reading them. I was high out of my mind. But it wasn't drugs. Drugs had never come close to making me feel euphoric. It was something else: it was Jenna. I was high on Jenna.

The next day, I started calling her as soon as I got off work. Her line was busy. It stayed busy. I called the operator. She told me there was apparently trouble on the line. I was getting kind of desperate. All I'd been able to think about all day long was how good I'd felt after being with her. It wasn't the sex, though that had been great; and it wasn't that I'd fallen in love with her again, which I hadn't. It was just the mental state she'd somehow put me in. For several hours after leaving her, I'd been able to transcend all my petty human problems. While I'd been raised poor, I'd been a pretty happy kid. And I'd been kid-happy again last night, after being with Jenna.

I spent another useless hour trying to contact her on the phone. Still busy. I drove over there.

There was a group out in front of her shabby old apartment house. People of all ages, colors, social stations. Maybe fifteen in all. A couple of the older women held candles, as if this were a religious service.

Nobody seemed to mind the cold night. Or the snowfall.

"What's going on?" I said.

They all just looked at me. Said nothing.

Their eyes told me how much they resented me.

I pushed past them and went inside.

A few residents were in the hall. "You see any cops out there yet?" a black man asked me.

"No."

"The bastards. I wish they'd hurry up."

"What's going on?" I said.

A heavy man shook his head. "They think she's some kind of angel or something."

"Who is?"

"Your friend," the black man said. "Jenna."

"They're all outside because of Jenna?"

The heavy man nodded. "The cops ran them off earlier tonight. But now they're back again."

"Is Jenna upstairs?"

"Far as we know," the black man said.

We'd long ago swapped apartment keys. I went upstairs and knocked softly. No answer. Stained wallpaper hung loose from the hallway walls. A country-western CD competed with the rap CD across the hall. Ancient steam heat radiators clanged and banged busily.

I let myself in. Darkness.

She said, "Close the door. And please don't turn on the light."

I sat down on the couch next to her.

"You all right?"

"Sure. I love having mobs of people out on my lawn waiting for me."

"What happened?"

"I don't know." She sighed. "That ship. The spaceship or whatever it was. I know you don't believe me—"

"I believe you now."

"You do?"

"Yeah. Something really did happen to you on that ship." I told her about the bliss I'd felt last night.

"Well, they must've felt it, too."

"Who are they?"

"Oh, you know, just people I met today. The guy in the

expensive topcoat and the homburg—he's my banker. The woman in the wheelchair runs the cash register at the beauty shop. The teenager is a bag boy at the supermarket. I somehow gave them the same kind of euphoria I gave you. And now they want more of it. They're addicts. I was just trying to be nice, was all."

I went to the window and looked out. A police car had just arrived. Two cops got out and made their way up the snowy walk to the apartment house. Took a while, but they managed to break up the people who stood dumbly staring up at Jenna's apartment window.

"Can I stay at your place?" she said. "I'm afraid to be here alone."

I got blissed out every night.

By the fourth night, I didn't want to get up and go to work. I just wanted her to focus on me, find that spiritual part of myself that made me happy (thinking of my boyhood never failed), and then make me euphoric. It was kind of like telepathy, I guess, her ability to read you and find the aspect of memory that released all that lovely happiness. And it wasn't even illegal.

The people she'd blissed out the other day had taken to quieting down. In their fervor, they'd managed to alienate a lot of their friends. The town was uncomfortable enough with all this talk about alien abductions. The prospect of an alcoholic woman who could work emotional miracles was downright embarrassing.

I knew better, and so did she. Several times, she tried to describe what had happened to her when she'd been taken aboard the ship. Unlike the experiences of most people, she reported a gentle and lovely time, not unlike those reported in many near-death experiences, when a soft, foggy atmosphere was filled with a warmth and security that imbued not only her body but her mind and soul as well. And during her fourth abduction, she returned from the ship carrying the blissful state with her. And shared it with anyone she had the time to concentrate on. Not passing strangers, but people she spent at least a few minutes with. When she focused, Jenna relieved them temporarily from all their anxiety and apprehension, filling them with tender and exultant feelings.

I wouldn't have believed any of this if I hadn't experienced it myself. I would have said that she was back on the bottle again and into fantasy and self-delusion.

But I knew better.

She kept me pretty well blissed out. I rented a lot of Abbott & Costello movies, and we watched a lot of late-night old movies, and ate a lot of pizza, and kept ourselves happy. I had to go to work, but it was difficult to concentrate. Several times the boss ragged on me. I wasn't exactly his favorite, anyway. That dubious honor belonged to Kenny Wayman, who did everything except wash and wax the boss man's car.

I couldn't wait to get home, to disappear inside that cocoon of well-being she created.

I was whistling as I came through the door. Usually, I heard the sound of the TV or the CD player as I came into the apartment. But now there was only silence. Suddenly a brief burst of light in the sky visible through my kitchen window caught my attention. My first thought was of the ship, the aliens she had talked about. But that was ridiculous. As quickly as it had appeared, the light was gone, and I gave it no more thought.

I stood on the threshold, knowing something was wrong. It was more than just the silence. It was the absence.

Jenna's beatific presence had changed the air. It really had. There was a freshness, the way the air is fresh and clean after a rain. But now the air was just air, apartment air, with faint food smells and the homey scent of furniture polish.

No note. No message on the phone machine. She was gone. I sat in the dark for many hours. The pizza got cold. I opened a couple of beers but didn't finish either of them. I fell asleep on the couch. The two cats slept on my back.

Around nine a.m., somebody pounded on the door. Two guys in moving uniforms.

"We're supposed to pick up some stuff that belongs to Jenna McKay."

I'd trekked over to Jenna's apartment during her stay here and had brought back a considerable number of her things. This is what they were picking up. I asked where they were delivering her things. They said they weren't supposed to tell me.

It wasn't much of a weekend. I cruised past Jenna's place at least twenty times, hoping she'd show up there. She didn't.

I used my car phone to check my home machine every twenty minutes in case she'd called. She hadn't.

I even drove out to the company the movers worked for. The place was locked up.

I didn't sleep well either Saturday or Sunday night. I couldn't bring myself to lie in the bed where we'd made love. Too lonely. The cats got to use my couch-prone body as a mattress again.

Monday night, just after work, she called.

She said, "How you doing, Randy?"

So, I told her how I was doing, and I wasn't very nice about telling her.

She waited until I finished and then she said, "It's going

to happen, Randy. Finally." I'd never heard her this happy.

"What is?"

"He's going to get a divorce and marry me."

I didn't need to ask her who "he" was.

"When did this happen?"

"He stopped by to see you last week, and I was there. And we just started talking—and he said he wanted to set me up in my own place—a real nice place. And that'd give him time to think of how he was going to handle the divorce. He doesn't want to hurt his wife."

Dumping his wife for another woman. Now how would that hurt his wife? "Yeah, he's a real sensitive guy."

"C'mon, Randy. We all grew up together. You should be happy for us."

"Remember what happened the last time he dumped you? Remember how bad you got?"

It was kind of funny. Even though I was no longer in love with her—and I wasn't—I had this proprietary feeling about her. She was like my kid sister now. I wanted to protect her. "You know how he is. He's fickle. He wants everything. And he figures he deserves it, too. You have to be very careful, Jenna."

"He loves me."

"That's the only dangerous part of you being blissed out. You've taken your guard down. You used to be very protective of yourself. And with Sean, you need to be."

"I know love when I see it, Randy. And he loves me. He really does."

What was the point of arguing? And how could I be sure that he didn't really love her? Maybe he'd changed. I've lived long enough to know that some people really do change.

"I'm happy for you, Jenna."

"Oh, thanks for saying that, Randy. It means a lot to me."

"I hope it all works out."

"I should've left a note or something. I just didn't know what to say. It all happened so fast."

"No problem. But let's keep in touch."

"Of course we will."

A few days later, I was eating lunch at The Big Table when I saw Sean's Mercedes pull up outside. He appeared to be headed to the bank down the street. I threw a five and my lunch bill on the counter and hurried out the door. I caught him at a red light.

He didn't seem happy to see me. "I'd appreciate it if you wouldn't talk to Jenna anymore."

"She called me, Sean."

"Oh, yeah. I guess that's right." He nodded to a diner. "Let's have some coffee." After we'd been served, and were sitting at a window table watching all the bundled-up people hurrying red-nosed and red-cheeked through the sunny Midwestern winter, he said, "I don't want anything to upset her."

I was shocked. I couldn't ever recall Sean saying anything like that before, being so protective of somebody else. I was not only impressed; I was moved. Maybe Jenna was right, after all. Maybe this time, he really was going to marry her.

"I mean, I don't know if all that UFO bullshit actually happened to her," he said. "But something did." He looked around and then spoke in a half-whisper. "The happiness stuff. She said she did it to you."

"Yeah," I said, "she did." I wondered if she'd told him we'd slept together. I hoped not.

"I haven't felt this good since I scored that thirty-yard touchdown pass against the 49ers in the playoffs. Won the fucking game," he said. The way he said it, I could tell he'd been with her pretty recently. He was still blissed.

But he was also something else, something far more recognizable: he was selfish. He was already addicted to the state of bliss she infused in him and he meant to keep her all to himself.

He said, "I'm just afraid she'll lose it somehow."

"Maybe it's religious."

"What is?"

"You know, her power. Maybe the things on that ship are religious beings. Maybe they showed her how to key in on her own innocence and to share it with other people."

"That's the dumbest fucking thing I've ever heard of."

"Thank you."

He smiled. "I'm sorry. That came out harsher than I'd intended. I just mean it sounds like some dipshit sci-fi show or something."

Actually, it was. A similar idea had been done on an invasion-from-outer-space anthology show called *Beings*.

"Well, she developed this power somehow."

He shook his head. "How she got it doesn't matter. It's keeping it that counts. That's why I'm taking good, good care of her. I'm putting her somewhere nobody knows about. I've convinced her there're these rumors all over town about her power and that she'll be treated like a freak if she ever walks the streets. That scares her. She wants to hide out."

"She says you're going to leave your wife and marry her." I wanted to see how he'd respond.

He smiled. It was close to a smirk. "Well, you know how the ladies are, Randy. They like you to whisper sweet things in their ear."

"Even if the sweet things aren't true."

The famous Sean temper was there instantly. "What the fuck are you? Her lawyer or something?"

"I just don't want to see her hurt again, Sean. I don't think she could handle it. The last time, she ended up in detox."

"Her choice, my man. Her choice entirely. Lots of people get dumped and don't end up in detox."

He was absolving himself of all guilt. He didn't have time for guilt.

"And if she loses her gift, you'll dump her again."

"You think I don't care for her, Randy? I do. I really do. She's a sweet, sweet girl. A lot of problems, but very sweet nonetheless. And you know what? She loves this idea of being hidden away. She picked the house and the furnishings—everything. It's a hideout for her. She's never been able to deal with people anyway. And now she doesn't have to." The smile again. Not a hint of smirkiness this time. Just the coldness that was always there. "She gets what she wants, I get what I want. I've cornered the market on bliss."

Every once in a while during the next month, I'd run into one of the people I'd seen standing on Jenna's lawn that night. They come up and grab my arm and plead with me to tell them where she was. Sad people. Junkies, really. Bliss junkies. I didn't feel superior to them. I had a physical ache in the pit of my stomach; I wanted the bliss, too. I don't think they believed me when I said I didn't know where she was. Our conversations were held in whispers. They didn't want the town to think they were still pursuing their wild claims.

A lot of nights, I'd sit home and watch TV and stare at the phone, kind of willing it to ring. And one night, it did.

She spoke quickly, in a whisper. "I need to get out of here."

"Then leave."

"I'm—afraid."

"Where are you?"

She told me. She said he was upstairs, sleeping. "If I leave, he'll just come after me."

"He can't hold you against your will."

"Yes, he can. In this town, he can."

I told her I'd pick her up in half an hour. She said she'd be ready.

The house was a chalet-style affair in the center of a tree-encircled meadow. No mailbox out front to announce it, and a road that would be impassable for most vehicles in deep winter.

She was out on the road, looking anxiously around, when I arrived. Winter dusk had rouged the sky the color of pink salmon. A quarter moon was crisply outlined against the night.

I didn't notice it right away, her walking to the car. Only when she was three or four feet away did I realize what was different about her.

When she got in, I said, "You're not limping."

She looked over at me and grinned. A kid-grin, it was, and it was gorgeous. "Yeah, isn't it great?"

"What happened?"

"I don't know. It just went away."

I smiled. "You must've 'blissed' it away."

"I know you're making a joke. But I think that's actually what happened."

By the time we got to my apartment, she'd told me all about it. Sean was quite literally hooked on being blissed out. That's all he wanted, the bliss. He rarely went to work. He rarely even watched TV or read a newspaper. He'd demand that she bliss him up and then he'd go lie on his Playboy-style round bed and lie there for hours until the blissful mind-state had finally faded. Then he'd be at her again, demanding that she bliss him again. If she didn't do it, he'd get violent with her. He was smart enough not to bruise her face, she said. But her body was covered with cuts and bruises. Power had made Sean's already consider-able temper even worse. She was now really afraid of him. He kept demanding that she could put him in an even higher state of bliss, if only she'd concentrate more. New, Improved Bliss—more potent than ever. Jenna said she feared for his sanity.

The first twenty-four hours were nice. It being a weekend, I didn't have to go to work. I rented some videos and or-dered in some pizza. I watched her slowly relax. She blissed me, but it was incidental. She said she hadn't even tried. But her own joy and purity just naturally worked its way into me. I spent a couple of hours reliving some of the great times with my younger brother and sister whom, I learned in retro-spect, I should have been a whole lot nicer to. But there were great memories nonetheless, good enough in fact to streak my cheeks with tears. She held me while I cried.

Toward dawn, she said, "I still love him."

"I know."

"Really?"

"Sure. It's in your voice. Even when you're angry with him, there's a kind of melancholy in your tone."

"He scares me."

"He scares me, too."

We didn't say anything for a long time. Then, "Maybe if he actually gets a divorce, and we have a chance to live a normal life, maybe he won't be so hung up on being blissed out, as you call it."

It didn't make much sense to me either, what she'd just said—I mean, she'd run to me because she was scared of him; now she was talking about going back with him—but I let it drift away, her words like wisps of smoke, and let myself slide into sleep.

I don't know what time the door-pounding started. I jerked awake at the first heavy thud.

Jenna whispered, "It's him."

"Sean?"

"Yeah."

"I'll take care of him."

"No; I've been thinking." Her tone of voice said it all. "I've been awake all night. I love him, Randy. I really do. I can help him through this thing. I really can. Being so hung up on being blissed out, I mean."

The pounding kept on.

She slipped from the bed and opened the door.

He did a Rhett Butler. They didn't say a word to each other. He just swept her up in his arms, her mussed in my ancient, blue, threadbare K-Mart bathrobe, and carried her out to his Mercedes. Then they were gone.

I guess the rest of it, you pretty much know. You do if you watch TV or read the papers, anyway.

She called me the night before it happened, one of her frantic, whispered calls. "I've got to get out of here. I think this phone is tapped. He doesn't want me to talk to anybody he doesn't know about. He's afraid somebody's going to take me from him. I want my own life, Randy. He doesn't love me. He just wants to stay blissed out. I can see that now. And that makes it easier for me. I just want to get out of town, so he can't find me."

The phone line clicked a few times: a phone tap, as she'd said. Then the connection went dead. I doubted she'd hung up. Someone had broken the connection for her.

I drove out to their aerie that night. No lights. No cars in the driveway. I parked up on a ridge for a couple of hours with a pair of field glasses. I didn't see anything moving inside the house. Not even shadows.

He was sitting on my couch in the darkness when I got back home around midnight. He scared the hell out of me when he spoke. I hadn't known he was in there.

He said, "Don't turn the light on."

"It's my place, Sean. I can do what I want."

"I—want to wash up first." He hesitated. "I've got blood all over my hands and shirt."

"You sonofabitch."

I started to lunge at him. But then moonlight outlined the pistol he raised and pointed at me. "No heroics, Randy. I don't want to kill you, too."

"We grew up together. The three of us."

"I know."

"We were as close as you could get without being kin."

"She was going to leave me."

"You didn't give a shit about her. It was being blissed out you were worried about."

He didn't say anything. "I'm never going to have it again. Being high like that."

"Maybe you should've thought of that before you killed her."

"She was going to leave me." He said, "I couldn't let her go."

"Well, I guess you stopped her, all right."

"Take me down to the police station, will you?"

I sighed. "Maybe I better call your lawyer first."

"I don't give a shit about lawyers. Just take me to the station, all right?"

I took him to the station. I knew the night man and told him everything that had happened and how Sean was out in the car. The night man called the Chief and, after spending a full minute apologizing for wrestling the Chief from his beauty sleep, told him what was going on. Then he hung up.

"We better go get your friend," the night man said.

I had just started to open the front door of the station when the gunshot sounded. Just one. Ordinarily, a 9mm wouldn't make that much noise, but it was late and the streets were empty and quiet, and Sean had the window rolled down because of the heat. It was still in the eighties and it was after midnight.

The car was a mess. I guess I focused on that so I wouldn't have to focus on the dead man in my front seat or the dead woman he'd left back at his aerie. They took an ambulance a while later and got her.

Sean's wife came down to the station after half an hour. I hadn't seen her in years. She didn't seem as icy as I remembered her. She hadn't aged especially well—three kids and all the despair over Sean's affairs had taken their toll—and when she saw me, she came over and hugged me and started crying. I thought of all the times this girl had snubbed me when we'd been growing up. But then I realized how petty I was being and held her tenderly and let her cry. I even told her I'd help any way I could with the funeral arrangements.

I tried to cry myself that night. I guess I've learned the male syndrome too well. Boys don't cry. It's funny. I see movies and TV shows all the time that make me cry. But when it's something personal—I tried but I couldn't cry. And then the hot, raw dawn broke and I slept fitfully.

A couple of months after Jenna was murdered, I heard

the first rumor. Somebody told me there was a Jenna Internet site. I logged on and looked it over. Seems Jenna hadn't really been murdered. That was just a cover story for the aliens who'd taken her back up to the mother ship, where she was now residing.

I went out there one Indian Summer night, out to the meadow where the people said they saw the ship every once in a while. There was a crowd of thirty or so. I recognized some of them. They were the people who'd stood in her yard that time, hoping to see her again to get high on the joy merely seeing her brought them.

I suppose I felt superior to them. My mind wasn't filled with all their delusions; I was brave enough to face reality. There had been no ship, no abduction. She was simply one of those people who'd developed a power to make people feel better. Such people were celebrated throughout history. Jesus was certainly one of them. And Jesus did not come from a spaceship.

But late that night, in the darkness of my bed, I didn't feel superior to them at all. I envied them. On our trip through the universe, the lonely and unknowable universe, they had something to cling to, anyway. I didn't have anything at all.

Survival

1

A lot of people in the hospital were still mad at me about last night . . .

. . . but then they'd been mad at me before and they'd be mad at me again . . .

. . . the problem was, what got them mad, was that he was more crazed than dangerous, the dreamduster who'd broken into the supply area on the first floor. He was also nine years old. They'd wanted me to kill him, but I'd declined the honor and handed my .38 auto Colt to Young Doctor Pelham and said, you want him killed, you kill him yourself. Pelham just muttered some bullshit about the Hippocratic oath and gave me my weapon back. What I ended up doing with the little bastard was putting a chute on him and then taking him up in a skymobile and pushing him out somewhere over Zone 1. He'd be lucky to survive forty-eight hours. There was some new kind of influenza taking hold there. It had already buried something like two thousand people in less than a week. Maybe I would've done him a favor, killing him quick the way Pelham wanted me to. Being a dreamduster, his life was over anyway. . . .

After dumping the kid, I went back to the hospital and walked the ten flights up to my room. There's an elevator, but since all our power comes from the emergency generators Pelham figured out how to soup-up, we use the elevators only when it's absolutely necessary.

My little place is on the same floor as the mutants that our two resident bio-engineers are studying, with the belief that one of the pathetic wretches will someday yield a vaccine useful to what remains of the human race. Tuesday, March 6, 2009—six long years ago now—the Fascist-Christian party got their hands on several nuclear warheads (helped considerably by several Pentagon generals who were also part of the plot) and proceeded to purify our entire planet of its sins and sinners. What the Christers in all their wisdom didn't understand was that twenty of the warheads also carried some pretty wild germ warfare devices, devices that had killed many of the workers who'd helped create them.

Tenth floor of the hospital used to be the psych ward. Each patient had his own room, with a heavy door and a glass observation square built in.

I used to hurry past the doors on the way to my room, but now I stopped most times and peered in through the squares.

They're pretty repulsive-looking, no doubt about that, none older than five years old, none resembling a real human being in more than a passing way, not unless you consider three arms and no vertebrae—or a completely spherical body with a head the size and shape of a pincushion—or a squid-like creature with heartbreaking little hand-flippers—human; definitely not the kind of folk you'd like to see at your next family reunion.

They were used to seeing me now and, as I waggled my fingers and smiled at them, they made these sad, frantic, little noises, the way puppies do when they want to be picked up. So, exhausted as I was, I spent a few minutes with each of them. By now I was not only used to looking at them, I was also used to smelling them. Poor little bastards, they can't help it.

I went to my room and got some sleep.

What I am, you see, is what they call an Outrider. Back in the Old West, this was a person who rode on ahead of the wagon train to make sure everything was safe.

A year ago, after my wife and two daughters died from one of the variant strains of flu that had claimed half the people in Fort Waukegan, I tried to kill myself with my trusty .38 auto Colt. Oh, the bullet went in all right, but it managed to traverse the exterior of my skull without doing serious or permanent damage.

A scout from Fort Glencoe found me out on the periphery of Zone 2 and brought me back to the hospital. Once they had me on my feet again, they asked me what I'd done before the Christers got their bright idea of "purifying" the planet. When I told them I'd been a homicide detective, they asked me how I'd like to stay in Fort Glencoe permanently, as an Outrider—scouting Zones 1 through 5 surrounding Fort Glencoe and making sure no bands of warriors were headed here—and doubling as a hospital security guard. Dreamdusters—the junkies who got off on synthetic powder that was cheap to make and more powerfully addictive than any heroin ever concocted—were always breaking into hospital supply rooms in search of toxins and vaccines that would give them the ultimate kick till they got some real dreamdust.

They kept telling me how lucky I was to be alive.

I wasn't sure about that.

But I stayed on as their Outrider and Security man, and it was in that role that I first heard of Paineaters, even though I didn't quite believe in them, at least not as described by my boss and nemesis, Young Doc Pelham.

Troubled sleep. But then it usually is. I dream of Joan and the girls and I wake up with a terrible sadness upon me. Usually I throw my legs off the side of the bed and sit there with my head in my hands, remembering faces and voices and touches and laughter.

Then there's the nightmare. It started a few months back when I—well, when I got in some trouble with the staff here. . . .

Today, though, there wasn't any time for reveries.

Not with somebody pounding, pounding, pounding on my door.

"Yeah?" I said, rolling, still mostly asleep, from bed.

She didn't say anything. Just came through the door.

Nurse Polly. Coppery hair; big, brown, melancholy eyes; sweet little wrists and ankles; and a kind of childlike faith that everything will always work out.

"Pelham."

"Oh, great," I said.

"Emergency, he says."

"Isn't it always?"

She gave me a look I couldn't quite read. "You slept through it."

"Slept through what?"

I stood up, giving her a good look at my hairy legs in boxer shorts. (Nurse Polly and I had made love several times in a conveniently-located storage closet on the third floor. We always did it standing up. She was very good, sexy and tender at the same time. She seemed to sense that I always felt guilty about it. "You're thinking about your wife, aren't you?" "Yeah, guess I am." "That's all right." "It is?" "Sure. I'm thinking about my husband. He died pretty much the same way." And then we'd just hold each other, two lonely animals needing comfort and solace.)

"We had two people die in surgery last night. He couldn't operate because—Well, you know."

"God."

"We've got three operations scheduled today and no Paineater."

"I won't go alone. I want somebody to go with me."

"I'll go."

"Really?"

"Uh-huh."

"I don't know."

"Why?"

"Polly, you've got a great big heart. And you can get so involved with them. . . ." I shook my head. "You know what happened to me, what I did."

I didn't know if she felt like being held by a hairy guy in white boxer shorts with red hearts on them but I figured I'd give it a try.

I held her and she seemed glad I did, snuggling into me and putting her arms around my waist.

Then she took my hand. "C'mon. Let's go see Pelham."

But I held back. "You know what I did—He shouldn't send me out to get a new one." I was getting spooked. I didn't want to go through it all again.

She looked at me and shook her head. "You want me to take you down and show you the patients waiting for surgery? One of them had his eyes cut out by a dreamduster."

"Shit," I said.

2

Young Doctor Pelham might not be so bad under normal circumstances—where a doctor had the staff and facilities to do his best work—but here he's always stressed out and usually angry. I might be that way myself, if I was losing sixty percent of my patients on the table.

A day or two after the Christers dropped the bombs, the looting and raping and murdering began. I hate to be cynical about it, but the human beast was a much darker one than I'd ever imagined. Made me regret all the times I'd been civilized about it and spoken up against the death penalty.

A couple of things became clear to all citizens good and true—man and woman, white and black, Christian and Jew, straight and gay—that there were a whole lot of really terrible people out there meaning them great malice. The good folk would have to band together. The concept of a Fortress came along soon after.

Most Forts comprise five or six miles inside a wall of junk cars. The walls are patrolled twenty-four hours by mean humans and even meaner dogs. Zoners, those living in the outer areas, sometimes sneak through, but most of them end up as little more than blood and flesh gleaming on the teeth of the Dobermans.

Most Forts are also built around hospitals. The good citizens had to quickly decide which was the most important of all buildings. Police station? Courthouse? Hospital? Indeed. With the bio-engineered warheads continuing to do their work, life was a constant struggle, not only against violence—once every three months or so a small army of Zoners would take a run at the various Forts and inflict great casualties—but also disease.

Inside the walls of scrap metal, the citizens lived in any sort of shelter they could find. Houses, garages, schools, roller rinks—it didn't matter. You lived where you could find room for you and your family.

Then there was the hospital. I know how you probably imagine it: ten floors of the various units that all modern hospitals have—maternity, pediatric, surgical, psychiatric, intermediate care, intensive care—all staffed by crisply-garbed interns and residents and registered nurses and practical nurses and nurses' aides, many of whom spend their time walking between the pharmacy, the central service department, the food service, and the laboratories.

But forget it.

This hospital is ten floors of smashed windows and bullet-riddled walls and bloodstained floors. Before the Fortress wall could be erected, some roving Zoners staged a six-day battle that cost a thousand people their lives, and nearly resulted in the Zoners taking over the hospital.

Patients are brought in on the average of fourteen a day. On average, eight of those are buried within twenty-four hours.

"There isn't any time for your usual bullshit," Young Doctor Pelham told me when I stood before his desk. "In case you want to give me any, I mean."

The glamorous Doctor Sullivan, dark of hair and eye, red of mouth, supple and ample of figure, sat in a chair across the room, listening. Everybody knew two things about the good doctors Pelham and Sullivan. That they'd once been lovers. And that they now hated each other and that Sullivan wanted Pelham's job. She was always telling jokes about him behind his back.

"They're kids," I said, wishing Polly had stayed. Her presence would have made Pelham less harsh. She had that effect on people.

"I know they're kids."

"Little kids."

"Little kids. Right. But I don't have a lot of choice in the matter. I have to do right by my patients."

Much as I dislike him, Pelham's arguments about the Paineaters are probably sound. Ethically, he had to weigh the welfare of his patients against the welfare of the

Paineaters. He had to choose his patients.

He sat behind his desk, a trim man in a white medical smock that had lost its dignity to spatters of human blood and other fluids. He looked up at me with tired, brown eyes and a face that would have been handsome if it didn't look quite so petulant most of the time. "I've got what he wants."

He reached down behind his desk and lifted up a leather briefcase. He set it on the desk.

"It's a shame we have to deal with people like that," Doctor Sullivan said.

"Do you have a better idea, Susan?" Pelham snapped.

"No, I guess I don't."

"Then I'd thank you to stay out of this."

She really was twice as beautiful when she was angry. She got up and left the room.

"I want one understanding," I said.

"Here we go," he said, "you and your fucking understandings."

"I won't bodyguard her. Don't forget what happened last time."

The brown eyes turned hostile. "You think I could forget what you did, Congreve? You think any of us could ever forget what you did?"

"I was thinking of her."

"Sure you were, Congreve, because you're such a noble sonofabitch." He shook his head. "You did it because you couldn't take it anymore. Because you weren't tough enough."

He pushed the briefcase across to me.

"We need one right away. I've got seven patients ready for surgery. They're going to die if I don't get to them in just a few hours."

I picked up the briefcase. "Just so we understand each

other, Doc. I won't bodyguard her."

He smiled that smirky, aggravating smile of his. "It's not something you have to worry about, Congreve. You think after what you did, we'd even want you to guard her?" I guess he probably had it right. Who the hell would want me to guard her?

I went outside and got in my skymobile.

3

Polly was in the passenger seat. She'd changed into a green blouse and jeans and a brown suede jacket.

"I don't remember inviting you."

"C'mon, Congreve. I won't be any trouble."

"I get downed somewhere and surrounded by a gang of Zoners and you won't be any trouble? Then I have to worry about you as well as myself."

She brought an impressive silver Ruger from somewhere inside her jacket. "I think I can take care of myself."

If you've ever seen photographs or film of Berlin right after World War II, you have some sense of what Chicago looks like these days: skyscrapers toppled, entire neighborhoods reduced to ragged brick and jagged glass and dusty heaps of stone. With no sanitation, no electricity, no official order of any kind, you can pretty well imagine what's happened: the predators have taken over. Warlords divided up various parts of each Zone. You do what they say or they kill you. Very simple.

We were headed for the eastern sector of Zone 2, which had once been the inner-city.

"I disappointed you today, didn't I?" Polly said.

"A little, I suppose."

"I know how you feel about Paineaters."

"I can't help it. I just keep seeing my own daughters."

"We don't have any choice, Congreve. You have to understand that."

"I'll take your word for it."

"You can really be an asshole sometimes."

"But Pelham can't?"

"We weren't talking about Pelham."

"I was. Pelham and all the other Pelhams who run these Fortresses and use Paineaters."

"You should see the patients who—"

"I've seen the patients," I said. "That's the only reason I'm doing this. Because I don't have the stomach or balls or whatever it takes to see all those people lying there and suffering. Otherwise I wouldn't help at all."

She leaned over and touched my hand. "I shouldn't have called you an asshole."

I smiled at her. "Oh, what should you have called me?"

She smiled right back. "A prick is what I should have called you."

"I guess that's a promotion of sorts, anyway."

"Of sorts," she said.

Sometimes when you're up there, you can forget everything that's happened in the last six years. Dawn and sunset are especially beautiful, and you can feel some of the old comfort and security you knew, and that awe you found in the beauty of natural things. That's why I took the skymobile every chance I got . . . because if I didn't look down, I could pretend that the world was the same as it had always been. . . .

The last twenty miles, we went in low. That's when you get a sense of the daily carnage, going low like that.

Bodies and body parts strewn all over the bomb-blasted Interstate. And not just warriors either: children, women, family pets. Families try to leave a Zone area when there's a war going on. Too often they make the mistake of following the Interstate, where bandits wait. These are not the gentlemen bandits of Robin Hood fame. A doc told me once he'd seen a ten-year-old girl that ten adult bandits had gang-raped. I'd kill all of them if I got a chance.

Originally, Jackson Heights had been a nice little shopping area for upscale folks. But those upscale folks who didn't get killed by the Christers' bombs got their throats slashed by the Zoners who took the place over and renamed it after one of their old-time leaders.

There was a block of two-story brick buildings. On the roofs you could see warriors with powerful binoculars and even more powerful auto-shotguns. I imagined, if I looked hard enough, I'd also find some grenade launchers.

Six black men raised their shotguns.

"God," Polly said, "are they just going to shoot us down?"

"Hopefully, one of them will recognize the mobile here and realize it's me."

"Yeah," she said anxiously, "hopefully."

I circled the roofs one more time and in the middle of the circle the shotguns lowered and two of the men started waving at us. Somebody had radioed headquarters and described our skymobile and headquarters had okayed us.

"Feel better?" I said.

"Sorry I was such a candy ass. I was just scared there for a minute."

"So was I."

Hoolihan is a black man.

I know, I know—his name is Irish; as is his pug nose, his freckled and light-skinned face; his reddish, curly hair; and his startling blue eyes. But he's Negro—which you can tell, somehow, when you see him.

Hoolihan, by my estimation, has personally killed more than two thousand people.

I reach this conclusion by simple mathematics: 365 x 6 = 2190.

He's been the warlord of East Zone 1 for the past six years. I figure, probably conservatively, that he's killed one person each day. As I say, simple math.

This day Hoolihan sent his own personal vehicle for us, an ancient Army jeep painted camel-shit green with a big red H stenciled on the back panel. He uses the H the way cattle barons used to use their brands.

Hoolihan lives in a rambling two-story red brick house. Easy enough to imagine a couple of Saabs in the drive, a game of badminton going on in the backyard, steaks smelling wonderful on the outdoor grill. Suburban bliss. The effect is spoiled somewhat, however, by the cyclone fencing, the barely-controllable Dobermans, and the armed guards in faded Army khaki.

In case none of that deters you, there's one other surprise: a front door that detonates a tiny bomb just big enough to render the visitor into several chunks, if he doesn't know the password.

The guard knew the password. "Your Mama," he said.

Hoolihan had a nasty sense of humor.

The door was buzzed open and we walked in.

What Hoolihan's done with the interior of his house is pretty amazing. He's turned it into a time-travel exhibit: the world as it was before the Christers got hold of it. Sore, sad eyes can gaze at length upon parquet floors and comfortable couches sewn in rich rose damask and Victorian antiques and prints by Chagall and Vermeer; and sore, sad ears, long accustomed to the cries of the dying, can be solaced with the strains of Debussy and Vivaldi and Bach.

Hoolihan, whatever else he is, is no fool.

He made us wait five minutes.

He enjoys being fashionably late.

He also enjoys looking like a stage fop in a Restoration comedy. Today he swept in wearing a paisley dressing gown, and his usual icy smirk. Oh, yes, and the black eyepatch. Dramatic as hell until you realize that it keeps shifting eyes. Some days it's on his right eye and some days—

"Nice," he said, referring to Polly. "I don't suppose she's for sale."

"I don't suppose she is," Polly said.

"Too bad. I know people who'd pay a lot of money for you."

That was another thing about Hoolihan. He had a sophomore's need to shock.

"Martini?" he said.

"Beer would be fine," I said.

"The lady?"

"Beer," she said.

He nodded to a white-haired man in some sort of African ceremonial robe. The man went into the next room.

"We found a supermarket that had been contaminated so long, people gave up on it," Hoolihan said. "I sent some men in last week. And now we have enough beer to last us for a long, long time."

"The land of opportunity," I said.

He said, "The palm of my hand is starting to itch."

I had to smile. He was a melodramatic sonofabitch but he had the brains to kid himself, too.

"I wonder what that means," I said.

"It means my right hand wants to just walk over there and grab that briefcase."

"We need to cut a deal first."

"I take it you don't want drugs, little girls or boys for sex, or the latest in weaponry my men took from that National Guard Armory in Cleveland last month."

"None of the above. Why don't we just cut the bullshit and you tell me if you've got one for sale."

The elderly man with the intelligent, dark eyes returned with our beers. I've never been much for servants. I felt funny accepting it from him, as if I should apologize.

"Please," Hoolihan said, "let's sit down and make this all very civilized. We're not making some back-alley deal here."

We sat. But I'm not sure how civilized it was. Not considering what the product happened to be.

"I've got five on hand at the moment," he said from his throne-sized leather chair, across the room from where Polly and I sat on the edge of an elegant couch.

"We need one right away."

"I've got them out in a shed."

Polly muttered something nasty under her breath.

Hoolihan smirked. He'd aggravated her and he loved it. "Don't worry, pretty one. It's a perfectly civilized shed. Clean, dry and protected not only from the elements but from Zoners. They're much better off in my shed than they would be wandering free."

With that I couldn't argue.

"Now how much is in that briefcase?"

"A hundred thousand dollars. It's all yours, as long as you don't dicker."

"A hundred thousand dollars," he said. "My, my, my, my. I wish my poor, old broken-down nigger daddy could see me now."

That's the funny thing about the warlords. Even though they know that the currency is absolutely worthless, they still revel in getting it.

Hoolihan's father had served three terms in prison for minor crimes and had never known a day's happiness or pride in his entire life. Hoolihan had told me all this one night when he'd been coasting on whiskey and drugs. And he'd broken down and cried halfway through. He was bitter and angry about his father, whom he felt had never had a serious chance at leading a decent life.

He was probably right.

His old man would have been damned proud of his one and only son.

One hundred thousand was now his. Didn't matter that it was worthless. It still had an echo, a resonance, money did, at least to those of us who could remember how everything used to be before the Christers went and screwed it all up.

A tear rolled down Hoolihan's cheek. "I miss that old fucker, you know?"

Not even Polly, who obviously didn't care much for Hoolihan, could deny him this moment. Her own eyes teared up now.

"Let's go get her," I said, "before it gets dark."

Kerosene torches lit the blooming gloom of dusk; a chill started creeping up my arms and legs and back; a dog barked, lonely. You could smell and taste the autumn night, and then smell the decay of bodies that hadn't been buried properly. Even though you couldn't see them, their stench told you how many of them there were. And how close.

The shed was a quarter mile through a sparsely-wooded area that a dog—maybe the same one that was barking—had mined with plump, squishy turds.

Two guards in khaki stood guard in front of the small garage that Hoolihan called the shed. Hoolihan, by the way, had traded his foppish robe for an even more foppish military uniform. He had epaulets big enough to land helicopters on.

The guards saluted when they saw Hoolihan. He saluted them, crisply, right back.

"C'mon in and you can pick one," he said merrily enough, as if he were inviting us on to a used car lot.

We went inside. He'd been telling the truth about the tidiness of the place. Newly whitewashed walls. Handsomely carpeted floor. Six neat single beds with ample sheets and blankets. At the back was a table where food was taken. The place even smelled pretty good.

There were four of them and they sat on their beds watching us, their outsize heads tottering as they gaped at us. For some reason I don't understand—this sort of thing I leave to Young Doctor Pelham—their necks won't properly support their heads. They were all female and they all wore little aqua-colored jumpsuits that resembled pajamas. They're mute, or most of them are anyway, but they make noises in their throats that manage to be both touching and disgusting. They were little and frail, too, pale and delicate, with tiny hands that were always reaching out for another human hand to hold.

"Where the hell's the dark-haired one?" Hoolihan said.

The guard got this awful expression on his face as his eyes quickly counted the little girls.

Four.

There were supposed to be five.

"Where the hell did she go?" Hoolihan said.

The children couldn't answer him; they couldn't talk.

And the guards were no help. They'd somehow managed to let one get away.

Hoolihan walked over to a window at the back of the garage. A small wooden box had been placed directly under it.

Hoolihan put pressure on the base of the window. It pushed outward. It was unlocked.

The kid had gone out the window.

As he was turning around to face us all again, Hoolihan took a wicked-looking handgun from his belt and shot the guards in the face.

Nothing fancy. No big deal.

One moment they were human beings, the next they were corpses.

Anxiety started working through me—surprise, shock, anger, fear that he might do the same to me—and then, as I looked at the children, I felt the turmoil begin to wane.

They stared at us.

They said nothing.

They started doing their jobs.

A few moments later, the worst of the feelings all gone, we followed Hoolihan out into the dark, chilly night.

"We're going to find that little bitch," Hoolihan said.

4

Well, we found her all right, but it took two hours, a lot of crawling around on hands and knees in dark and tangled undergrowth, and a lot of cursing on Hoolihan's part.

The little kid was a quarter mile away, hiding in a culvert.

When we found her, got the jostling beam of the flashlight playing across her soiled aqua jumpsuit, she was doing a most peculiar thing: petting a rat.

This was a big rat, too, seven, eight pounds, with a pinched, evil face and a pair of gleaming, red eyes. He probably carried a thousand kinds of diseases and an appetite for carrion that would give a flock of crows pause. After the Fascist-Christians had their way with the world, rats became major enemies again.

But there he sat on the little girl's lap, just the way a kitten would. And the little girl's tiny white hand was stroking his back.

There was some semblance of intelligence in the girl's eyes. That was the first thing that struck me. Usually the saucer-shaped eyes are big and blank. But she seemed to have a pretty good idea of who and what we were.

Then Hoolihan shot the rat and the little girl went berserk.

The rat exploded into three chunks of meat and bone and gristle, each covered with blood-soaked flesh.

The keening sound came up in the little girl's throat and she quickly got on all fours and started crawling down the culvert as fast as she could.

Hoolihan thought it was all great, grand farce.

I wanted to kill him—or at least damage him in some serious way—but I knew better. He had too many men eager to kill anybody white. With Hoolihan gone, Polly and I would never get out of here.

Polly went after the kid.

I was still trying to forget the kid's terrible expression. They establish some kind of telepathic link with their subject, that's what the kids do, and so the relation becomes intimate beyond our understanding. Rat and little girl had become one. So then Hoolihan goes and kills it.

"You look pissed, man," Hoolihan said.

"You're scum, Hoolihan."

"Just having a little fun."

"Right."

"I like it when you get all judgmental and pontifical on me, Congreve. Kinda sexy, actually."

"You knew what the little girl was doing."

"Sure. Linking up." The smirk. "But maybe I have so much respect for her I didn't want her to link up with some fucking rat. You ever think of that?"

I grabbed his flashlight.

He started at me, as if he was going to put a good, hard right hand on my face, but my scowl seemed to dissuade him.

I didn't find Polly and the girl for another fifteen minutes and I probably wouldn't have found them then, if it hadn't been for the dog.

He was some kind of alley mutt, half-boxer and half-collie, if you can imagine that, and he stood on the old railroad siding barking his ass off at the lone boxcar that stood on the tracks that shone silver in the moonlight.

I could hear her now, the kid, the mewling deep in her throat. She was still terrified of the rat exploding.

I climbed up inside. In the darkness the old box car smelled of wood and grease and piss. A lot of people had slept in this, no doubt.

Polly was in the corner, the kid in her lap.

Polly was sort of rocking the kid back and forth and humming to her.

I went over and sat down next to her and put my hand to the kid's cheek. It was soft and warm and sweet. And I thought of my own daughters when they were about this age, how I'd see their mother rocking them at night and humming the old lullabies they loved so much.

I thought of this and started crying. I couldn't help it. I just sat there and felt gutted and dead.

And then Polly said, "Why don't you take her for a little while? She's calming down. But my legs are going to sleep. I need to walk around."

I took her. And rocked her. And sang some of the old lullabies, and it was kind of funny because when my voice got just so loud, the mutt outside would join in and kind of bark along.

Polly jumped down from the boxcar. I imagined she needed to pee, in addition to stretching her legs.

When she came back, she stood in the open door, the night sky starry behind her, and the smell of clean, fresh, rushing night on the air, and said, "God, that'd make a sweet picture, Congreve, you and that little kid in your arms that way."

And then I got mad.

I put the kid down—I didn't hurt her but I wasn't especially gentle, either—and then I stalked to the open door and said: "No fucking way am I going to go through this again, Polly. I don't want anything to do with this kid, you understand? Not a thing."

She knew better than to argue.

She went back and picked up the kid.

She came back to the open door.

I'd jumped down and stood there, waiting to lead the way back to Hoolihan.

Polly was pissed. "You think you could hold the kid long enough for me to jump down?"

"Don't start on me, Polly. You know what I went through."

"I love it when you whine."

"Just hand the kid down and get off my back."

She handed the kid down.

I took her, held her, numbed myself to her as much as possible. It wasn't going to happen again.

Polly jumped down. "That Hoolihan is some piece of work."

"Dreamdust."

"That's an excuse and you know it. He would've done that if he was straight. It's his nature."

"Nothing like a bigot."

"I'm not a bigot, Congreve. There're lots of white people just like him. I'm starting to think it's genetic."

"Here's the kid."

She didn't take her right away but put her hand on my arm. "I know how hard it is for you, Congreve, after what happened and all, with the little one here, I mean."

"I appreciate you understanding, Polly. I really don't want to go through it again."

"I'll take care of her."

"I appreciate it."

"We're saving lives, Congreve. That's how you have to look at it."

"I hope I can remember that."

Now she took the kid. Cuddled her. Looked down at her. Started talking baby talk.

It was sweet and I wanted to hold them both in the brisk night wind, and then sleep warm next to them in a good clean bed.

When I got Polly and the kid in the skymobile, Hoolihan said, "I heard about what you did."

"Yeah, well, it happens."

"You're a crazy fucker."

"Look who's talking."

"Yeah but I got an excuse. I'm a warlord. I got to act crazy or people won't be afraid of me."

"I guess that's a good point."

He nodded to the kid inside the bubble dome. "You think you'll do it again?"

"This time I won't have anything to do with her."

"I'd still like to buy that chick."

"No, you wouldn't. She's too tough for you. You want somebody you can beat into submission. You couldn't beat her into submission in twenty years."

He laughed. "She sounds like a lot of fun, man. I love a challenge."

I got in the skymobile.

He leaned in and looked at Polly, who was completely captivated by the small child in her arms.

"I'll see you both soon," he said, wanting to get one more shock in. "You know them little ones never last very long."

5

Young Doctor Pelham and his number two, Doctor Sullivan, put her right to work.

Polly gave her the name Sarah and fixed her up a nice, cozy, little room and then proceeded to wait on her with an almost ferocious need.

She also dressed her differently, in jeans and sweatshirts and a pair of sneakers that Polly had dug up somewhere in the basement.

Pelham started Sarah on the most needful ones first, which only made sense. He knew not to ever yell at her or push her—as I'd seen him do with a couple of them—but he was never tender with her, either. To Pelham, she was just another employee.

Polly, Sarah, and I started taking meals together in the staff mess on the lower level.

Polly fussed with everything. Made sure Sarah's food was heated just-so. Made sure her drinking glasses were spotlessly clean. Made sure that with each meal—which was usually some variation on chili—there was at least a small piece of dessert for Sarah.

In that respect, Sarah was a pretty typical kid. She lusted after sweets.

But that was the only way Sarah was typical. Autism is the closest thing I can liken her condition to. She was with us in body but not in spirit. She would sit, staring off at distances we couldn't see. And then she would start making a kind of sad music in her throat, apparently responding to things far beyond our ken.

She hadn't been used much before we'd gotten her because she didn't exhibit any of the usual symptoms of deterioration. They start with the twitches and then graduate to the shakes and finally they end up clasping their heads between their hands, as if trying to fight a crushing headache.

After that, they're not much good to anybody.

And after that . . .

I didn't see much of Polly for the next few weeks. Not that I didn't go up to her room. Two or three times a day, I went up to her room. But she was always busy with the kid. Bathing the kid. Fixing the kid's hair in some new, pretty way. Singing to the kid. Reading to the kid . . .

A few times I tried it real late at night, hoping that she'd want to lean against the wall with me the way she sometimes did.

But she always said the same thing. "I wouldn't feel right

about it, Congreve. You know, with Sarah in the room and all."

I just kept thinking of what had happened to me with the kid before this one. . . .

How fast you can get attached. . . .

I felt responsible for Polly: I never should have taken her along to Hoolihan's. . . .

"Pelham says we can have a holiday party."

"Good old Pelham," I said. "What a great guy."

"You don't give him his due, Congreve. Maybe you'd be more like him, if you were responsible for this whole hospital."

"Maybe I would."

She stood in my doorway, natty as always in her nurse whites.

"You know why I brought up the holiday?" she said.

"Huh-uh."

"Because we need a Santa."

"Aw, shit."

"Somebody found an old costume up on the sixth floor."

"Aw, shit."

"You said that."

"I don't want to play Santa."

"That nice little beer belly of yours, you'd be perfect."

"You haven't seen me naked lately; my little beer belly is even littler now."

I said it in a kidding fashion but I think she knew that there was some loneliness, and maybe even a bit of anger in it, too.

In the three months since Sarah had been here, I'd seen increasingly little of Polly.

No more standing-up lovemaking.

Not even the occasional hugs we used to give each other.

Sarah was her priority now.

"I'm sorry we haven't gotten together lately, Congreve."

"It's all right."

"No it isn't and you know it. It's just that between my two shifts and taking care of Sarah—"

"I understand."

"I know you think I'm foolish. About her, I mean."

I shrugged. "You do what you think's best."

"You think I'll get too attached to her, don't you?"

I looked at her. "You know how much you can handle."

"She's not going to be like the others."

"She's not?"

"No." She shook her coppery hair. I wanted to put my hands in it. "I think I've figured out a way to let her rest up between the visits she makes; I think that's what happened to the others."

"That doesn't sound real scientific."

"Simple observation. I saw how she was when Pelham was scheduling her. She started to twitch and shake and do all the things the others did. But two weeks ago I convinced Pelham to let me make up her schedule—and you wouldn't believe the difference."

I saw how excited and happy she looked. She was one damn dear woman, I'll tell you.

"I'm happy for you, Polly. I hope this works out for you."

"She isn't going to end up like the others. That I can promise you."

I stood up and went over to her. I wanted to make it friendly and not sexual at all, but I guess I couldn't help it. I slid my arm around her shoulder and held her to me and felt her warm tears on my face. "You'll do just fine with her, Polly. You really will."

We stood like that for a time, kind of swaying back and forth with some animal rhythm coupling us fast, and then she said, sort of laughing, "You know, we never have tried it lying down the way most people do, have we?"

"You know," I said, "I think you're right."

And so we tried it and I have to admit I liked it fine, just fine.

6

A few days after all this, I saw a miracle take place: I was walking down a dusty hall, half the wall hoved in from a Christian-Fascist bomb, when I saw Young Doctor Pelham break a smile.

Now understand, this was not a toothpaste commercial smile. Nor was it a smile that was going to blind anybody.

But it was a) a real smile, and b) it was being smiled by Young Doctor Pelham.

He was talking to Nurse Ellen, on whom I'd suspected he'd long had some designs, and when he saw me the smile vanished, as if I'd caught him at something dirty.

By the time I reached the nurse, Pelham was gone.

"I think I just had a hallucination."

"Pelham smiling?"

"Yeah."

"You should have been here a minute earlier. He slid his arm around my waist and invited me up to his room tonight. It's the kid."

"The kid?"

She nodded her short-cropped blonde head. "The Paineater."

"Oh."

"She's the best one we've ever had."

"Really?"

"Absolutely. She did three patients last night in less than two hours. Then she went into surgery with them this morning." She angled her tiny wrist for a glimpse of her watch. "In fact, that's where I'm headed now. Somebody got caught by some Dobermans. He's a mess. I'm not sure we can save him. They've been prepping him for the last ten minutes."

"The kid going to be in there?"

"Sure. She's already in there. Trying to calm him down."

"Guess I'll go take a look at her."

I started to turn away but she grabbed my arm. "I want to say something to you, Congreve, and I'm going to say it in terms you'll understand."

"All right."

"You're full of shit about Doctor Pelham."

"You're right. Those are terms I can understand."

"He works his ass off here. He's the only surgeon in the whole Fortress. He suffers from depression because he loses so many, and when he can't sleep, he spends time with all the wounded and injured. That's why he needs the Paineaters, Congreve. Because he doesn't have anybody else to help him and because he's so damned worried about his patients." She was quickly getting angry. "So I want you to knock off the bullshit with him, all right? The only reason he was mad about what you did was because of the bind you left him in with the patients. Or can't you understand that?"

The funny thing was, I did understand it and, for the first time, what Young Doctor Pelham was all about. I guess I considered him cold and arrogant, but what I missed seeing was that he was just a very vulnerable and overworked guy doing an almost-impossible job. And it took Nurse Ellen to make me see it.

"He isn't so bad, is he?" I said.

"No, he isn't."

"And he isn't just using those Paineaters because he likes to see them suffer, is he?"

"No, he's not."

"Maybe he feels sorrier for them than I do."

"You're a stupid fucker, Congreve. You know the first three of them we ever had in here?"

"Yeah."

"When they—Well, after they died, he took each one out and buried her."

There wasn't much I could say.

"So knock off the 'Young Doctor Pelham' bullshit, all right?"

"All right."

"And one more thing."

"What's that?"

Now she gave me a great big smile of her own. "He's not so bad in the sack, either."

On my way back down the hall, I saw Doctor Sullivan and one of the nurses laughing in a secretive sort of way. They were probably telling jokes about Sullivan's boss, Pelham. It almost made me feel sorry for him.

I borrowed a book from Pelham's library once on the history of surgery. Pretty interesting, especially when you consider that the first operations were done as far back as the Stone Age. Using a piece of stone, the first surgeons cut holes in the skulls of their patients, so that they could release evil spirits thought to cause headaches and other ailments.

But over the centuries, doctors had gotten used to slightly more sophisticated methods and equipment: X-rays and CAT scans and scalpels and clamps and retractors and sutures and hemostats and sponges and inverts among them.

And anesthesia.

Before 1842, when anesthesia came into use, all doctors could give patients was whiskey or compounds heavy with opium. And then the operations couldn't last too long, the sedative effects of the booze and opium wearing off pretty fast.

These days, Pelham and all the other doctors in all the other Fortresses faced some of the old problems. Anesthesia was hard to come by.

A few years back, a sociologist named Allan Berkowitz was out making note of all the mutated species he found in the various Zones, when he was shot in the arm by a Zoner who robbed him and ran away.

Berkowitz figured he was pretty much dead. The blood loss would kill him if he didn't get to a doc. And the pain was quickly becoming intolerable. The blood loss had also disoriented him slightly. He spent a full half-day wandering around in a very small circle.

He collapsed next to a polluted creek, figuring he might as well partake of some polluted waters, when he noticed a strange-looking little girl standing above him. His first thought, given the size and shape of her head, was that she was just another helpless mutant turned away by her parents. You found a lot of freaks in the Zone, just waiting for roaming packs of Dobermans or genetics to take them from their misery.

This little girl made strange, sad sounds in her throat. She seemed to be looking at Berkowitz and yet seeing beyond him, too. The effect was unsettling, like staring at someone you suddenly suspect is blind.

He dragged himself over to her. A fine and decent man,

Berkowitz decided to forget his own miseries for the time and concentrate on hers. Maybe there was something he could do for her.

He took her little hand and said, "Hi, honey, do you have a name?"

And realized again that somehow she saw him, yet didn't see him. The autism analogy came to mind.

And realized, also, that she couldn't talk. The strange, sad noises in her throat seemed to be the extent of her vocabulary.

He wasn't strong enough to stand, so he gently pulled her down next to him, all the time keeping hold of her hand.

And then he started to feel it.

The cessation of his pain, of his fear, even of a generalized anxiety he'd known all his life.

His first reaction was that this was some physiological trick associated with heavy loss of blood. Maybe the same kind of well-being people noted in near-death experiences, the body releasing certain protective chemicals that instill a sense of well-being.

But he was wrong.

He sat next to the girl for more than three hours and, in the course of it, they made a telepathic link and she purged him of all his grief and terror.

He knew this was real because each time he opened his eyes from his reverie-like state, he saw animals nearby doing their ordinary animal things—a squirrel furiously digging a buried acorn from the grass; a meek little mutt peeing against a tree; a raccoon lying on his back and eating a piece of bread he'd scrounged from some human encampment.

The wound didn't go away—she didn't heal him—but he

felt so pacified, so whole and complete and good unto himself, that his spiritual strength gave him physical strength, and allowed him to find his way out of the Zone and back to his Fortress in Glencoe.

He brought the girl with him.

He took her straight to the doctor at the hospital and told the doctor what had happened and, skeptical as the doctor was, the little girl was allowed to audition, as it were.

They put her in the ER with a man whose arm had been torn off. You could hear his screams as far up as the sixth floor. They were prepping him for surgery.

The girl sat down and took the man's lone good hand.

He was in so much pain, he didn't even seem to notice her at first.

Nothing happened right away.

The strapped-down man went on writhing and screaming.

But then the writhing lessened.

And then the screaming softened.

And the doctor watched the rest of it, bedazzled.

Berkowitz's discovery made it possible for hospitals to keep on functioning. All they had to do was hire Outriders, men and women willing to take the chance of searching the Zones for more youngsters who looked and acted like this one. And while they were out there, like the Outriders of old, they could also note any gangs of people who seemed headed for the Fortress to inflict great bodily harm.

To date, these were a few observed truths about the Paineaters, as they'd come to be called:

Generally between the ages of three and six.

Generally put out to die by their families because of their mutation.

Unable to speak or see (as we understand seeing).

Generally useful for only a three- to four-month period.

Afterward, must be sent to Zone 4 for further study. At this stage, dementia has usually set in.

They could be used up, like a disposable cigarette lighter. They could absorb only so much of other people's pain, and then that was it. A form of dementia set in. Fortress Northwestern had a group of doctors studying the used-up ones. By doing so, they hoped to increase the chances for longer use. There was a finite number of these children and they were extremely important to the survival of all Fortress hospitals. There were two other observations I should note:

Extended proximity to these children has been known to make human beings overly protective of them, leading to difficulties with hospital efficiency.

Extended proximity to these children has led to difficulties with normal human relationships.

I thought of all this as I stood in the observation balcony and watched the operation proceed.

The man who'd been attacked by the Dobermans was a mess, a meaty, bloody, flesh-ripped mess.

There would have to be a lot of plastic surgery afterward and, even then, he would always be rather ghastly looking, a D-movie version of Frankenstein.

There were six people, including Pelham, on the surgery team. Even though he didn't have the equipment he

301

needed—or in truth, the ability to completely sterilize the equipment he did have—Pelham tried to make this as much like his old surgery days as possible. There was the large table for instruments; the small table for instruments; and the operating table itself.

Above the line of her surgical mask, I could see Doctor Sullivan's beautiful eyes. Disapproving eyes. She obviously felt she should be in charge here, not Pelham.

They started cleansing the man's wounds, the surgical team, with Pelham pitching in. Surgeons were no longer stars. They had to do the same kind of work as nurses now.

The kid sat in a chair next to the operating table, holding the hand of the patient.

He was utterly tranquil, the man.

The kid had been working with him for some time now. The kid and the patient faced me, as did the surgery team.

I spotted Polly right away, behind her green surgical mask. She was supposed to be helping with the cleansing, but she spent most of her time glancing at the kid.

You really do get hooked into them, some kind of dependence that you ultimately come to regret.

But then she was snapped back to the reality of the operating table when another nurse nudged her roughly and nodded to the patient.

Polly needed to clean a shoulder wound.

She set to work.

And just as she pulled her attention away, I saw the kid do it.

Go into a spasm, a violent shudder ugly to see.

And then I knew how foolish all Polly's talk had been about resting the kid, so she didn't ever get used up the way all the other ones did.

I got out of there.

I didn't want to be there when Polly noticed the kid go into a spasm, and realized that all her hopes had come to nothing.

7

The argument came three days later. Even two floors up, you could hear it.

I was walking up the stairs to my own room when I heard the yelling and then heard a door slamming shut.

Eighth floor, two down; eighth floor being Polly's. I decided I needed to check it out.

Pelham was in front of Polly's door. So was Nurse Ellen. They were speaking in low voices so nobody except Polly could hear them. Then Doctor Sullivan appeared, swank even in her dusty medical smock.

"What's going on?" I said.

Pelham frowned and shook his head. Of late I'd been nicer to him and was surprised to find that he'd been nicer to me, too.

He walked me down the hall, away from the door, to where a small mountain of rubble lay beneath the smashed-out windows.

Doctor Sullivan and Nurse Ellen stayed by Polly's door.

"Have you talked to her lately?"

"Not for a couple of days. She keeps pretty much to herself."

"That's the trouble. Herself—and the kid."

"I know."

"The same way you got, Congreve." For once there was sympathy in his voice, not condemnation. "Have you seen the little room she fixed up for the kid?"

"Huh-uh."

"It'll break your heart. Polly's convinced herself that she's the kid's mother."

"What's wrong with that? We're all pretty lonely here."

The frown again. But the dark eyes were sad, understanding. "She won't let us use the kid."

"Oh, man. Then she really is gone on her."

"Far gone. Maybe you can help."

"Not if she's this far along. You get hooked in."

"The same way you did."

I nodded. "The same way I did."

Nurse Ellen was getting mad. Raising her voice.

"Polly, we've got a ten-year-old boy down there who was shot by some Zoner. We have to operate right away. We need her, Polly. Desperately. Can't you understand that?"

"Let us in," Doctor Sullivan said in a voice that implied she expected to be obeyed immediately.

But the door didn't open.

And Polly didn't respond in any way at all.

"She said the kid has started twitching," Pelham said. "You know what that means."

By now, Nurse Ellen was shrieking. "Polly, we have to have the kid and we have to have her now!"

"C'mon, Congreve," Pelham said. "Try your luck. Please."

"Then you three go back downstairs."

"We don't have long. The boy's lost a lot of blood."

"I'll do what I can as soon as you two leave."

He wasted no time. He collected Ellen and Doctor Sullivan, went to the EXIT door, and disappeared.

"They're gone, Polly."

"You can't talk me into it, Congreve."

"Polly, you're not being rational."

"And you are?"

"There's a little boy downstairs dying."

"Well, there's a little girl in here who's dying, too, and nobody seems to give a shit about that."

"She won't die. She's got a long way to go."

"You know better than that. You know how they are after they start twitching. And getting headaches."

"She'll be all right."

"I can't believe you're talking like this, Congreve. After what you did and all."

"They don't have any choice, Polly. They'll come and take her from you."

"I've got a gun in here."

"Polly, please, please start thinking clearly, will you?"

Three of them came through the EXIT door now, two men and a woman. The men were nurses. The woman was an intern. They all carried shotguns.

They were in a hurry.

They swept up to me and forced me to stand aside.

They meant to get Polly's attention and they did.

No warning. No words at all.

Two of them just opened fire. Pumped several noisy, echoing powder-smelling rounds into the door.

Polly screamed.

The kid was making frantic animal noises.

"You going to bring her out?" one of the male nurses shouted.

"No!" Polly shouted back.

This time they must have pumped twenty rounds in there. They beat up the door pretty good.

"We're coming in, Polly!" the second nurse shouted.

Pretty obviously, she didn't have a gun. Or she would have used it.

Because now they went in. Booted in the door. Dove inside the room. Trained all three shotguns right on her.

She had pushed herself back against the corner in the precious pink room that she had turned into a wonderful bedroom for a little girl.

The girl was in her arms, holding tight, all the gunfire and shouting having terrified her.

Polly was sobbing. "Please, don't take her. Please, don't take her."

She said it over and over.

But take her they did, and without any grace, either. The moment Polly showed the slightest resistance—held the kid tight, so they couldn't snatch her—one of the nurses chunked Polly on the side of his head with the butt of his rifle.

I grabbed him, spun him around, put a fist deep into his solar plexus.

Not that it mattered.

While I was playing macho, the other two grabbed the kid and ran out of the room with her.

I dragged the lone nurse to the door and threw him down the hall.

Then I went back and sat on the small, pink single bed where Polly was sprawled now, sobbing.

I sat on the bed and let her hold onto me as if I were her daddy and knew all the answers to all the grief of the world.

I was sitting up in my room, cleaning and oiling all the weapons, when Pelham showed up, knocked courteously—I told you we were trying to be nice to each other these days, Nurse Ellen's irate words taking their toll on me—and said, "Polly took the kid in the middle of the night and left."

This was two days after the incident at Polly's door.

"Maybe they just went out for a while."

"She took food, two guns, and some cash."

"Shit."

"I've got a woman downstairs who won't see tonight, if I don't get that kid back."

"Damn."

"I know how much you like Polly, Congreve. I like her, too. But I have to—"

"—think of the patients."

"I'm sorry if you get tired of hearing it."

I sighed and stood up. "I'll go get her."

"She tried to start the skymobile. Smashed in the window and then tried to hotwire it."

"She isn't real mechanical. On foot, she won't be hard to find. Unless something's happened to her already."

I tried not to think about that.

"You have to hurry, Congreve. Please."

8

Took me two hours.

She was up near the wall in what had formerly been a public rest stop. There were three semis turned on their sides in the drive, the result of the initial bombing, and they looked like big, sad, clumsy animals that couldn't get to their feet again.

Apparently, the rest stop had been pretty busy at the time of the bombing, because from up here you could see the skeletons of maybe a dozen people, including that of a family—mother, father, two kids.

When I first spotted her, she was sitting on a hill, resting, with the kid sitting next to her.

She heard me about the same time as I saw her.

She stood up, wiped off her bottom from the grass, picked up the kid like a football, and started running.

There was a deep stand of scrub pines but they weren't

deep enough to hide her for long. I waited till she came running out of the trees, and then I put the skymobile down not far away and started running after her.

She was in much better shape than I was. Even holding the kid, she was able to stay ahead of me for a good half-mile. I stumbled twice. She didn't stumble at all.

We were working up the side of a grassy hill when her legs and her wind gave out.

She just dropped straight down, as if she'd been shot in the head, straight down with the kid still tucked in her arms, straight down and sobbing wildly.

I stood several feet away and said nothing. There wasn't anything to say, anyway.

Pelham took the kid away from her and then put Polly up in one of the observation rooms in a straitjacket. He wouldn't let me see her for a couple of days.

By the time I got up there, she was a mess. She had a black eye from me having to wrestle her into the skymobile, and her coppery hair was shot through with twigs and dead flowers and her face was streaked with dirt. It was as if she'd been buried alive.

I took a straight-backed chair and sat next to her.

"You fucker."

"I'm sorry, Polly."

"You fucker."

But there was no power in her voice. She was just mouthing words.

"I'm sorry I got you involved in this. I never should have taken you along to Hoolihan's that day. I was being selfish."

"I don't want to live without her."

"You have to stop thinking that way, Polly. Pelham doesn't have any choice. He has to use Sarah for the sake of the patients."

"She's near the end."

"You need to get on with your life."

At one time, this room had been small and white and bright. Now it was small and dirty. The only brightness came from the kerosene lantern I carried, its flame throwing flickering shadows across Polly's face, making her look even more insane.

"Pelham's a fucker and Ellen's a fucker and you're a fucker. You're killing that little girl and none of you give a damn."

A knock. Just once. Curt.

The door opened and Pelham came in. He walked noisily across the glass-littered floor.

He stood next to me and looked at Polly in her chair and her straitjacket.

"You're doing better today, Polly. You're verbalizing much more."

"You're killing that little girl. Doesn't that matter to you?"

This time her voice was heartbreaking. No curses. No anger. Just a terrible pleading.

"Another few days and maybe we'll be able to take off the straitjacket."

He was breaking her, the way cowboys used to break horses. By keeping her in this room long enough, in the straitjacket long enough, alone long enough, she would eventually become more compliant. She would never again be the fiery Polly of yore. But she would be a Polly who was no longer a threat to the hospital.

At least that was Pelham's hope.

"Would you like some Jell-O, Polly?"

But her head was down.

She was no longer willing to verbalize, to use Pelham's five-dollar word.

He nodded for me to follow him out.

"You get some sleep, Polly," Pelham said. "Sleep is your friend."

I took a last look at her.

No matter how long Pelham kept her in here, she would never forgive me and I wasn't sure I blamed her.

I followed him out.

9

That afternoon, over coffee, Pelham made me talk about it again and I resented it but I also understood that he was simply trying to help Polly and I was the nearest equivalent to Polly in the hospital.

Eight months ago, the hospital in need of another Paineater, I'd taken the skymobile over to Hoolihan's and bought myself a kid.

I got hooked. I wasn't even aware of it at first. The simplest explanation is that the kid became a substitute for my daughters. When she'd get back from downstairs, from consuming the pain of the patients that day, I'd find myself rocking her to sleep with tears in my eyes.

Soon enough, I saw her start to twitch. And then the headaches came. And night after night she made those same muffled, screaming noises in her throat.

And Pelham, it seemed, was always at the door, always saying, "We need her again. I'm sorry."

And all I could do was watch her deteriorate.

"I know you hated me," Pelham said. "And I'm sorry."

I nodded. "You didn't have much choice."

He sipped his coffee. "So what finally made you decide to do it?"

"I guess when you started talking about her future and everything. How she'd be studied and tested, so that we could get a better grasp on how to make the future ones last longer. 'New, Improved' models, I guess you'd call them."

"Unless things change a whole hell of a lot, Congreve, we're going to need even more Paineaters in the future. And better ones."

"I guess that's what I was against. I don't think we have the right to use anybody that way. We get so fucking callous we forget they're human beings, and incredibly vulnerable ones."

"So you killed her."

"So I killed her."

That's what the nightmares were all about. Seeing little Michelle sleeping in my bed and creeping up to her and putting the gun to her chest and pulling the trigger and—

"I loved her," I said. "I felt it was the right thing. At least at the time. Now, I guess, I can see both sides."

"I really am going to let Polly go free in the next week or so. I just hope she's as rational as you are."

I sighed. "I hope so, too. For everybody's sake."

"We're doing the right thing, Congreve. The goddamned Christians took out half of Russia and China. We have to rebuild the species, what with all the mutation taking place. We normals have to survive. I don't like what we're doing with Paineaters but we don't have any choice. It's just survival is all."

He clapped me on the shoulder and went back to work. He looked exhausted, but then he always looked exhausted.

10

She didn't get out in one week or two weeks or three weeks. It took four weeks before Pelham thought she was ready.

Mostly, she stayed in her room. They brought her food because she didn't go down to the mess. She was not allowed to see Sarah.

I stopped by several times and knocked. I always identified myself and always heard her moving about in there. But she would not acknowledge me in any way.

One day I waited three hours at the opposite end of the hall. I knew she had to come out eventually. But she didn't.

Another day I found her room empty. She was down the hall in the bathroom, apparently.

I hid in her room.

When she came back, I surprised her. Her face showed no response whatsoever. But her hand did. From a small holster attached to the back of her belt, she pulled out a small .45 and pointed it at me. I left.

A week after this she went berserk. This happened down in the mess. She was walking by and saw people staring at her and she went in and starting upending tables and hurling glasses and plates against the walls. She wasn't very big and she wasn't very mighty, but she scared people. She wandered, sobbing and cursing, from the mess and went back upstairs to her room. After a while, Pelham went up to see her. He decided against confining her again.

11

"She's near the end. The spasms—I can barely stand to look at her. She won't last past another couple patients."

This was Pelham in his office two weeks after the incident with Polly in the mess.

Doctor Sullivan, lean, hungry, and gorgeous as ever, sat to the left of Pelham, watching.

"Can you get ahold of Hoolihan?"

"Sure. Why?"

"Get another one lined up."

"She's that close to burning out, huh?"

Doctor Sullivan said, "Doctor Pelham is right. A few more patients at most. Sarah takes on trauma and grief and despair and frenzy as her own. She is a very small vessel. She can't hold much more. The situation is actually much more urgent than Doctor Pelham is letting on."

A deep, bellowing horn-like alarm that signals Pelham that ER has a patient very near death rumbled through the ground floor of the hospital.

Pelham and Sullivan were off running even before I got out of my chair. I followed.

"Used some kind of power saw on him," one of the techs said as the three of us reached the ER area.

Indeed. His neck, chest, and arms showed deep ruts where some kind of saw had ripped through his flesh right to the bone. He wasn't screaming. He was unconscious.

"Get surgery set up!" Pelham shouted after one quick look at the man on the gurney.

"Things are just about ready to go," the tech said.

"We need the Paineater, then," Pelham said.

"She's in there, too," the tech said, "but she's not doing real well. You know how they get near the end—all the shaking and shit."

Five minutes later, we were all in surgery. One of the techs was sick today and I was asked to assist, as I did on occasion.

Operating table and instruments and staff were prepared as well as could be expected under these frantic conditions.

And Sarah was in place.

She sat, staring off at nothing, holding the bloody hand of the man on the table. Her entire body shook and trembled—and then went into violent seizures that would lift her out of her chair.

The screams in her throat kept dying.

"Your job is to watch her, make sure she stays linked to the patient," Pelham told me.

I went over and sat next to her. Just as she held the patient's hand, I held her free one. I kept cooing her name, trying to keep her calm.

She'd peed all over herself. The deep sobbing continued.

The operation started.

The patient was totally satisfied. You could see the pleasure on his face. Sarah was cleansing him not only of his physical pain but of all the grief and anxiety of his entire life. No wonder he looked beatific, like one of those old paintings that depicted mortal men looking on the face of an angel.

One thing you had to say for them, Pelham and Sullivan worked well together—quickly, efficiently, artfully. You'd never know they hated each other.

They had started doing the heavy-duty stitching when the rear door of the operating room slammed open.

I looked up and saw her there. Polly. With an autorifle. Face crazed and streaked with tears.

"You're killing her and you don't even care!" she screamed.

She worked left to right, which meant that Pelham was the first to die and then all the staffers standing next to him. This gave Sullivan and a few others the chance to hide behind the far side of the operating table.

By now I had my gun out and was crouched behind a small cabinet.

She kept on firing, trying to hit Sullivan and the others where they were hiding.

"Polly! Please drop your gun!"

If she heard me, she didn't let on. She just kept pumping rounds at the operating table, hoping to hit at least a few of them.

I started to stand up from my crouch.

She must have caught this peripherally because she suddenly turned in my direction, still firing, as one with her weapon.

"Polly!" I screamed. "Put it down!"

But she didn't put it down, of course, and then I had no choice. I put a bullet into the middle of her forehead.

She managed to squeeze off a few more shots but then her gun clattered to the floor, and soon enough she followed it.

Silence.

And then Sarah was up and tottering over to Polly's fallen body.

Sarah knelt next to her and made the awful, mewling noises in her throat—the saddest sound in her entire repertoire—and then she was touching Polly's face reverently with her tiny white hands.

We all stood around and watched because we had never seen this before. Paineaters took on all the physical and psychic pain of others. Here was a Paineater who had to take on her own pain.

After a time, Sarah still kneeling there, rocking back and forth and twitching so violently I was afraid she might start breaking her own bones, I went over and picked her up and carried her out of the room.

12

There was a funeral for Polly the next day. Some fine, sincere, and very moving things were said.

Nurse Ellen announced that Doctor Sullivan would now be in charge of the hospital and that people should now come to her with any questions they had.

Afterward, I put Sarah in the skymobile and got ready to take off.

Doctor Sullivan came over to say goodbye. "The doctors at the school will be very interested in this one especially. Studying the effects of her own trauma. With Polly."

Sarah had made no sound since I'd carried her from the operating room yesterday. She just sat there in the throes of her shaking and jerking and trembling.

"I appreciate you doing this," Doctor Sullivan said. "I know you don't think we should prolong their lives or their suffering. But it's necessary if we're to survive."

"That's what Pelham said."

She smiled her beautiful, icy smile. "Well, at least he was right about something."

It took three hours to find the school, a rugged, stone castle-like building that had once been a monastery sitting in the middle of deep woods.

"Well, this is going to be your home for a while, Sarah," I said. I'd tried not to look at her. The spasms were really getting to me.

Survival, Pelham had said.

I started circling for my landing, finding a good open area near the west wing to put the machine down.

And that's when the cry came up in her throat and her hand reached over and grabbed mine.

She shook so violently that I couldn't keep my hand around hers. Tears filled her dead eyes.

By now a couple of the docs below had come out and were waving to me. They knew who I was and what cargo I brought.

I waved back—or started to.

I pulled the machine up from the landing I'd started and swung away abruptly from the school.

I could hear them shouting below.

That night, in the mess, Doctor Sullivan came over and sat by me. "I really appreciate you taking her over there this afternoon."

"No problem."

"You doing all right?"

"Doing fine."

"I'm looking forward to working with you, Congreve."

"Same goes for me."

"Thanks."

Then she was off to do some more PR work with other people she felt vital to her new post as boss.

Being tired, I turned in early.

Being tired, I slept at once and slept fine and fast, too, until that time in the middle of the night when everything is shifting shadows and faint, disturbing echoes. I was awake and that meant I'd think back to this afternoon.

I'd tried to do it fast. I'd landed and carried her out of the skymobile and set her down on the grass and put one bullet quick and clean into the back of her skull. And then I held her for a long time and cried, but the funny thing was I wasn't sure why I was crying. For her. For me. For Polly. For Pelham. For the whole crazy, fucking world, maybe.

And then I buried her and stood over the little grave and said some prayers and a feisty little mutt from the forest came along and played in the fresh dirt for a time. And I thought maybe she'd have liked that, little Sarah, the way the puppy was playing and all. And Polly would probably have liked it, too.

Darkness. Shadow. My own coarse breathing. I didn't

want to think about this afternoon anymore. I just wanted sleep.

"You look tired," Doctor Sullivan said cheerfully at mess next morning.

"Guess I am kind of."

"You're going to see Hoolihan today, aren't you?"

"Uh-huh."

She looked at me hard then. I hadn't been properly enthusiastic when she brought the subject up. "You know how important this is, don't you, Congreve? I mean, for the whole species. Just the way Pelham said."

"Right," I said, "just the way Pelham said."

Three hours later, I fired up the old machine and flew over to see Hoolihan.

About the Author

ED GORMAN has written eighteen novels and published seven collections of short stories. *The Oxford Book of American Crime Stories* noted that "Gorman's novels and stories provide fresh ideas, characters, and approaches." *Voya* said "His work will appeal to a wide audience." *The San Francisco Examiner* said "Gorman has a wonderful writing style that allows him to say things of substance in an entertaining way."